Take a Chance on You

The Chances
Book 11

Emily E K Murdoch

© Copyright 2026 by Emily E K Murdoch
Text by Emily E K Murdoch
Cover by Dar Albert

Dragonblade Publishing, Inc. is an imprint of Kathryn Le Veque Novels, Inc.
P.O. Box 23
Moreno Valley, CA 92556
ceo@dragonbladepublishing.com

Produced in the United States of America

First Edition March 2026
Trade Paperback Edition

Reproduction of any kind except where it pertains to short quotes in relation to advertising or promotion is strictly prohibited.

All Rights Reserved.

The characters and events portrayed in this book are fictitious. Any similarity to real persons, living or dead, is purely coincidental and not intended by the author.

AI Statement: No AI or ghostwriting was used in the creation of this story, or any story, published by Dragonblade Publishing. All text, structure, content, ideas, and concept are 100% human generated solely by the author whose name appears on the cover. It is prohibited to use this material, or any copyrighted material, for AI engine training.

ARE YOU SIGNED UP FOR DRAGONBLADE'S BLOG?

You'll get the latest news and information on exclusive giveaways, exclusive excerpts, coming releases, sales, free books, cover reveals and more.

Check out our complete list of authors, too!

No spam, no junk. That's a promise!

Sign Up Here

www.dragonbladepublishing.com

Dearest Reader;

Thank you for your support of a small press. At Dragonblade Publishing, we strive to bring you the highest quality Historical Romance from some of the best authors in the business. Without your support, there is no 'us', so we sincerely hope you adore these stories and find some new favorite authors along the way.

Happy Reading!

CEO, Dragonblade Publishing

Additional Dragonblade books by
Author Emily E K Murdoch

The Chances Series
A Fighting Chance (Book 1)
A Second Chance (Book 2)
An Outside Chance (Book 3)
Half a Chance (Book 4)
A Chance in a Million (Book 5)
Not a Chance in Hell (Book 6)
An Eye for the Chance (Book 7)
A Sporting Chance (Book 8)
Any Chance You Can Take (Book 9)
Chance Would Be a Fine Thing (Book 10)
Take a Chance on You (Book 11)

Dukes in Danger Series
Don't Judge a Duke by His Cover (Book 1)
Strike While the Duke is Hot (Book 2)
The Duke is Mightier than the Sword (Book 3)
A Duke in Time Saves Nine (Book 4)
Every Duke Has His Price (Book 5)
Put Your Best Duke Forward (Book 6)
Where There's a Duke, There's a Way (Book 7)
Curiosity Killed the Duke (Book 8)
Play With Dukes, Get Burned (Book 9)
The Best Things in Life are Dukes (Book 10)
A Duke a Day Keeps the Doctor Away (Book 11)
All Good Dukes Come to an End (Book 12)

Twelve Days of Christmas
Twelve Drummers Drumming
Eleven Pipers Piping
Ten Lords a Leaping

Nine Ladies Dancing
Eight Maids a Milking
Seven Swans a Swimming
Six Geese a Laying
Five Gold Rings
Four Calling Birds
Three French Hens
Two Turtle Doves
A Partridge in a Pear Tree

The De Petras Saga
The Misplaced Husband (Book 1)
The Impoverished Dowry (Book 2)
The Contrary Debutante (Book 3)
The Determined Mistress (Book 4)
The Convenient Engagement (Book 5)

The Governess Bureau Series
A Governess of Great Talents (Book 1)
A Governess of Discretion (Book 2)
A Governess of Many Languages (Book 3)
A Governess of Prodigious Skill (Book 4)
A Governess of Unusual Experience (Book 5)
A Governess of Wise Years (Book 6)
A Governess of No Fear (Novella)

Never The Bride Series
Always the Bridesmaid (Book 1)
Always the Chaperone (Book 2)
Always the Courtesan (Book 3)
Always the Best Friend (Book 4)
Always the Wallflower (Book 5)
Always the Bluestocking (Book 6)
Always the Rival (Book 7)
Always the Matchmaker (Book 8)
Always the Widow (Book 9)
Always the Rebel (Book 10)
Always the Mistress (Book 11)

Always the Second Choice (Book 12)
Always the Mistletoe (Novella)
Always the Reverend (Novella)

The Lyon's Den Series
Always the Lyon Tamer

Pirates of Britannia Series
Always the High Seas

De Wolfe Pack: The Series
Whirlwind with a Wolfe

Noble titles throughout English history have, at times, been more fluid than one might think. Women have inherited, men have been gifted titles by family or gained them on through marriage, and royals frequently lavished titles or withdrew them as reward and punishment.

The elder Chance brothers in this series agreed to split the four titles in their family line during the Regency era, rather than the eldest holding all four. It is a decision that defines their brotherhood, and their very different personalities.

Now with the next generation, one Chance father has allowed his son to inherit his title before his own demise, echoing kings and queens who have abdicated their titles throughout history. Perhaps his brothers, the uncles of this next generation, will follow suit...

Get ready to meet a family that is more than happy to scandalize Society...

Chapter One

January 2, 1841

Miss Rosemary Morgan, famous actress, fabulously wealthy patron of the arts, woman beloved by all, was not having a good day.

Fine. She was not famous, Rose acknowledged darkly as she pulled on another scarf around her shoulders, a meager attempt to keep out the bitter Brighton wind.

And fine. Perhaps, based on an absolutely accurate definition of the world 'fabulously,' she was not fabulously wealthy, Rose conceded as she stepped off the pavement to cross the busy street and discovered her boot had a hole in it. In the bottom of the sole.

As water soaked into her threadbare stockings and she cursed all rain, Rose tried not to think about how cold she was. She really needed to purchase a proper winter coat, but her summer one had always been suitable in Italy and honestly, she had almost forgotten how freezing these English winters were.

Fine. Not fabulously wealthy. Perhaps not even wealthy at all.

Patron of the arts, then!

Rose shivered as she marched as swiftly as she could down the busy Brighton street, the scent of saltwater in the air. Well, not exactly patron.

If anything, she *needed* a patron.

As she thrust a hand into her coat pocket in search of a coin, any coin, Rose was not surprised but greatly disappointed to discover that there was a great dearth of gold guineas to be found.

In fact, as she pulled out her fist and looked into her palm with sinking spirits…she discovered there was very little silver. Very little of anything.

Well, there was nothing for it. She had to eat, didn't she?

"Ah, Rosy." The pie stall owner grinned, his teeth black thanks to all the sugar he clearly consumed. "The usual?"

Rose flinched.

The usual. It was a benign enough term for a horrible habit she had fallen into—but really, what other option had she? Until the play opened, and it *would* be a huge success, *everyone* was saying so, she would have little coin at her disposal. Truly, it was a small miracle that her landlady had been an actress herself and knew the ebb and flow of income for those in such a profession.

The stall owner was still grinning. "Come on. You know the bargain we struck."

Rose tried to smile. She was an actress, for goodness's sake. She could at least pretend this wasn't mortifying and degrading.

"Of course," she said lightly. "Just gathering my thoughts."

His leer was most pronounced, and so was the stench of him as she grew closer. But they had come to an arrangement, and she was not the sort of person to rescind an agreement that was so beneficial.

Even if it was most unpleasant, in the moment.

Rose leaned forward, ensured she displayed her most sultry expression—pouted lips and hooded eyes—and as she always did, moved to kiss the man on the cheek.

As he always did, the man turned his face so that their lips touched.

Rose tried not to breathe. *Three, two, one—*

"There," she said, leaning back and forcing herself not to take a few actual steps back. "My pie, sir."

That was demeaning. That was what it was, she thought darkly as the man wriggled his eyebrows suggestively and he bundled a slightly dirty pie into a brown paper bag.

"Only fell off the cart for a moment." He slowly, disgustingly, ran a hand down his bulky thigh as he maintained prolonged eye contact.

Rose tried her best to keep her smile intact. And she did. She was an actress, after all—but more than that, she was a woman down on her luck with no family to speak of and no friends who would own her.

If a woman in her position couldn't smile at a man despite his disgusting behavior, who could?

"Thank you," she simpered, allowing a hint of warmth in her eyes but nothing more. Then she turned around and started down the street.

Rose waited until she had turned a corner before stopping, ripping open the paper bag, and stuffing the first piece of pie into her mouth.

Her eyes closed, just for a moment.

Food.

It wasn't that good. After one had spent time living in Rome, with the delicious herbs they used in their lasagna and the way there was a red wine to perfectly complement every meal, one could not find palatable delight in a pie poorly baked and still dusted with street dirt.

But when it was the most recent thing one had eaten in two days... Well. It was ambrosia.

The pie disappeared far more quickly than Rose would have liked. The thing had been almost larger than her fist, but within four mouthfuls, the dry pastry and soggy meat filling was gone.

Rose looked down at the empty paper bag in her hands—well. Empty save for the crumbs.

She looked around surreptitiously. Would anyone judge her, perhaps, for licking out the paper bag? There was surely almost no sustenance within it, but her stomach was craving something, anything, and she had almost no coin until opening night, which was three days away.

Three days on a pie-a-day from that man would not be enough. Besides, she could catch something from the revolting man, and then where would she be?

Rose inhaled deeply, looked once again at the paper bag, and slowly lifted it to her mouth. Ignoring the passersby on the pavement and hoping to goodness none of them recognized her as the great Miss Rosemary Morgan, success and darling of the Italian stage newly arrived back in England, she licked the crumbly remnants of the pie.

She stopped within a heartbeat, her stomach revolting against the action.

No—no! She would not stoop that low. Dear Lord, she was not that desperate!

Crunching the paper bag and placing it in her pocket, Rose strode forward. She would be a little early for rehearsal at the Grand Theatre, but there was no harm in that. Besides, her costume for the leading role—one she had easily won through her acting prowess, Rose told herself firmly—should be finished by now. She had not yet had the opportunity to try it on with the coronet, and there was a full-length looking glass in the wings, something Rose had not been able to use in... Well. Weeks? Months?

The icy wind got up, bringing with it its briny smell, but Rose was just a few steps away from the theater as she pulled her two scarves around her neck. *This blessed winter!* When the warm weather came, she would be relieved.

"Morning, Ted," she said brightly as she stepped through the stage door and into the corridor that led to the rooms behind the stage.

The bushy-browed man stared. "Rose—Rose?"

"That's my name," Rose said with a smile, her spirits lifting as they always did whenever she was within a theater. "One day, you'll see it in the Society pages, Ted, mark my words."

"But—"

Rose did not wait to hear an argument. She would one day be in the Society pages, she was sure of it. Her talent was not something that could be hidden under a bushel, after all—she was going to be one of the most famous actresses in all of England.

Dukes would wish to see her. Earls would fawn over her. There may even be a foreign prince or two who wished to dine with her, Rose daydreamed wistfully as she meandered through the maze of corridors, Ted following her chattering about some sort of nonsense. Yes, within a few weeks, news of her talent would reach London, and she could go there and—

"*Rose!*" shrieked Annabelle as Rose entered the dressing room.

Rose halted. There were two things wrong here, and for a moment, her mind could only suggest one.

Annabelle. What was Annabelle doing here?

"Annabelle," Rose said, confusion etching her tone. "But you—your rehearsal isn't until this afternoon! Chorus isn't needed for anything this morning, are they?"

Annabelle's cheeks had flushed and yet despite that, she was still very pretty.

Of course she is, Rose tried not to think. The woman was a full seven years younger than her and still had that maidenly beauty that only a girl of just turned eighteen could possess.

True, but she does not have your acting ability, that resolute little voice at the back of her mind reminded her.

Rose's shoulders relaxed, though she had not noticed when they had grown so fraught with tension. Perhaps when she had turned the corner and seen Annabelle in—

The gasp that left her lips was truly impressive. Honestly, Rose was a tad disappointed she had not performed it on the stage. It would certainly have reached the very back of the theater here in Brighton, and that was no small feat. One really needed excellent projection to do such a thing.

The cause of such a gasp, however, was not nearly so delightful.

"You—You're wearing my costume," Rose said, her heart racing. "Why are you wearing my costume, Annabelle?"

The younger woman looked like a rabbit being pinned down

by a fox, all wide eyes and gaping mouth—but no words came from those pink lips.

Rose could do nothing but stare. It was a truly gorgeous costume; she was to be Titania, Queen of the Fairies, in Shakespeare's *A Midsummer Night's Dream*, and so the most lavish materials had been used to construct a gown worthy of such a character. Brocade and velvet and lace and gold thread... Even some glass jewels had been found to embroider into the—

But why on earth was Annabelle wearing it?

Rose stared as the younger woman remained silent and Ted gabbled some nonsensical thing from behind her that she paid no attention to. It was inexplicable! There was absolutely no reason for it, no reason at all. Unless...

Her shoulders relaxed. "Ah, I suppose it needed adjusting, and as we are essentially the same size, they asked you to stand in for me? That was kind, Annabelle, with you having the morning off."

Yes, that was it. Well, that was all to the good. *It is right and proper*, Rose thought as she shrugged off her scarves and pelisse to place them over her chair, *that the underlings are made useful when the true stars—such as myself—are busy.* After all, they had not expected her this early, had they?

That was what Ted was saying, anyway. "It's just—well, with everything—and we didn't expect you this early, y'see... And I thought, tell you later, when it was quiet like—"

"Please do not worry yourself, Ted," Rose said kindly to the gangling stage manager, who appeared to be getting himself into quite a flap. "You did not need to inform me that Annabelle was assisting with the costume fitting. As long as it is ready for me on opening night—"

"But that's just the thing, y'see—"

"And I can see that you're testing the shoes too. And the coronet, my, my," said Rose lightly as she turned to examine the young woman. "And... And has someone done your hair, Annabelle?"

The girl flushed. Ted's stammers petered out into nothing.

Rose looked between them slowly, her pulse starting to race as though it knew something she did not.

There was something...wrong here. Something definitely wrong, though she could not entirely put her finger on it. Annabelle was not dressed up like Rose, she was dressed like...like Titania. And Ted was still gibbering, and he was not a man to lose track of his words.

And their expressions. Furrowed brows, pinched lips. Their expressions looked very worried, indeed, which was odd, because she was here now. Their greatest star had arrived. Rose would have presumed that their worry would have diminished now that she was here, not intensify.

Something was not right...

Annabelle, her cheeks flushed crimson, managed to say, "I-I thought they had told you."

Rose frowned, some of the warmth of being back in a theater diminishing. "Told me what?"

The young woman looked at Ted. Rose followed suit.

Ted was sweating, rivulets of perspiration trickling down his temples, and he was still wringing his hands together before him as though he were standing in the dock for murder.

As though he were guilty.

Rose took a slow step toward him and he backed up immediately, taking three steps for her one.

Very guilty. And there was only one crime that one could commit against an actress of such prestige and talent such as herself, Rose knew. She knew because she herself had committed it against the great Italian talent, Miss Margolotta. And the woman had never forgiven her.

Rose had not understood why at the time. She understood now.

"Am I to understand," she said coldly, driving ice into every syllable, "that I have been...replaced?"

Annabelle gave a whimper of nerves behind her, but that did

not interest her. No, Rose had fixed her steely expression upon Ted and poured into it as much loathing and imperious disgust as she possibly could.

And she was an actress. A good one.

The man looked as though he was about to wet his drawers. "N-Now *replace*, replace now, that is a strong word. I wouldn't say *replace*—"

"You did not say anything," Rose said sweetly, though no tenderness reached her eyes. She made certain of that. "You did not speak to me at all about any problems or concerns about my performance."

"It's just, well, Titania, Queen of the Dairies, you know. She must be—"

"Regal," Rose said impressively, ensuring that she projected the word around the large dressing room. "Impressive. Majestic. Experienced in the arts of the stage."

Even as she'd said the words, she could see that it would make no difference.

It never did. How many times had she seen this scene play out, but she was the one wearing the costume? She had been the one staring awkwardly, surprised that the older woman had not been told—but then, Rose recognized with searing guilt, she had always presumed that the older woman would have realized she was no longer suitable.

She had thought those older women... When she had been as fresh-faced as Annabelle, as idiotic, as naïve, she had believed those older women should have examined themselves in a looking glass and realized they were past their prime. They had seemed so...so *old*. Miss Margolotta had seemed ancient, now that she came to think of it, at eight and fifty.

And now Annabelle was looking at her not just with discomfort, but with...pride. It was that slight thrust forward of her chest, the straightened back. Pride, Rose could see, that she had been chosen to replace her.

Her.

"You must have seen this coming," Ted was blabbering. "I mean, you are a spot old—"

"I am five and twenty!" Rose hissed, the pretense of calm swiftly abandoned. "Dear God, man, you cannot tell me that is old!

"Five and twenty!" Annabelle's head recoiled as Rose cast her an irritated glance. "Goodness, and you are still acting!"

"I will still be acting when you are in the grave, you child," Rose shot over, unable to keep down her anger any longer. "What, you think you will not age? You think you will never reach such heady heights of experience as five and twenty?"

Annabelle drew herself up, which Rose had to admit—in the privacy of her own mind—looked rather striking in the Titania costume. "I shall be married by then," she said commandingly. "One day, I will be in the Society pages!"

The words echoed around the small room, but mostly, they echoed within Rose's mind.

*Dear Lord...*had she not thought that exact statement mere minutes ago? How was it possible that her dreams could so quickly be subsumed by a younger woman? A woman, moreover, barely out of the nursery?

"—must have predicted this," Ted was saying incoherently behind her. "After all, we could not cast you as one of the young women in the play, could we?"

Rose turned to him, directing her ire at the man who had made the decision. Yes, that was whom she should be angry at. "What do you mean, you could not? I chose to play Titania!"

"Titania was the only role that would suit a woman of your...your advanced years," Ted said awkwardly, swallowing rapidly, no doubt truly worried she would fly at him with a stage sword.

She hadn't completely discounted the notion. "'Advanced years'?"

The man was an imbecile. How could he think that a woman still in her prime, not even close to thirty years of age, was advanced in years?

Rose pushed aside all thoughts that contradicted her, all memories that a woman's prime in the theater was closer to twenty and that almost all the women who passed that age left the theater.

She had presumed...perhaps foolishly, she had always thought they had chosen to do so. That they had gone on to something better. Married well, or earned so much money, they did not need to work.

The very idea that they had been forced out, not slowly over time, but abruptly, turning up to the theater one day and discovering some chit of a girl in their own costume...

Rose slowly sank onto the chair that held her coat and scarves. "You did not cast me as Helena or Hermia because I am too *old*?"

"It would have been embarrassing," Annabelle said haughtily.

"You stay out of this, child," Rose shot back, temper sparking.

But the girl did not back down as she had expected. Perhaps it was the coronet that gave her strength. Perhaps she had realized that now she was the most impressive person in the room. Perhaps she gained comfort from the knowledge that she would be performing on opening night, and not this has-been woman before her, sitting on a chair.

Rose swallowed. *Opening night.* She needed that money—she needed *any* money, but she would not get paid until she had performed on opening night. If she was not performing on opening night, then she would not get paid.

All threats to her vanity and pride disappeared beneath the weight of reality.

She needed money. She needed this job—no. *Any job.*

"So. Annabelle and I will switch roles," Rose said stiffly, hardly believing she was saying this. "She will... She will play Titania. I will become a fairy, part of the chorus."

There was an awkward silence, and it grew more awkward the longer it continued.

Rose turned to stare at Ted. "Tell me you are keeping me in the chorus."

"Lots of young girls...looking to make a name, lots of them...very pretty, lots of—"

"Damn it, man, you cannot tell me that you are firing me!" The words tasted wrong in her mouth. They could not have been true. And yet why had she said them?

Rose's mind was spinning, or the room was spinning, and her lungs were tight and they weren't getting enough air because this could not have been happening. She had been forced to kiss a disgusting man for her first food in two days just minutes ago. Surely, she could not fall any farther than that?

Annabelle was looking pleased with herself. "You told me you would inform her, that I wouldn't have to!"

Ted grimaced. "I didn't expect her so early. She wasn't supposed to be here for hours yet."

"I can hear you, you know." Rose left the chair and straightened up with as much dignity as she could muster—which, in truth, was not much. "But I will not be able to hear you for long. If you truly think you can have a chit of a girl with no true acting experience play the momentous role of Titania—"

"*Rose!*" Ted said wretchedly.

"—then you have proven to me that your theater is in fact not interested in true art. You are interested in farce, mere coin," Rose said coldly.

The stage manager blinked as though she had started speaking nonsense. "Of... Of course I am interested in coin. Why do you think I run a theater?"

It was not what Rose had wished to hear, but then, none of today had been particularly uplifting. *At least,* she thought viciously as she pulled on her coat and bundled her two threadbare scarves around her neck, *the day cannot get any worse.*

"Goodbye," she said coldly as she turned to leave. Then she paused as a thought struck her, and she walked slowly up to the young woman.

Annabelle leaned back, but she was prevented from escaping by the wall behind her.

Rose grinned as she reached her. "And you. You haven't noticed, have you?"

Bless the child. She at least attempted to put up a fight. "'N-Noticed'?"

"Yes," Rose said sweetly. "You think this is your lucky chance, your moment to shine, your opportunity to become a celebrated actress, don't you? Society pages and all that."

The girl jutted out her chin. "Yes. Yes, I—"

"Then why hasn't Ted," whispered Rose darkly, knowing she shouldn't be enjoying this, "cast you as Helena or Hermia? The leads, Annabelle. Why has he given you, as he calls it, *the older woman's* role'?"

And there it was; the fear in her eyes. It flashed in Annabelle's pupils, full of panic, as her gaze flickered from Rose to Ted in growing concern.

Rose smiled, though the expected gratification did not feel nearly so sweet. In fact, it was replaced by guilt as she stepped away from the young woman before she swept out of the dressing room.

She had presumed she would feel...better, somehow. But the barbed words—true though they were—only made her feel even more empty.

The freezing-cold air was her only welcome as Rose stepped out of the Grand Theatre. It was a brutal reminder that she had little coin for firewood for her lodgings—and no hope of food.

What on earth was she going to do?

Panic, and fear, and terror, and anger… They all swirled in her stomach, causing a cacophony of thoughts to overwhelm her and all Rose could think to do was get to the beach as soon as possible and stare out at the waves and the emptiness of it all and remember that she was alone.

Alone, and she would have to think of something.

Not permitting any further thoughts, not even looking where

she was going, Rose stepped out in a rush and crossed the road, busy with carriages, and hastened down the pavement before turning a corner and—

A mountain stood in her way, the sudden collision crashing her to the ground. The hard, slightly damp, absolutely freezing ground.

Rose attempted to prevent herself from being unwittingly garroted by her own scarf and glared up at the mountain. "How dare you attack me, you brigand!"

The mountain blinked down at her. "That's a rather salty tongue you've got on you."

Chapter Two

Lord Samuel Chance, eldest son of the Marquess of Aylesbury and not a complete fool, was not the sort of person to stare. So he was not staring.

He was gaping.

"You... You... You just said... Would you mind saying that again?" he asked weakly.

The pear-shaped, square-jawed solicitor gathered his papers together and shuffled them into a neater pile. "I think you understood me the first time, my lord."

"But—" Samuel could not believe it. He could not believe it because it was entirely unbelievable...and it was clear that he was not the only one who thought so.

"The whole lot?" His younger brother, Benjamin, a tall man with sandy-blond hair, sounded incredulous and more than a little hurt. "Everything—it all goes to Samuel?"

"Absolutely everything," said Mr. Todd calmly, as though he had to give bad news to people all the time.

Which, now that Samuel came to think about it, he probably did.

"I'm sorry. I think this is hilarious." Frank grinned from the other end of the table. She had the sharp beauty that a woman with her brains resented, but no amount of apathy could turn her hair anything less than spectacular. "Samuel, the great heiress!"

"Hush, F-Francesca," admonished their mother, her silvering hair still brilliant and paired with a beautiful pair of sapphire earbobs.

"Call me 'Frank'!"

"It is indeed a sudden legacy," said John Chance, the Marquess of Aylesbury, calmly, as though his eldest son inherited a great deal of money every day of the week. He rubbed his graying temples then tugged at his cravat. "What we need to understand is why."

"But Great-Aunt Tessie barely knew Samuel!" Benjamin continued, as though their father had not spoken.

"Samuel was very g-good at v-visiting your Great-Aunt T-Tessie, weren't you, dear?" Florence Chance, Marchioness of Aylesbury, said fondly. "I s-s-suppose this is h-how she wished to reward y-you."

Samuel could see his brother getting redder and redder as Benjamin said, "But why on earth would she leave a small fortune to him, and only him? He's already heir to Father's title and estate!"

Mr. Todd cleared his throat. "Not precisely a *small* fortune, Lord Benjamin. I think you will find that along with the estate in Scotland, the palazzo in Rome—"

"Dear God!"

"—and a great number of investments in a wide and varied portfolio—"

"We're never going to hear the end of this," muttered Benjamin darkly, pushing back his hair in a harried movement. "Never."

"—your elder brother and his wife will be coming into a fortune of approximately one hundred and twenty thousand pounds," finished the solicitor gravely.

The chatter continued, most of it astonished, some of it irritable. Samuel was not able to take in much, for his ears were ringing and his mind had wandered out of his head to cry in a corner.

One hundred and twenty thousand pounds. One hundred and twenty thousand pounds. One hundred and twenty thousand pounds.

Twenty thousand pounds would have been a legacy far beyond his expectations. Two thousand! When was the last time he had seen Tessie—a month? Longer than that?

He had always intended to schedule another visit, but life had grown busy and then there had been Cousin Irene's wedding and the time had gotten away from him and now...

Now his great-aunt was gone. But she hadn't taken all her wealth with her.

One hundred and twenty thousand pounds.

"Yes, you and your wife are to take possession immediately," said Mr. Todd from a long way off.

"Well, there's nothing for it," came a calm, low, and measured voice that nonetheless captured the attention of all.

Samuel blinked as he looked up. The solicitor's office in Brighton came into view: a dark room, though that, of course, was the time of year, not helped by the dark-wooden paneling that lined the walls and the small number of candles. The large, mahogany table around which the Aylesbury branch of the Chance family was gathered only added to the sense of darkness in the room.

Though perhaps that is the point, Samuel thought wildly. Perhaps in a solicitor's office, where usually only bad news was delivered, it was right to have the place feeling a little somber.

It had been his father who had spoken. He was seated by Samuel's mother, the two of them with matching O-shaped lips, looking a mite surprised but just as fair of face as ever.

They were holding hands. Samuel prevented himself from snorting. They had been in love like that since as long as he could remember.

His brother, Benjamin, only two years younger and seated to his left, snorted. "'Nothing for it'? Yes, there's nothing for it. Samuel will go off and be rich—"

"You are hardly p-p-poor, d-dear," said his mother fondly.

There was something scratching at the back of Samuel's

mind. He couldn't put his finger on it, but there was something. Something someone had said, which had not been quite right...

"And just think what use I could put a *fraction* of such a fortune to," said Frank wistfully. "More copper piping than a girl could want!"

Samuel suppressed a smile at the solicitor's rapidly blinking eyes, the way the man's prominent jaw dropped. Most people reacted that way when they met his sister.

"I was going to say," said their father slowly, "that I have been thinking of doing something for some time, and what with this news, and the fact we are here at a solicitor's..."

Benjamin groaned. "I knew it."

Samuel looked between his brother and father. "Knew what?"

"It was only a matter of time." Frank sighed, shaking her beautiful head with an expression of deep discomfort. "We'll just have to hope he doesn't lord it over us."

Samuel cocked his head, not in on the joke, evidently. "Who? Lord what?"

"I am minded to pass on my title to my eldest son," said the Marquess of Aylesbury with a wry look. "Now. Before my death. Just as my elder brother has done for his own son."

And that was when Samuel's ears decided to simply stop working at all.

No. No, he wouldn't. His father had always said that he admired what his brother William, Duke of Cothrom, had done in prematurely handing over the title to Samuel's cousin Thomas, but that he would not do the same—and to be quite honest, Samuel had been relieved.

Being Lord Samuel Chance, eldest son of a marquess, was fun. He could have even more fun as Lord Samuel Chance, eldest son of a marquess in possession of one hundred and twenty thousand pounds.

But being the Marquess of Aylesbury? All that responsibility, and duty, and—here Samuel gulped—requirement to marry?

Oh, Lord. The mamas of good Society already hounded him

enough. He didn't need the addition of one hundred and twenty thousand pounds and a more notable title.

"I th-think it is an excellent idea," Samuel's mother was saying fondly. "Like a ret-t-tirement—I've been s-saying for years, you s-spend far too m-m-much time locked away in that study, w-working on the estates. It's d-difficult and compl-plicated work!"

Samuel groaned.

Benjamin crossed his arms over his chest and leaned back but still managed to send a smirk in Samuel's direction. "Oh, well, if you're going to have all that money to prop up the estate…"

"Your f-father has the p-place in very g-good financial h-h-health!" their mother said hotly.

"I'm just saying, it's not like Samuel won't be spending it on wine and women."

"A bold decision, but I know the Chances are renowned for such choices," Mr. Todd interjected with reddening cheeks. "My lord, I will need you and your wife to come back to the office in a week to sign the paperwork. There will be a great deal to be done."

Samuel looked at his father. John had rather been looking forward to returning to his London townhouse, his eldest son knew. The last thing he would want to do was linger in Brighton, of all places.

The strange thing was, everyone was looking at Samuel.

Samuel blinked. "What is it?"

"When M-Mr. Todd says, 'm-my lord,'" said his mother with a dry smile, "he m-means you."

It was a good thing Samuel was seated, for he would surely have suffered with weak knees had he been standing in that precise moment.

My lord was now…him? Well, once the formal abdication paperwork was completed.

Oh, he'd been Lord Samuel as a courtesy because of his father…but to be *a* lord in his own right?

Frank was giggling. "Your face!"

"The new Lord Aylesbury's face, I think you'll find," teased Benjamin. "Oh, goodness, Lilianna will be in hysterics when she hears!"

Samuel supposed their absent sister would find the thing amusing. The whole family would. Despite his brother's accusation earlier, Samuel wasn't particularly spendthrift or wasteful; he wasn't particularly bad at managing his accounts or anything like that. But to become a marquess in the matter of minutes...

And that was when his mind finally caught up with him, and he realized precisely what it was that had been nagging at him these last five minutes.

"Mr. Todd," Samuel said formally, "I will be happy to return in a week to sign any paperwork that needs seeing to, but I will not be able to bring my wife."

The solicitor blinked through thick spectacles. "She is not in Brighton?"

"She is not in existence," said Samuel with a wry expression. "I am unmarried."

It was not so much a confession as a declaration. He had never seen the problem with being unwed; he was, after all, only seven and twenty. There was plenty of time to find a wife if he so chose—though now that he came to think about it, now that he'd inherited the damned title, he should probably think more seriously about it.

In five years or so.

Which was why it was so odd that Mr. Todd should look so stricken. "No—No wife?"

"No wife. Not yet, anyway," Samuel added, seeing his mother's eyes lighting up. "I am sure, one day—"

"'One day' will be insufficient," interrupted the solicitor. "That won't do at all!"

It was not in Samuel's nature to grow irritated with tradespeople, and he supposed being a solicitor was not quite a tradesman. But he was hardly a gentleman, and to be spoken to in such a fashion! The cheek of the man!

Ah.

Dear Lord, it was remarkable how quickly one took on airs and graces. He'd only been a marquess for five minutes. Not even officially one until papers were drawn up.

"'Won't do'?" repeated Samuel.

The solicitor chewed his lip as he quickly rustled through the papers before him. "No, no, let me see... Yes, the precise wording is 'And I leave all my otherworldly goods and possessions to my eldest great-nephew and his wife.'"

The man looked up at Samuel, his eyebrows drawing together as he grew still, as if to observe the new marquess before him. Samuel waited for the rest of the sentence, which would surely explain why the man was so troubled.

"And?" he said eventually, when Mr. Todd said no more.

The solicitor took off his spectacles and looked seriously at Samuel. "My lord, the wording is quite specific. If you are unmarried by the time the estate must be passed over, one week from today... Well, I cannot sign it over to you. It must go to the late contessa's eldest great-nephew and wife. Without the wife, there is no fortune of one hundred and twenty thousand pounds."

There was a great deal of silence in the room as everyone attempted to take in the man's words.

Samuel blinked. Then he blinked again. The solicitor was saying more, but he could not hear the man.

This... This could not be. It was a trick of the law and could somehow be undone, could it not? Surely, he would not be prevented from accessing the greatest fortune in the family merely because he was unmarried?

The silence was broken by his sister.

"Contessa? Great-Aunt Tessie was a contessa? And what was that name you referred to her as... So are you telling us," Frank said slowly, as though weighing every word carefully, "are you saying that...that Great-Aunt Tessie's name was not Tessie, but that it was a nickname due to her title?"

"*Frank!*" cried the whole family in censure.

Well, the whole family save for Samuel. He was still reeling from the news that due to a lack of wife, there would soon be a lack of fortune.

"M-My aunt has always b-been—*was* always—that way," said the marchioness. "She spent almost her whole life abroad, d-doing who knows what. At one point, she b-became a c-contessa and visited home. W-Wouldn't tell us why she'd g-gotten the title, muttered something about a brief marriage. We d-d-didn't ask an-ny questions. It b-became a bit of a joke with my family."

Mr. Todd nodded, but his smile didn't reach his eyes, as if this tidbit of family history were hardly worth considering. "I am afraid the wording is precise and the stipulation specific." He put his spectacles back on as he re-examined the paper before him. "I suppose, if you were to marry in the next week, though a special license would need to be procured and the Archbishop of Canterbury—"

And that was when the stupidest words that Samuel had ever uttered slipped from his mouth, so fast, he could not catch them back.

"I *am* married."

Samuel froze, almost horrified at what he had said. His father's eyebrows rose, Frank's mouth fell open, Benjamin merely stared, immobile, and his mother cleared her throat.

"S-S-Samuel, dear, the m-money does not matter. It will st-stay in my family, after all. I b-b-believe my cousin's son m-married only last year. P-Perhaps he will inherit."

"I am married. Secretly. I got married secretly." With every syllable, Samuel knew he was making the situation worse and yet he did not appear to be able to stop himself. The lies kept slipping out, more and more. "I didn't wish to tell anyone because... because... Well. I didn't want a fuss. Look at Lilianna, such a large wedding. No, I didn't want—"

"You mean to tell me that *you are married?*" his father interrupted him with wide eyes.

"Rubbish!" said Benjamin at the same time. "When would this have happened? Where has she been?"

"It's not like you're ever long from home, *brother dear*," said Frank with a tad of mockery added to the term of endearment. "When have you been seeing this bride of yours?"

Samuel ignored his siblings and focused on his father. He did not know how he'd explain away this story, but he'd spent time away from his family over the past year. Even a couple of days would explain it. And his wife, well... He'd come up with some reason why she'd stayed away from the Chance family home.

Samuel opened his mouth and then hesitated. He had never lied to his father. He was not a liar. But now that he had said the words, and with a solicitor—and more importantly, his mother—present, there did not appear to be a way to escape. "Yes. Yes. I'm married."

Silence once again fell in the solicitor's office, until Mr. Todd cleared his throat. "Well, that's that settled, then. If you and the marchioness will come in next week, we can finish the matter."

"But my mother will be returning to—" Samuel caught himself, though not quickly enough.

Of course. The damned man meant Samuel's own wife... The wife who did not exist. *Damn.*

"Yes, yes," he said instead, hoping to cover the blunder.

Benjamin was smirking. "So when do we get to meet the new Marchioness of Aylesbury?"

"Soon," said Samuel, hoping to goodness his mind would soon crank into gear and offer him solutions. "Soon."

His mind gave him absolutely nothing as the Chance family rose and shook hands with Mr. Todd, the marquess—the dowager marquess, Samuel supposed, if he followed his uncle dowager duke's odd titling convention—leaning close to discuss something that Samuel didn't hear. His mind appeared to have no thoughts whatsoever as they left the solicitor's office, his head numb and his fingers cold as they stepped out into the cold Brighton air.

"All right, then," said the dowager marquess as he led his wife to the conveyance awaiting the family. "Let me help you into the carriage, my dear, but I must stay a short while behind. Mr. Todd has agreed to draw up the paperwork transferring the title and estate to our son posthaste. Best to get it done before his other inheritance paperwork."

"Of-Of course," said the dowager marchioness. "The ch-children and I will just be returning to the hotel for a sp-pot of luncheon. S-Samuel, do you need to stay behind as well? Th-That is, I would like to hear more about where you've been keeping your wife, b-but…"

Samuel waved a hand, barely following along with what everyone else was talking about. "Yes. Yes, I suppose. All in good time. I, erm, I'll go for a walk along the seafront first."

"Good man," said his father approvingly. "Clear your head. We need some time to finish the paperwork regardless. All we'll need is for you to sign."

It isn't possible to clear my head any further, Samuel wanted to say, *because it was completely empty when I spoke and now I don't know what to do about this lie!*

Instead, he said, "Yes. Yes. Clear my head."

Clear his head. *As though my mind weren't already clear*, Samuel thought forebodingly as he stomped away from his family and toward where he presumed the sea to be. *Empty of all sense.*

What had possessed him to say such a thing? Telling his family—his mother!—that he was married?

It was a lie, a lie that would have consequences. He couldn't live in that lie forever. His family would expect to meet this mysterious wife of his. That lawyer man, Mr. Todd, would expect him, Samuel, to turn up next week and sign a document alongside his wife. A wife who did not exist.

Well, I will have to think of something, Samuel thought feverishly as he marched along the street almost without taking in his surroundings. He could hardly expect the solution to fall into his lap—

"How dare you attack me, you brigand!"

Samuel stared down at a woman who was lying on the pavement before him. Why was she doing such a thing? "That's a rather salty tongue you've got on you."

The words were instinctive, the sort of teasing jest that he would say to his sister Frank. Now he came to think about it, he rather thought he *had* said such words to Frank.

There was a strange ache within him. For a moment, Samuel thought it was the remnants of guilt for lying to his mother...then he realized that the woman, whoever she was, must have walked clean into him.

Honestly! Could she not look where she was going?

"Are you going to help me up," asked the woman peevishly, "or are you a complete cad?"

Samuel bristled but offered a hand. "I am not a cad."

"No, mountains cannot be cads," muttered the woman as she grasped his hand and used him to pull herself up. Now upright, she dusted herself down then glared up at him, as though he had committed a mortal injury. "What?"

What... What? What? "What?" Samuel repeated stupidly, his mind still panicking in a corner of Mr. Todd's office.

The woman rolled her eyes. "Lord save me from idiotic men today—what are you looking at, sir?"

Samuel swallowed.

You, he wanted to say. *You. You're... You're beautiful.*

She truly was. Oh, she was not dressed particularly beautifully; the coat had seen better days, and one of the scarves that had been around her neck had fallen to the pavement but had immediately blended in with the grey stone. But her hair...her hair was golden and beautifully pinned. Her figure was slight, but strong—he could tell even through the thick folds of the coat—and her face...

Samuel swallowed. He came from a family of particularly good-looking people, he knew, and so in a way, he was inured to the presence of beautiful women. His own sister Lilianna was a renowned beauty, but Samuel had never really noticed.

He was noticing this one. The woman's lips were pink and her face was flushed and there was such elegance in her appearance that it contrasted strangely with the unkempt clothing and the wrinkled nose and pinched mouth comprising her harassed expression. Why, she could be a countess!

"What, I say, are you looking at?" the woman snapped.

Samuel cleared his throat. "I do beg your pardon."

"And another thing, I—what did you say?" The woman took a swift step back, seemingly entirely taken aback by his swift apology.

Interesting, Samuel could not help but think. She did not expect kindness. She certainly was not experiencing good fortune. "What is your name?"

From the jut of her chin, the woman appeared displeased with the direction of conversation, but good manners evidently made her say, "Morgan. Rosemary Morgan."

She spoke the name imperiously, as though he would recognize it.

Samuel did not. "My name is—is Samuel. Where are you going in such a hurry, Miss Morgan?"

Her focus ranged over him, and Samuel could see that she was taking in the impressive great coat, the refined fit of his suit, the way he held himself. She could not have been more obvious in her appreciation for him—*for my money*, Samuel thought ominously.

Then his stomach jolted. *My suddenly increasing money.*

"I am an actress," Miss Morgan said grandly, as though he should have known and it was a mere kindness that she was reminding him. "I have graced the stage across Europe! I was feted for my Juliet, praised for my Katherine, adored for my—"

"'An... An actress'?" Samuel repeated.

Something in his mind was starting to percolate, and he hardly dared examine the thought in case it melted away.

Miss Morgan's shoulders sagged. "Yes, an actress. An actress out of work, for the present, for I have been callously and most scandalously cast aside by a—"

"'Out of work'?" echoed Samuel, his spine tingling.

Out of work. An out-of-work actress. A beautiful, aristocratic-looking woman who was clearly down on her luck, able to act...

"Yes, and it is something history will never forgive the Grand Theatre." Miss Morgan sniffed, as though she had been conned out of a great prize, but in fact she, herself, was the prize. "Looked over for being old!"

Samuel blinked. "'Old'?"

Old? The woman could not be more than... Well. Four to six and twenty? She was still young, and beautiful, and rather alluring, to tell the truth.

Miss Morgan held her head high. "That is what they tell me. For that, I am cast out of my latest production and now have no work at all to speak of! The audacity!"

Samuel grinned. "That is most excellent news."

His statement had clearly nettled her as a brisk, wintry breeze tugged at her hair, which she rapidly tried to keep out of her face as if pawing away the irritation Samuel had caused her. "It is most certainly *not* excellent news! It is an outrage! It is a scandal! It is an insult of the greatest measure!"

"Yes, yes, most unpleasant," he said hastily. *Goodness, but the woman can speak.* "But my point is, you are currently without employment and therefore looking for some. And you are an actress."

Yes, it might just work. *It is foolishness itself,* Samuel thought wildly, *but was it not foolishness that had gotten him into this mess in the first place?* Was it possible that an equally foolish act in the opposite direction would balance the whole thing out?

Miss Morgan was glaring, clearly highly suspicious. "Are you quite well?"

"Very well, thank you," Samuel said brightly. "Look, Miss Morgan, I may have a job for you. For an actress such as yourself. Out of work."

She took a hasty step back. "I don't do anything like that, sir, and you offend me by even suggesting I would—"

"No! No, nothing like that," he said quickly. He was no innocent; he knew the ways that many actresses found to make money when parts dried up. "No, this would be...different."

Still entirely unethical, Samuel could not help but think. *But not like that.*

"I think I have a part for you to play," he said slowly, his mind racing. *Could this work?* "Would you be willing to discuss it with me tomorrow?"

He would have to look into some of the legality of the thing—he couldn't talk to Mr. Todd, but there must have been another solicitor in this town who would be up for the task.

"Tomorrow?" repeated Miss Morgan, her expression curious but clearly wary. "Over... Over luncheon? You would pay?"

Samuel tried not to grin. Without work and clearly hungry. That was all to the good; he would need someone who could be relied upon, and there was no one more reliable than someone depending on the scheme for their next meal.

"Tomorrow, and I will pay for luncheon at—" Blast, there had to be a second hotel in this place. He could hardly meet the woman where he and his family were staying...

"Francois's Restaurant. Near the bathing huts," Miss Morgan said quickly, as though concerned he would lose interest. "At midday?"

Samuel smiled and held out his hand. "It's a bargain."

Chapter Three

January 3, 1841

T HIS WAS A mistake.
Rose was not normally one to focus on her instincts; she had never needed to. She could manufacture instincts on command. She was an actress.

Now, as she stood outside Francois's Restaurant, she was listening to her instincts, and they said, *Don't go in.*

There was surely something strange about the tall man—Samuel, though whether that was a first name or surname, Rose did not know. The man had not introduced himself properly, cad that he was, and precisely why she had bothered to agree to meet him here and then had actually turned up, she did not know.

Her stomach rumbled.

Well, Rose thought bleakly, *perhaps because of that.* But no other reason. She would listen to his ridiculous idea, whatever it was, eat as much as was physically possible, and then leave. She had to concoct a plan of survival, and no great ideas had arrived last night as she'd sat in bed all evening—that being the warmest part of the room—desperately trying to think.

So. Luncheon, hear his nonsense, then back to her lodgings. That was all.

The wonderful heat of the hotel filled her lungs as Rose stepped forward, and though her hunger could still not be ignored, her stiff shoulders loosened slightly as the warmth caressed them.

That was when the scent hit her.

Oh, goodness, there was roast potatoes, and red wine, and garlic, and—

"There you are," said a confident voice as a man stepped toward her. "I was starting to think you were going to be late."

Samuel... Mr. Samuel, or Samuel something, Rose did not know, but Samuel nonetheless. He smiled, and she felt her lips curling in an immediate response.

Which was foolish. The man looked just the same as he had yesterday, just as tall, just as broad, just as achingly handsome—

Which was ridiculous. Rose had met enough actors to know that anyone could ooze confidence if they put their mind to it, and there was nothing more attractive than confidence.

She returned his smile. *Confidence.* "Good afternoon, Mr....?"

"Call me 'Samuel,'" said the man, ignoring all etiquette and gesturing forward. "Shall we? I have booked a table."

Excellent—the man clearly had money. *Perhaps he is a patron of the arts*, Rose thought with a spark of joy as they stepped forward into the restaurant part of the hotel and the scents of food and delicious wine only increased. A man who perhaps sponsored a theater—a play! He was looking for the next Cleopatra. He wanted a Lady Macbeth. He needed—

"I need a menu," said Samuel, pulling out a chair for her but speaking to a waiter, who bowed his head immediately. "And a bottle of your best red wine."

Their best? Rose tried not to appear impressed as she sat down and allowed Samuel to push the chair in under her. Well, the man certainly had money to burn. If he made her an offer of a role, she was hardly in a position to decline...but still. There was something odd about him.

Rose examined her dining companion as Samuel took the seat opposite her. He was well dressed, certainly. His tailor had earned a pretty penny and the man's hair was elegantly coiffed, suggesting a valet. Oh, he was a gentleman, to be sure, but that did not answer the most important question.

Was he about to offer her the role of a lifetime?

"This place is pleasant," Rose said aloud, as the man did not appear to wish to say anything. In fact, he was gawping.

"Yes, very pleasant," said Samuel vaguely. "Have you any family, Miss Morgan?"

Rose stiffened, and for more than one reason. *Miss Morgan.*

What sort of a question was that?

The sort of question that a predator asked of its prey.

Well, at least she had been wise enough to meet the man in a public place. She would have to be certain he did not follow her to her lodgings, but then, Rose was the great Miss Morgan. She had fought off admirers for years.

Ha! For years. Yes, that was precisely why Ted had let her go, wasn't it?

"Miss Morgan? Ah, yes, I'll have the soup, then the salmon, and where is that red wine? Ah, here it is," said Samuel blithely, as though ordering people about and getting his own way was a tad pedestrian. "And you, Miss Morgan?"

Rose blinked. "Me?"

"What will you have? I hear the salmon is very good, but there's partridge and roast beef if you prefer," said the man companionably.

Salmon, partridge, roast beef... It would be too much to ask for all three, wouldn't it?

Just for a moment, Rose's stomach threatened to overwhelm her good manners. When was the last time she had consumed a hot meal? Not a pie, or a pasty from the street. An actual hot meal, on a plate, with a knife and fork?

Rose looked down at the knife and fork. A lesser mortal would have forgotten how to use a knife and fork.

She looked up at the silent waiter. "The partridge to start, then the roast beef. And all the trimmings. And extra potatoes. And gravy."

The slight tilt of his head, that tiny look of incredulity that the waiter gave Samuel, did not pass unnoticed. "But madam, the partridge, it is not a starter. It is a main course."

"I said what I wanted," Rose said imperiously, looking down her nose at the man who was standing above her, which was no mean feat. "Go along."

The waiter bowed, and bowed to Samuel—which was odd—before hurrying away.

When Rose turned back to her dining companion, it was to see that Samuel was not only smiling faintly but nodding to himself.

Nodding?

"Very good," he said aloud.

Rose frowned, her mouth watering as he poured her a glass of wine. A very large glass. "What is?"

"You are," he said brightly. "You are precisely the sort of person I was looking for. An excellent actress."

It was difficult not to preen, and so Rose did not attempt to. It was delightful, after that debacle with Annabelle, to be so praised. "You have heard of me, then?"

"Not in the slightest," came the slightly less flattering remark. "But I am already impressed by your talents. Might you regale me with a list of some of your roles on the stage?"

A sense of peace radiated over Rose, loosening the tension in her shoulders, as it felt more like a proper interview now. She listed a number of her roles, as well as the venues, her chest puffing more with each entry on her list.

Eventually, Samuel held up a hand. "Thank you. Impressive, but I've heard quite enough. At this point, I prefer to see more of your talents in action."

Rose opened her mouth to ask precisely what talents he was speaking of when their starters arrived. The partridge was...large.

"You did say," began the waiter.

"I know what I said," Rose replied eagerly, placing her napkin on her lap and trying not to salivate openly. Goodness, it smelled spectacular, with a plum dressing and crispy skin and—

Oh, dear God. It tasted even better.

Trying not to moan in delight, Rose swiftly consumed five

mouthfuls of the thing before looking up and realizing that Samuel was staring, soft eyes brimming with unbridled delight.

She bristled. "What?"

"You know, I thought for a moment that I should not suggest my...my plan to you," said Samuel, the corner of his mouth quirking upward. "And now I can see you are just perfect for it. You're pretty, too. That helps."

Vague passing compliments from gentlemen who did not even bother to properly introduce themselves were not supposed to be so pleasing. Rose tried not to flush. It did not work, which was most odd. She had always been expertly in control of her flushes. It had been what made her such a great Rosalind.

"Helps how?" she asked warily, trying not to swallow a roast potato whole.

Samuel leaned back in his chair and examined her for a moment. When he spoke, it was in a cautious tone. "I am in somewhat of a predicament and I believe you may be the person to help me."

"A predicament?" Rose repeated.

There were those instincts again. They were telling her to run—well, to finish her luncheon then run—and not give this man the time of day. They were telling her, in truth, that this was not a man to be trusted.

The man shrugged. "A vaguely complex legal matter. One I cannot overcome alone."

Rose glared. Well, she finished the last carrot, had a large swig of the heady wine, *then* glared. "I am not a thief, nor a liar."

"And I would not ask you to be one," Samuel said smoothly. "In fact, if you are able to help me in this...this delicate matter, you would actually make me less of a liar than I have already been to my mother."

To his mother? That was interesting. The lie, whatever it was, clearly bothered him. Rose was a student of the arts, an actress extraordinaire, and that meant she could read body language better than she could read a book.

The man was nervous. Unsure of himself, unsure of this plan, and certain, she could see it in the flinch of his jaw, that he had no other option.

Interesting. So he needed her.

"I think you had better tell me what sort of problem you have managed to get yourself into," Rose said slowly. "Then we can see just how my acting abilities—extraordinary as they are—can help you. *If* they can help you."

"Oh, they can help me," said Samuel blithely as Rose took another sip—fine, a gulp—of the delicious red wine. "I need you to become my wife."

Rose sprayed red wine across the white tablecloth.

"Oh, dear, did it go down the wrong way?" Samuel asked calmly. "Here, have my napkin."

It was a miracle she did not have red wine dribbling down her chin. Lifting her own napkin to frantically dab at her lips, Rose spluttered, "B-Become your w-wife? You cannot be serious!"

"Deadly serious, I'm afraid," said Samuel cheerfully. "I need a wife by the end of the week."

Rose stared at the man who was clearly insane. *Need a wife—by the end of the week?* "One does not proposition love and marriage to random women whom one accosted on the street!"

"No, they don't." His voice was low and level, and there was an expression of strange calm across Samuel's face. "But they do offer a financial arrangement that includes matrimony to an actress who will play the part well, with the understanding that an annulment would be sought after a year and a day, and there would be...financial recompense provided."

Rose ceased dabbing her chin and stared at the man.

He could not be serious. He wished to *buy* a wife? No sane woman would ever...

But then, he did not want a woman who would fall in love with him, did he? She could see that; this Samuel, Samuel whatever his name was, had clearly formed some sort of scheme that would require a wife, but only a momentary one.

To be sure, there were plenty of gentlemen who wished for the same thing. That was why they went to brothels.

But this man... This man wanted something different.

"Ah, you are finished," said the waiter, appearing out of nowhere. "Excellent."

He cleared away their first course as Rose stared in mute confusion at the man who was treating her to luncheon. He did not seem to be a madman. There was no frothing at the mouth, no staring at the ceiling and muttering, "Mad, mad, they called me!" He had not attempted to hurt her, if one discounted the crash in the street, and she supposed that might have been accidental.

Financial recompense provided.

"Tell me why you need a wife," Rose said slowly, "and why you won't need one after a year and a day. That's mightily specific."

Samuel shrugged. "I technically only need one for a single day, but the ruse will be impractical if it does not continue for longer."

"And you need a wife for a single day…because?"

His answer, whatever it was about to be, was interrupted by the arrival of their main course. Rose's mouth watered as she breathed in the beef roasted to perfection, a double portion of roast potatoes, peas, carrots, parsnips—

"And another bottle of red wine, please," Samuel was saying.

Rose blinked and looked at her wineglass. Goodness. She would have to slow down.

"Look," said Samuel heavily as he gestured to start eating. "I have come into some money, but it has been left to myself and my wife. Without a wife, I cannot collect it."

Rose narrowed her eyes and said, "A great deal of money, I suppose?"

At least, that was what she had intended to say. What actually came out, due to the fact that she had stuffed three forkfuls of delicious food into her mouth faster than she could swallow, was,

"A gwaff feel of funny, I spopose?"

She swallowed and tried her best to look dignified. "Is it a lot of money?"

Samuel hesitated, and that told her everything she needed to know. "Yes."

"And so you need a wife to collect the money. And then what, I wait about in a manor house you buy with the proceeds?" Rose asked, testing the waters as she had another sip of wine.

After all, one wished to know how one was to spend a year and a day in the company of this man. And whether they would...surely, they would not—

"A manor I buy with the proceeds? Oh, no, I believe my London townhouse will be sufficient," said Samuel with a shrug.

"You intend to buy one?"

"I already have one," said the man blithely, as though everyone did.

Rose tried not to gape, and thanks to over a decade in the theater, she managed it. She doubted someone like Annabelle could have heard such a thing with such sanguinity.

Besides, London... It had been a long time since she'd been there. Her family had rarely—and they wouldn't go now, would they?

"Oh, I see," she said, as though she did. "So you need a wife. For a day. You'll keep her for a year extra and then turn her out?"

It was almost laughable. Did the man truly think he could hire a wife?

"Oh, no, my wife will receive a lump sum and a generous pension," Samuel said calmly, as though negotiating for a wife were a daily occurrence. Lord knew, maybe it was. "An annulment, naturally, not a divorce. It would be imperative that my wife and I... Well. Not consummate."

His ears were red and yet he held her attention calmly.

Rose struggled to keep her giggles under control. This was surely a farce! A joke, a jest. Men did not meet women in the street and offer to marry them!

Her need to giggle faded away as she looked into Samuel's eyes and saw no laughter there.

"You think this a joke?" he asked quietly.

"It isn't?" asked Rose blandly. "Forgive me, sir, but you must admit this sort of scheme is beyond strange. There cannot be many people who plan a marriage to gain money—"

"In my circles, they do it all the time," interrupted Samuel with a droll smile. "They call it naught but custom. That is what they consider marriage is for."

Her eyes widened. *All the time?*

"My point is—your circles?"

The slight shifting in his chair, the way his eyes moved from her to his wineglass. "Yes."

Rose frowned. There was something more going on here, something more that she did not know—and that was something she did not like. "Precisely what sort of circle is that?"

Samuel looked at her again, and his gaze was not so much penetrating as examining. As though he could trust her, perhaps? He knew nothing of her, after all.

"Do you have any family, Miss Morgan?"

Rose bristled. "I asked—"

"I think you will find that I have already asked you that very question, before we even ordered our food, Miss Morgan," said Samuel politely—or as politely as one can when one is interrupting another, Rose could not help but think. It helped that he was so handsome. Handsome people always got away with things.

She should know. She was one of them.

"I have no family," she said curtly. Well, there was no harm in telling him that. "None who still live who will own me. I have not seen them for a very long time. I dare say they have all died now."

Samuel inclined his head. "I am sorry for your losses."

"Don't be. They were lost to me a long time ago," said Rose, ignoring the twitch in her stomach.

She was not going to think about them. She was not.

"So there is no one to defend your honor, should I seek an annulment," he continued, making clear precisely why he wished to know.

Rose stiffened. "Should I require someone to defend my honor?"

"Are you accepting my proposal?" Samuel returned without missing a beat.

Opening her mouth to retort that of course she was not, it was the most ridiculous thing she had ever heard, Rose found that she instead filled that open mouth with a bite of delicious and succulent roast beef.

This made it difficult to answer for two reasons. Firstly, because she had her mouth full. She was not so unladylike as to speak with her mouth full, even if the man was propositioning her.

Secondly, because it reminded her just how good food tasted. One did not appreciate the variety of good food, any food, until it had been absent. And it had been absent.

Rose inhaled deeply. "What is your name, Samuel? All of it, I mean."

The hesitation should have told her everything. "It is not important for you to know."

"Oh, I think it is. If you are proposing matrimony to me, which I think you are, even if it is by arrangement and by mutual agreement to cease in just over a year..." said Rose carefully. A little Rosalind, a little Lady Capulet... "I think I deserve to know what name I shall be known by for that year."

Samuel swallowed. She attempted not to notice the bob of his throat, or the edge of his jawline, or how his shirt was so tight. All of which she failed at.

"My name," he said quietly, "is Samuel Chance."

Chance. Chance—did she not know that name?

"Chance," she repeated quietly. "That is a name of some repute, is it not?"

The fact that he laughed did not answer her question, and

when the man saw her expression, he added, "Yes. Yes, it is. In fact it will be shortly announced that I am the new Marquess of Aylesbury."

Marquess of—

"Your father died and left you a title and money, but only if you are married?" Rose asked in horror.

Truly, nothing had changed in the nobility and aristocracy...

"Not exactly," said Lord Samuel Chance, newly titled Marquess of Aylesbury, man of mystery. "But when I find a wife—and I will find a wife, Rose—she and I will inherit my Great-Aunt Tessie's fortune. That wife will live in luxury, in warm and luscious homes, wearing fine silks and eating delicious food eight times a day if she wishes."

Rose leaned closer, despite herself. There was something truly seductive about the man's voice—and the man's words.

"She will take tea with my family, and smile, and act the perfect marchioness because that is what she will have to be," Samuel continued, his dark eyes raking hers. "And when she and I reach our first wedding anniversary—though if anyone asks, we must pretend we married weeks ago, for reasons I will explain in time—we will go to a solicitors and sign a few pieces of paper, and my wife will have never been my wife. She will, however, be in possession of ten thousand pounds and a pension of a thousand pounds a year. She can go off and live her life any way she chooses."

Rose swallowed.

Ten thousand pounds—and a yearly income of a thousand pounds, all gained if she sat around in fancy townhouses and played at marchioness?

Why, it was a role of a lifetime.

And then she asked the question which she was almost certain would lose her any hope of gaining access to such a role. "Why me?"

Samuel blinked. "Why not you?"

"I am a nobody. I am an actress without work, without support, without..." Rose's voice trailed away. "I will be in your debt."

"You will be unlikely to disagree with me, yes," said Samuel quietly. "I am willing to take a chance on you, Miss Morgan. I need a wife, soon, and an actress who can play the part well enough to fool my mother—at least for a time—is what I need. The question is, will you take a chance on me?"

Rose swallowed. Her mouth, so recently filled with enchanting and resplendent food, was somehow dry. The temptation to take another sip of the rich, berry-red wine was strong, but as she looked at her glass, she rather wondered whether this newly titled marquess had been topping it up without her noticing.

"*I am willing to take a chance on you, Miss Morgan.*"

It was a chance, a ridiculous one that no actress had surely ever received before. The role of a marchioness—even better, with all the trimmings. Why, Rose thought rapidly, she could order gowns and buy jewels and all sorts of things that surely this man would not want to keep. She could gain far more than a *mere* ten thousand pounds.

And all it would take was...marrying him.

"You wish to decline."

The man's disappointment was strange to hear. Rose looked up to see Samuel slumped back in his seat. So, he had no other options but herself. That meant she could negotiate—and the first rule of negotiation, as any actress worth her salt knew, was timing.

"I need time to think," she said quietly.

A flash of hope in Samuel's eyes told her that she had him.

Or perhaps not quite. "I don't have much time," he reminded her. "I need a wife by the end of the week."

"So a day will not matter," said Rose brusquely. "You start work on that special marriage license and I... I will think."

Just as soon as I work out precisely what to think, she could not help but wonder in the privacy of her own mind.

"And are there ices as part of this dinner?" she added, her

stomach rumbling despite the great amount of food she had shoveled into it. "I adore ices. Are there ices?"

"There can be ices. Well, your suggestion is fair. Until tomorrow, then," said Samuel with a laugh. "Now, would you like to see the dessert menu? Or shall I just order one of everything, doubling the ices?"

Rose grinned. "How well you know me already."

Chapter Four

January 4, 1841

SAMUEL TRIED NOT to tap on the table.

"Will you stop tapping on the table?" Frank muttered irritably from behind a large notebook splattered with ink. "You are fast becoming the most irritating of the family, you know."

Samuel glanced over at Benjamin, who was flirting with one of the waitresses at the hotel while their parents weren't looking.

"Yes, even worse than him," came his sister's voice over her scribblings with a drafting pencil.

That was not a good sign. By general agreement, the Chance family—at least, the Aylesbury side—knew that Benjamin was the most irritating. It had always been that way. Samuel could hardly recall a time when it was not.

And now he was worse?

"I'm sorry," he mumbled, leaning back in his chair and sitting on his hands. It appeared to be the only way he could stop himself.

A whole day. More, seven and twenty hours. That was how long it had been since he had last been sitting with Miss Rosemary Morgan.

Not that it was her presence itself that he was missing, obviously, Samuel tried to reassure himself. He was in no danger there! No, it was the fact that another day had almost completely passed, and he was no closer to finding a wife.

He needed a wife. That money would disappear off to some distant cousin, Samuel knew, whom Great-Aunt Tessie had never met and certainly would not like. And he had plans for that money. Big plans—plans that would require a wife.

And speaking of the need to find a wife...

"And when, p-precisely, are we going to meet this wife of yours?" his mother asked, turning her attention back to the table. "I am g-glad you are wed, of course, but to have n-never met her..." She shook her head.

"I suppose you got her in trouble," muttered his father.

Samuel flushed. "Not at all!"

"Then I d-do not understand w-why we have n-not m-met her." The Dowager Marchioness of Aylesbury was not usually one to raise her voice, but there was an element of pique in her tone. "But st-still, I am g-glad of her. I examined the f-f-family t-tree, and the heir is m-my second cousin, Ebenezer."

Though Samuel had never heard of the man, his mother's obvious distaste was enough. "An unpleasant man?"

"A slave owner," said his father shortly. "An owner of those nefarious mills in the north, the ones that only employ children. A brigand."

A brigand? Strong words from his father.

The dowager marchioness's breath hitched. "B-B-Benjamin Chance, p-put that woman d-down!"

The waitress flushed beetroot red, scampered away from their table, and left Samuel's brother sighing as he leaned back in his chair.

"Honestly, Mama, it was a *conversation*."

"It was just inviting scandal, that's what it was," snapped their father with a stern look. "Why can't you be more like your brother?"

Samuel winced as Benjamin muttered curses.

Why can't you be more like your brother? Yes, it was a valid wish for any parent...though as soon as his mother and father realized he had completely lied about the existence of a wife to gain access to a fortune... Well. They may reassess their preference of sons.

"My lord?"

Samuel looked up. A footman from the hotel was standing beside him with an arrogant expression on his face. "Yes?"

"A note for you, my lord," said the footman quietly.

As expected, Samuel's father looked up. "Ah, another post has arrived?"

"No, my lord. This was delivered...personally."

"'Personally'?" repeated Samuel, bemused. He had no acquaintance in Brighton, did he? From what he could recall, the family had never been to Brighton. Been through it, perhaps, but never stayed. It was only Great-Aunt Tessie's will reading which had brought them here at all. So who could it have been?

"'P-Personally'?" repeated his mother, her eyes lighting up. "S-Samuel, is it from your w-wife? W-Why are you h-hiding her from us?"

"Yes, why?" asked Benjamin with a wry grin. "Or are you hiding us from her?"

"*Frank!*"

The name was uttered in almost a shriek from their mother, and Samuel knew precisely why. It was because his sister had come down for afternoon tea before their parents, and so she had been seated by the time the dowager marquess and marchioness had joined them.

That meant they had not seen, until now, precisely what his sister was wearing...

"What have I told you about wearing trousers in public!" hissed their father, his brow furrowed. "Honestly, you'll never find a husband if you keep this up!"

"Trousers are far more practical for my work."

"What work could you possibly be doing here, at the Regent's Hotel, that would necessitate *that*?"

Samuel allowed the family's conversation—well, hushed argument while the other guests in the dining hall of the Regent's Hotel stared at them curiously—to wash over him as he slowly opened the envelope that had been presented to him.

His brother may only have been teasing when he'd asked

why Samuel was hiding her, but perhaps he was right. Perhaps this note was from his soon-to-be wife...

It was short. It was sharp. And it was to the point.

~~Sir~~ *My lord,*

I require a conversation. Now. I am outside.

Miss M

Well, she clearly could not waste money on paper. Samuel supposed he had to be grateful for something.

He rose from his seat just as Frank threatened to take off her trousers right there, right then if her father was so worried about her wearing them.

"I have an errand to run," said Samuel.

"I'll come with you," said Benjamin with a snort of laughter at their father's now puce expression. "I've got something to see to myself."

Samuel's heart sank as the two brothers walked together out into the wide hall of the hotel. The last thing he needed was for Benjamin to see Miss Morgan.

"Or rather," added his brother with a wink as the waitress with whom he had been speaking so fervently appeared, pink-cheeked, by a servants' doorway. "I have *someone* to see to. I'll see you for dinner?"

He did not want for a reply, disappearing off with the giggling woman who, Samuel saw in a flash of gold, at least wore a wedding ring. Well, they would have to hope she was a widow, though goodness knew what their father would do if Benjamin was discovered.

That was his brother's problem. He had enough of his own.

Miss Morgan was standing just outside the hotel, bundled up in that same old coat and the two raggedy scarves.

"You look...cold," Samuel said lamely. Dear God, he was Eton and Cambridge educated, a noble, a peer! Did he not have better conversation than that?

The trouble was, the mere act of looking at Miss Morgan was enough to clear all thoughts from his mind.

"I *am* cold," Miss Morgan said curtly. "Will you walk with me?"

"Of course."

Samuel held out his arm, as he would have done for any of his cousins, or sisters, or even his mother. Miss Morgan ignored it, marching forward at top speed as though they were being chased by something quite dreadful.

It was only when he managed to catch up with her—not an easy feat, even for his long stride—that he wondered whether she was walking at such a pace to keep warm.

His stomach twisted. Oh, one knew of the less fortunate. One knew of them. Lilianna always did a great deal for several families she knew, and their cousin Thomas and his wife financially propped up an orphanage that was working wonders.

But actually seeing the poor, up close, as it were… Well. That was simply not something that one did.

It wasn't something *he* had ever done.

"I thought we'd walk along the beach," Miss Morgan said as she stepped out to cross a street without intimating why. "It's where I go. To think."

"I tend to think while riding. Or playing billiards at Dulverton's," said Samuel without thinking.

A crease appeared across her forehead, he noticed, when Miss Morgan frowned. Just between her eyes. "What's a Dulverton's?"

"It's a private members club in London. For gentlemen. All us Chances are members there."

Miss Morgan snorted, though Samuel could not understand why. After all, most gentlemen were members of clubs. Weren't they?

They turned around a corner and there it was: the beach. In the dying sunlight of the day, the ocean was speckled with gold, its gentle tide a beautiful accompaniment to the screeching of the seagulls.

"I so rarely see the sea," said Samuel, desperate to fill the silence and utterly unsure what else to say. "Our homes are a smidgen landlocked—though my cousin Jessica recently married the Baron Llyne, whose estate looks out over the Kent coastline."

Miss Morgan slowed her pace and settled into a regular step as she glanced at him with a raised eyebrow. "Your homes? Plural?"

"The family's homes," he corrected, with a sense of pride and yet somehow, of awkwardness. "I come from a large family."

Well. It was all very well, discussing one's estates with other gentlemen who had estates. It was quite another thing to mention them to a person who, from what Samuel could tell, would only be able to eat when he himself fed her.

Quite different, indeed.

She did look a tad thin, Samuel thought as his eyes cast over her. Even in the voluminous coat and through the numerous scarves, he could see her collarbones. His gaze meandered down. She wore no gloves. Her hands were pale.

"I have questions."

Samuel's focus snapped back up to her face—her beautiful face. *Her face*, he corrected himself firmly. This whole scheme wasn't going to work if he was going to allow himself to be distracted all the time!

"I thought you might," he said aloud. "Ask, and I will answer in the most truthful way I can."

Miss Morgan smiled as she glanced at him, their feet crunching on stones. "So you will not necessarily tell the truth?"

Blast. She was a clever one, then. Samuel would have laid money on the fact that more than half the people in England would not have picked up on that.

"I cannot reveal secrets of my family, nor tell the truth from any other person's perspective," he said quietly. "But I will not lie to you, Miss Morgan. If I cannot answer to your satisfaction, you will have to trust me that I do not tell all for a good reason."

"And *should* I trust you?" came the gentle yet teasing question.

Samuel almost tripped over his own feet. His honor had never been questioned before! He was a gentleman! He was a lord! More to the point, he was a Chance!

He opened his mouth to say all these things, and more, then he caught the eye of Miss Morgan and realized...that did not matter.

To the Miss Morgans of the world, gentlemen were not always kind. Lords were a type of far-off person whom one almost never met. And a Chance? Why, no Chance had ever been in Brighton. What did she know of his family?

"You should trust me," he said finally, "because I give you my word. And that is a great thing. You will have to...erm...trust me on this."

This whole thing was getting away from him, but there appeared to be nothing for it.

Samuel grinned. "I know that is probably not very helpful."

"Not really, but the fact that you see that is perhaps half the battle," said Miss Morgan lightly. She crossed her arms—for warmth, Samuel would guess. Or perhaps as a natural defense. "As I said, I have questions."

"Ask away."

"You said... At luncheon, you said..." For some reason, Miss Morgan's face had gone pink. Had she truly warmed up so quickly? "You said that it was imperative that you and your wife, that you wouldn't... Well. Consummate."

Ah.

Now heat burned Samuel's cheeks, and he rather supposed his face was just as red, if not redder, than Miss Morgan's. Why, to the casual observer, they may even look as though they were courting!

Well, not courting. There was no chaperone, obviously. Though now Samuel came to think about it, did the lower classes even use chaperones?

"My lord?"

Samuel blinked, then shook his head as though in doing so, he could rid his mind from the question he would not ask: *had Miss Morgan ever been courted?*

"Consummation," he said aloud.

"Yes...consummation," repeated Miss Morgan, her expression serious. "I am sure you can understand that I am curious about how... How that would work."

Would work? Good God, was he about to give a biology lesson to a young lady while walking along Brighton beach?

"Ah," Samuel said aloud helplessly. "Right. Well... Well, when a gentleman and a lady...er...when they love each other very much... or are forced into a marriage, I suppose, of convenience or status, one they aim to secure for all their lives—"

He was interrupted by a vigorous whack on his arm, which would have hurt, if Frank had not been in that habit for several years now.

"I didn't mean—of course I know how to—*honestly!*" Miss Morgan looked pink again. "I meant, how do you intend to keep up the pretense without...without it actually happening, you dolt!"

Samuel laughed, the chuckle releasing some of the tension in his neck. "Oh, that's easy. Separate bedchambers."

Miss Morgan slowed to pick up a shell. When they started to walk again, it was more slowly, and her fingers twirled the shell around and around. "Will that not cause comment? For your servants, I mean—you have servants, don't you?"

"Oh, it's quite common among my sort of people for a husband and wife to have separate bedchambers," said Samuel with a shrug. "No one will think anything of it."

"And you wouldn't be...tempted?"

It was a good thing he was looking away at that moment at the cresting waves that scattered gold and red from the dying sun along the surf, for he was not sure what his expression would look like.

Tempted? Dear God, he was tempted. *He was tempted right*

now.

He may not have been the cad that Benjamin was, or the rake that Cousin Zander was reported to be, but Samuel had had his fair share of dalliances—widows only, naturally, and those who were fully aware that he would not be offering neither hand nor heart.

None of them had ever tempted him like Miss Morgan.

She was…delectable. Innocent and yet worldly, a heady combination Samuel had never known he wished to taste before. He wanted to know what it was to touch those lips, with his fingers, with his lips, with his—

"Samuel? My lord? What am I supposed to call you, anyway?"

Miss Morgan's tones wakened Samuel from his entirely inappropriate daydream.

He tried to smile. "'Samuel.' 'Samuel' is fine."

"Consummation," Miss Morgan repeated sternly, as though she were a schoolteacher and her prize pupil was misbehaving. "I asked you if you would be tempted."

Samuel cleared his throat. Well, here it was: time for that modicum of truth. "Right. Well, it's very important that doesn't happen. For when we seek an annulment."

"For when you and this mythical wife of yours seek an annulment," Miss Morgan corrected him with a wry expression.

A sharp pain, sharp and unexpected, seared through Samuel. Was she truly discounting herself from his clever…fine, his frantic scheme? But then why have this conversation—why seek him out and ask these questions?

"You do not wish to accept the role?" he asked quietly as the beach curved slowly to their left.

"It's not… It's not that. It's just…" Miss Morgan's voice faded away and she looked out to the water. Her footsteps halted and she stood there, utterly lost in her thoughts.

If it had been someone else, he might have interrupted her, but Samuel rather enjoyed taking the moment to look at her.

He could understand why she had become an actress. What

man would not wish to look at her? Why, on the stage as Ophelia, for example, she would have been magnificent.

And she was out of work. That should worry him, he knew, in case her skills as an actress would not prove up to his task, but was there not far more people who wished to be on the stage than... Well, room on the stage?

Anyone could be down on their luck. That was, Samuel had never been so. It did not happen to Chances, not even really to their poorest branch. But he had read about it. In newspapers. In novels.

"To be your wife...to take on the role of Lady Chance—"

"Lady Aylesbury, actually," Samuel reminded her with a sardonic smile.

Miss Morgan did not turn to look at him, and her voice continued on with a wistful air. "It would be the role of a lifetime. To actually inhabit the peerage, to meander through Society, to gain entrance to such places and—and hold court for you, as your wife..."

Samuel swallowed. Yes, he hadn't really thought that bit through yet.

Miss Morgan lifted her face to him. "To lose oneself in such a part. It would be magnificent."

"But you would not be able to lose yourself within it," he reminded her quietly. "It is very important you understand—this is not a permanent position." Well, he supposed, he had initially been insistent on that. Surely, *she* would prefer that?

"A year and a day," she said with an incline of her head. "Like a fairy tale."

"This is not a fairy tale," Samuel said decisively. It was imperative—crucial she understood. He would not be accused of forcing a lady—a stranger—into a lifetime of matrimony. "You appear to be a very nice woman, Miss Morgan, but we hardly know one another. Committing to one another for a lifetime would be ridiculous." He swallowed, almost wishing that weren't true. Would the future marchioness—the *real* marchioness—

captivate him as much as Miss Morgan?

"'Nice'?" she said, her mouth agape, as though that were the only word he'd spoken that mattered, as if he had mortally wounded her.

A seagull screeched overhead as the tide continued to come in and the sun dipped, finally, below the horizon. The dusk air was cold, yes, but there was a cordiality here Samuel had not expected.

"More than nice, I am sure," he amended with a laugh. "But my point is that this is not the end of the story. This wedding will be quick and perfunctory. You will play a part, as my wife, to get me the money. We will live as partners, not husband and wife, though to the outside world it must appear to be true—and after three hundred and sixty-six days, we will go our separate ways, never to see each other again. Do you understand?" There. That was the proper way to go about this, wasn't it? Wasn't that the best way to get her to agree to the job?

There was no way an actress would want to spend any longer than that as a marchioness, away from the actual stage.

Miss Morgan looked up at him with brilliant, sparkling intelligence in her eyes. Or Samuel supposed it could have been the reflection of the stars. "Why do you want the money so much?"

Samuel swallowed. He didn't know, exactly. Or at least, he knew, but he wasn't going to tell her.

Think what he could do with such a fortune! Such good he could do, such changes he could make to the family. Investments to secure them for generations, support for the family's charities, an additional input into Frank's dowry—if she was going to persist in wearing trousers, she was going to need it.

Not that he could say all that to Miss Morgan, a relative stranger.

"I admit the distant relative to whom the money would go otherwise is not of the most commendable reputation," he said aloud. "But more than that... Money brings freedom. I want freedom."

Something glittered in her eyes, and this time, he was almost certain it was not the stars. "And you are not worried about my past?"

"Should I be?"

Miss Morgan laughed as she slipped her hand through his arm and turned so that they started back toward the town. "I meant that I am an actress. It is not the most respectable profession—indeed, you may find yourself embarrassed if my past resurrects itself."

But Samuel could not concern himself with such things. What on earth could possibly be in such a nice girl's past that he would have to worry about?

"No one in London will know, and that is all that matters," he said brusquely. "Besides, I would rather marry an actress than an actual... I mean... Oh, blast."

Miss Morgan was far too intelligent to miss that. The arm that had rested so pleasantly in his own was immediately withdrawn. "An actual what?"

"Don't mind me. I talk nonsense all the time," said Samuel helplessly, his stomach churning with embarrassment at the slip. "In fact, just the other day, I—"

"No, you were going to say that it was better to marry me, an actress who no one cares about, than an actual lady from Society. Weren't you?" Miss Morgan asked with painful accuracy. "As though I am not an actual lady? Was that not what you were going to say?"

Samuel swallowed.

Well, yes, he would have said in different circumstances. After all, surely, she could see that he could not sully a debutante or a Society lady with an annulled marriage? He would never hear the end of it from her family! And he would have to marry a lady among the *ton* someday, he supposed. Best not to make enemies.

But a woman like Miss Morgan, someone with no family, no prospects, who would eagerly take the money and leave...

A Miss Morgan who was still glaring with a sharp expression.

Samuel's shoulders slumped. "Yes. Yes, I was going to say that."

For a moment, her ire seemed to increase in temperature, her foot tapping and her inhalation becoming deep. Then the feeling faded, as though it had never been there. "Thank you."

He had most definitely heard that wrong. They stepped off the beach and back onto the pavement. The bustle of Brighton had returned, all rumbling carriages and muffled conversations and shouting hawkers. "I beg your pardon?"

Miss Morgan grinned, though there was no mirth in such an expression. "You told me the truth, even though it embarrassed you. Good. I need honesty for this to work, Samuel."

His spirits lifted. *Yes.* "So you agree?"

"I will…think about it," she said evasively.

It was not in Samuel's nature to be demanding—at least, he did not think so—and therefore, it was far beyond his own comfort to speak as he must do.

"I am sorry, Miss Morgan, but that will not do," he said quietly, holding on to her elbow to prevent her from continuing to walk. She looked up with confusion. "I need to be with the solicitors in just a few days."

"But I had hoped for a week to decide if—"

"No." Samuel swallowed. "This is not an ultimatum because I gain pleasure in pressuring you, Miss Morgan, but in less than a week, the scheme itself will be immaterial. Useless. Defunct."

Irritation flared in her gaze. "I know what immaterial means."

He winced. "Ye-Yes, I believe you do." Was it just him, or had he suddenly stuttered like his mother would have? "Let me be plain. You appreciate honesty, and there are two more things you need to know that you have no reason to understand as of yet. Firstly: my father is alive and well."

She tilted her head. "But you are the marquess? Is your father a duke?"

"No, my uncle is—*was*. My cousin, his eldest son, is now the duke. We are the Chances, and you'll find we do things a little differently than most. My uncle and father have stepped down from their titles prematurely so that they might enjoy a retirement of sorts. We've been calling them the 'dowager duke' and 'dowager marquess' respectively."

"I see." Miss Morgan nodded slowly, very slowly, as if she did not quite see. Perhaps she didn't. He'd have to explain at some point about how he had two more uncles with titles and how that family estate split had been quite odd at the time it had happened as well.

"Secondly, my father and mother and siblings are quite eager to meet you. I told them... Well, I can't even rightly explain *why*, perhaps to fend off any suggestions of a rushed *ton* marriage, but I told them I was already wed days ago. Implying the marriage had taken place at least a few weeks prior. So we—that is, my year-long wife and I—would have to come up with a story about how we met and married during one of the trips I took without any of them present. And where she's been since then. And why I've kept it all secret."

"Hmm, interesting," said Miss Morgan, a bounce in her step now. "I suppose I'm used to that. When inhabiting a role, I like to know the character's background. Every detail. Even if it never comes up during the performance."

Samuel wanted to keep laying out his terms, but he had to pause to smile at that. She was *perfect* for this role. "I have applied for the special license and a friend of mine is close to the archbishop. It should be here in a day, on a fast rider," Samuel said hurriedly, keeping his voice low, as if they could be overheard.

Not, he told himself confidently, *so that Miss Morgan will have to step closer to me. Not at all. That is just a convenient consequence.*

"'A day'?" Miss Morgan breathed.

"I will need your answer tomorrow," said Samuel, tension cracking up his jaw as he spoke. "Or this whole plan will be for naught. I will have to admit to my parents that I have lied about the existence of a wife, and the whole fortune will go to a man who is most unpleasant and I am sure will use the funds for nefarious deeds."

Miss Morgan inhaled slowly. "'Nefarious deeds'?"

"Indeed."

She looked down and so did he. The shell was still in her hands, being turned around and around.

"Tomorrow, then."

The words were so faint, Samuel almost did not catch them. "I beg your pardon?"

"Tomorrow." Miss Morgan looked up, and her smile was wistful. "I will give you your answer tomorrow."

Chapter Five

January 5, 1841

Rose looked around the meager possessions she had managed to accumulate over the last nine years.

The fact that they all fit into one small trunk was in and of itself a small indictment. Three gowns, a coat, two scarves. Enough underthings—just—to last her. One heavy shawl, her mother's. She probably should not have stolen it. Three books, though no Shakespeare, as she knew the Bard by heart. A small drawing of Rome on which she had spent far too much money. A pair of pearl earbobs, borrowed from Annabelle and now, Rose thought somberly, never to be returned. One pair of shoes, one bonnet, three hair ribbons, enough soap to last her a week, one glove—where the other had gone, she did not know...and that was all.

Her life. In a trunk.

Her eyes flittered around the room, which she had taken for a month and ended up staying in for six. She had always told herself that she would take somewhere better, once the play opened at the Grand Theatre and she was being feted.

But the play had been put off, and put off, and now she had been summarily shoved off the stage, for want of a better description.

And now...

Rose bit her lip as she glanced at the door. It had been the right decision, she knew. It had to be. There was no other option.

But in the minutes before he arrived, there was still the opportunity to run. To simply pick up her trunk, take the two shillings her landlady had given her back out of pity, which was the worst sort of coin, and take the stagecoach to...

And that was where her plan ran out. And that was why any moment now, a certain gentleman would be knocking on her door, ready to take her to her new life.

She wasn't entirely happy about it. The man did not understand the ways of the stage, and he had offered her an agreement that in many ways was only just short of prostitution. Not that she had anything against the women she met, waiting outside the stage door in the hope of picking up some custom. But it was not the sort of life she would choose.

And now...

The knock at the door was polite, and respectful.

Rose sighed. He was an enigma, this man. Who *hired* a wife?

"You are late," Rose snapped as she opened the door to glare up at Samuel Chance.

"And you," he said lightly, "are beautiful. Do you need a hand with... a hand with..."

His voice faded away as his attention slipped past her face, over her shoulder, and to something which evidently had him transfixed.

Rose turned around and cringed so hard, it was a miracle she was still able to remain upright.

Of course, a gentleman like this Chance fellow had probably never seen squalor like this.

Not that she lived in squalor. Not exactly. The room was clean, mostly, but it was bare. Rose had grown accustomed to the wooden panels boarding up half the window because it had broken before she had arrived. The fact that the mattress was not on a frame had never bothered her; she had always returned exhausted from the theater, and so what difference would it make whether it was on a cheap frame or on the floor?

Only now that she stood here, looking at the place with Samuel's eyes, did she notice the lack of carpet, the paint that was peeling off the walls, the fact that other than her trunk, there appeared to be no other furniture.

She turned back to Samuel with blazing cheeks. "Yes? You have something to say?"

"You have been living like this?" he exhaled, as though unable to be polite.

Rose bristled. "I'll have you know I once lived in a manor! I know what I am and I know where I am—and I am supposed to be in your coach!"

Samuel's expression—that slight tilt of his head, the hitched breath—was more than pitying, it was disbelieving, which was the most irritating part.

I don't know. You tell the truth and no one believes you...

"I am sorry." And he truly sounded sorry, which was unusual. Rose was not accustomed to men actually meaning what they said. "I just—I thought—well. I would not wish my wife to live in such...such circumstances."

And he meant it, too. Oh, Rose could see that the man was horrified, in a way, but he did not transfer his horror of her locale to herself. He did not judge her for living here. Perhaps he judged her landlady?

But no. There was no judgment in his eyes. Just pity.

"If I had my way, no one would have to live like this," Samuel muttered, his ears pinking at the tips.

"Well, perhaps that is something you can put our stupendous fortune to," Rose said in a bright attempt to lighten the mood. Yes, think Rosalind. Think Hermia—she was always able to transform the mood of a room. "I'll have you know that plenty of people live in worse abodes than this one."

Samuel's expression was kind. Too kind. "*My* stupendous fortune, I think you'll find."

Ah. Yes. "Just getting into the spirit of the thing," she said meekly. The last thing she needed was the fool to change his mind. Besides, did he not think the ten thousand pounds sum and thousand pound annuity was not a stupendous fortune to her?

How great his own fortune must have been in comparison.

"You have decided, then? You will marry me?"

If Rose had ever spent any great time thinking about her future husband, and she rarely had, the proposal itself would never have been quite like that.

A gentleman on bended knee, flowers—roses, for preference—a glass of champagne in her hand and a string quartet somewhere... She had visited Venice once and had been quite taken with the idea of being serenaded on a gondola. Not that her purse had stretched to it.

Not standing in a dank, almost-bare room with a man behind her tapping his foot in a very tangible reminder that she was, by not replying immediately, wasting his time.

Rose drew herself up. "I... I will marry you if—"

"There is simply no room, or time, in this matter for you to set conditions," Samuel said, in a tone that told her quite clearly that this was not a man accustomed to negotiation.

She smiled, pouring as much prettiness into the motion as she could. "Would you deny me even the possibility of a request?"

That was when she saw it: the flare of the nostrils, the shifting of the feet to give enough space between his thighs. Yes, he was attracted to her. *Interesting*.

"A... A possibility?" The man's voice was hoarse.

"Come on in," Rose said sweetly. The last thing she needed was an audience for this. "It's just one request. You can deny me, of course."

There it was again, those hints of desire at the word 'deny.' *Most interesting*.

Samuel glanced over his shoulder, presumably at a man he had waiting in a coach, but evidently considered his own time more important, for he stepped into the room. He even made to wipe his boots, Rose noticed with a grin, though to his evident surprise, there was no mat. He settled for scraping them along the wooden floor, as if to cover his blunder.

"Well, then?"

Rose stepped around him and closed the door. Tempting as it were to lock it, she was not certain she would achieve much more by penning him in.

No, this had to be asked delicately—most delicately.

She inhaled deeply. "I need to know if there is any attraction between us."

Perhaps she should not have been standing so close to him. Rose had not taken in that her position by the door meant that she was mere inches from the man, and when he whirled around with wide eyes, it was a mere coincidence that his hip did not bump into hers.

"'Attraction'?"

Rose nodded. "If we are to pretend to be husband and wife—"

"No one will need to know about the—the lack of consummation," Samuel said hurriedly, cheeks pinking as though this were simply not the right sort of conversation between a gentleman and a lady.

And perhaps it wasn't. But Rose wasn't a lady.

Not anymore.

The walls appeared to creep in as she looked up and said, "We are agreed this is no love match—"

"I sh-should think not!" Samuel choked. Then he grinned awkwardly. "No-No offense meant."

It is always just when a man had given offense, Rose thought darkly, *that he will inform a woman that she is not allowed to take offense.*

Outwardly, she smiled sweetly. "Of course. So I repeat, this is no love match, and yet we will need to convince not only your family, but Society at large that this is a true marriage, and most of all, this solicitor of yours."

Ah, *that* got his attention.

Samuel tried to step closer to her. As it was, there wasn't a full step's gap between them. So he shuffled. "I need Mr. Todd to believe this—and he will, because there will be a marriage certificate."

Damnation. Rose had almost forgotten. His kind—his own phrasing—were accustomed to loveless marriages. Marriages made for convenience, for alliance, for wealth.

She should have remembered.

Though she wondered how such a supposedly whirlwind courtship and marriage he'd kept secret from his family would have occurred without a romance. Still, he was clearly embarrassed to even discuss the matter. The details of their supposedly weeks-old marriage's origins would have to wait.

"Oh, well, that's all right, then," Rose said lightly, stepping around Samuel toward her trunk. "I will just merely pretend attraction should it ever become necessary."

She picked up her trunk and turned to face him, ready to leave—at least, that was what she wanted him to believe. And damn Ted and the whole pack of them because this Samuel was obviously taken in.

Taken in by her acting genius, naturally.

"You cannot do that," he said woodenly.

Rose raised an eyebrow. "Cannot do what? Carry my own trunk? I quite agree, it is beneath the new Marchioness of Aylesbury, but if you are not willing to carry it, I shall have to or you can summon your coachman."

"I mean, you cannot just—just pretend attraction! It is either there or it is not," spluttered Samuel, his eyes wide. "You cannot be in earnest!"

Rose carefully lifted her other eyebrow. "I am sorry. Are you doubting my acting skills?"

Samuel snorted as she placed down her trunk. "I have never *seen* your acting abilities, Miss Morgan."

"You are seeing them right now as I continue to smile at you and not look as though I wish to stab you through the eye with a pencil," she said sweetly.

His eyes, if possible, widened even further. "Y-You are?"

Rose almost laughed. Goodness, she had always known that gentlemen were absolutely foolish when they were in the presence of a beautiful woman—like herself—but to see it so clearly played out before her... She was rather enjoying it.

And now to make absolutely sure...

"I am," she said calmly. "And when I say that I can convince the world that I am deeply, passionately attracted to you, Samuel Chance, I speak the truth. I am Cleopatra. I am Juliet. I am Helena and Hermia and if you are not careful, I will be Katharina."

It should not be so attractive to see how the man immediately understood her implication. An intelligent man—at the very least, a well-read man—however, was always going to be alluring to someone like her.

"I...I don't believe it. Such things... Such emotions are pure. They cannot be aped on a stage," said Samuel, his voice hoarse.

Rose shrugged. Was he no fan of the arts, then? Had he never seen a play with lovers? "Love? Love is different. But it is not of love which I speak. I speak of attraction, Samuel. I am sure you know what I mean."

His throat bobbed.

For some reason, her own throat wished to swallow, but Rose did not permit it. Instead, she tilted her head to one side, mimicking the motion in reverse with her hips. She did not grin as Samuel's gaze darted down then immediately back up, as though desperately trying to pretend he had not looked.

But she had him.

Rose knew this was wrong—probably. It was wrong to use one's feminine wiles in this way, and most certainly wrong to use her acting ability to tie the silly man in knots.

But this man had power, and money, and friends clearly in high places. *An in with the Archbishop of Canterbury, indeed!*

No, she would need some power of her own and there was only one way she knew how to do that.

Short of taking a pencil to his eye, obviously.

"Desire," Rose breathed, and she heard with satisfaction how Samuel cleared his throat with a rough cough. "Need. That is what I speak of, and that is most certainly something that I can create. All I need to do is channel the right skills and act accordingly."

She shrugged again as though this were merely a formality and turned once again to pick up her trunk.

"I don't believe it."

Rose froze.

Samuel's words, though brief, had encapsulated a great deal of something that she could not quite explain. There was a...a request buried in there somewhere, but Rose would be damned if she was going to help him articulate it.

Straightening up once again, she turned to face him and raised a quizzical eyebrow.

This time, when Samuel swallowed, it was more of a gulp. "Prove it."

"I beg your pardon?" Rose asked in her most silky tone.

She knew what he meant, and in a way, she should have expected it. Despite her best attempts to make clear to the fool that she was not about to offer...offer *those* sorts of services, she should have known no man could be trusted to keep his wits about himself when she was displaying her most potent skills.

Yet despite her most potent skills, Samuel was still able to speak. She must have been slipping. "I said, prove it. Our love story—it will have to be a love story to explain my impulsiveness. So you shall have to seem attracted to me. Show me this attraction of which you speak—which of course you do not feel. Neither of us is attracted to the other." He swallowed thickly.

Of course. Rose nodded curtly, glad that she did not have to trust her tongue to deny it. Who would be attracted to tall, dark men with more money than sense?

"But you say that you can act attraction, that you can pretend it? Well, that, I would like to see." Samuel crossed his arms and looked expectant.

It was all Rose could do not to roll her eyes. The man had spent the last two days moaning about there being no time for decisions, and now he wanted to loiter in a room that, truly, had seen better days—and debate about her acting skills!

Well, she would have to put this to bed, as it were, once and for all. One single performance, and the man would never doubt her abilities again.

Rose did not immediately smile. Smiles were distrusted, she knew, and rightly so. A smile could hide anything; it was a basic technique used by beginner actresses who had no other strings to their bow.

So she allowed her eyes to soften, slowly, slowly, until her face was a blank slate.

Then she poured warmth into it. Warmth and heat, and hunger—something that thankfully she did not need to pretend.

"Wh-What are you doing?" Samuel asked in a low voice.

Rose said nothing in reply. Instead, she inhaled. Slowly. This gown was particularly convenient for such a display, low in the bust as it was. Samuel's gaze, as she knew it would be, was immediately drawn to her décolletage. She may not have had much as some other actress she might name who merely thrust out her chest and let her nipples do the acting, but it was on full display, and she had yet to meet a man who would complain about the size of the view as long as he had one.

When the inhalation was over, she sighed, allowing her lips to part—once she had wet them, naturally.

"You... You're just standing there," came Samuel's words.

Just standing there, indeed—the man had no subtlety!

Rose took a hesitant step forward, then another. She allowed herself—just for a moment—to glance up at Samuel's eyes but darted her eyes away quickly, as though she had been burned.

When Samuel spoke again, it was in a hoarse voice. "Miss Morgan."

Ah, she was getting somewhere then. Rose said nothing but gently allowed a hand to rise until it was a mere inch from his own, resting on his elbow as his arms remained folded.

They did not remain so for long. Taking care to move slowly,

slowly, Rose interlocked her fingers with his own and carefully untangled his arms. One fell to his side. The other remained lifted by her own hand.

Rose slowly turned it over and stared down into his palm. Remember, heat, hunger, desire... Three, two, one...

"What are you—Miss Morgan." Samuel exhaled her name with such surprise and yet such longing that she was almost distracted from what she was doing.

She finished kissing his palm, however, and when Rose looked up, curling his fingers inward as though capturing the kiss between them, Samuel's expression was a picture.

There it was: heat, hunger, desire. But instead of her drawing them up inside of her to display on her face, they were in his eyes.

"M-Miss Morgan," Samuel said in a jagged voice. "That is quite enough."

Rose made her breath falter. "Is it?"

The distance between their lips was almost nothing, and it was nothing when she pushed herself up on her tiptoes and pressed her mouth firmly against his own.

For a heart-stopping moment, nothing happened. Had she lost her touch?

And then Samuel's free hand was around her waist, pulling her in, the hand grasping hers was pulled forward, trapped between her breasts and his wide chest as Samuel's tongue plunged through her lips and into her mouth, *demanding* pleasure, not asking for it—and Rose surrendered.

Dear God, this man was incredible. The hesitancy, the dryness of his words at times, they were nothing compared to the appetite and heat pouring between them. Bliss sparked as his tongue trailed a teasing line through her mouth, and his powerful frame surrounded her petite one as she was swallowed up within him.

But of course, she had to reply. Rose pushed the man back and Samuel stumbled, his back hitting the door, and she was pinning him between her quivering body and the unyielding wood and he groaned, tilting his jaw to deepen the kiss.

And Rose opened her eyes wide in panic.

Dear God, this was not supposed to happen! She was not meant to feel pleasure—she was not supposed to *feel* attraction. She was supposed to be acting!

She broke the kiss, tugged herself free, and tried to say in a calm voice, "There."

Samuel blinked as though he had been struck by lightning. "Wh-What?"

"There," Rose said resolutely, looking away from the handsome man to smooth down her skirts with fingers that were not quite shaking. "That is how I would act as though…as though I were attracted to you."

He was leaning against the door as though his mere legs would be insufficient to hold him. Rose would have been flattered, if she were not attempting to quieten her frantically beating pulse and tell it that she was not aroused by the man.

The very idea! Despite his evident attraction to her, he had made it clear he had no plans to make her his marchioness for life. No doubt he'd take his time to find a more *suitable* bride after they parted, one with a doting father with wealth or title. Or both.

"That… That was acting?" Samuel asked weakly.

Rose cleared her throat as she looked up at him.

She was not a liar. Despite what her father had said—and he had said a great deal on the subject—acting was not lying.

But in this particular circumstance, she could think to do nothing but lie.

"That was acting," she said, completely falsely as her body thrummed and ached for another kiss like that.

Samuel tugged a hand through his hair as though wildly attempting to remember his own name.

It was flattering, in the main. *If only I did not want to throw myself at the man again*, Rose thought bleakly.

"Well, that… That will certainly be sufficient," Samuel said brusquely. "If needed. Which it probably won't be. I mean, certainly not *that*. I'm sure doe eyes in the presence of others will do."

"'Doe eyes'?" Rose had to stifle a chuckle as she forced herself to nod in as much of a business-like manner as she could. "Excellent."

She ignored the small part of her—the very small part of her—that railed against the idea that they would never share a kiss like that again. How could they not? When one found someone whose body was so in tune with one's own...who could spark such sensuous decadence in mere moments...surely, it was a crime to walk away from such a connection?

Rose cleared her throat again. "So we are agreed? A fake marriage for you to gain a fortune, absolutely no more kissing in any circumstance—"

"Not at all," agreed Samuel, his breathing still a little ragged.

"—and in a year and a day, we'll part ways, never to see each other again, with a fortune in my pocket and a greater fortune in yours," Rose said decisively.

Her gaze sought his out and she wondered...*hoped* he would disagree.

Samuel nodded curtly. "Agreed."

Chapter Six

January 6, 1841

"You," Samuel told his reflection sternly, "are going to be absolutely fine."

There was a giggle behind him and he whirled around, trying not to flush at being caught.

Miss Morgan—soon his wife, soon Lady Aylesbury, Samuel reminded himself sternly—was placing a pair of pearl earbobs in her ears. "Do you always start your mornings with such a lecture?"

"No," lied Samuel with a wry expression. "Sleep well?"

It had been the first point of order when the carriage he'd hired had arrived at the Regent's Hotel last night. He had chosen that time of day—while his family would be dining—so he could hurry Miss Morgan upstairs through a servants' corridor. It was a wonder how much a few shillings could do.

"Sleeping arrangements," Miss Morgan had said. "Ah."

"I've got it all sorted out," Samuel had said hurriedly. "You'll take the bed—"

She had grinned. "Most generous, for your wife."

"And I'll take the sofa. It's only for one night, after all," he had added with a shrug. "I'll speak to the hotel manager about getting you your own suite."

If she had been surprised at the ease at which he could spend money, Miss Morgan had not said anything. "I see."

"And, Miss Morgan—"

"*Rose*, I think, is best," his soon-to-be temporary wife had said as she had placed down her trunk she had insisted on carrying herself and looked about his hotel room. "And you are to be Samuel to me, are you?"

His stomach had twisted last night, and it twisted now as Samuel looked at the woman with whom he would be spending the next year in close quarters. Strange. In all his schemes, and in truth he had spent far too much time thinking about this, he had never quite considered just how much time they would be spending together.

A great deal of time.

A great deal of time not kissing Rose Morgan...

Rose *Chance*. Soon enough. Even if just for a short while.

Pushing the thought, and the memory of that toe-curling kiss, far from his mind at once, Samuel nodded. "I am glad you slept well."

"I do not think I have slept well in all my life." Rose yawned.

Samuel grinned. "And yet you yawn."

"Well, I am about three weeks' short on sleep," she said with a shrug. "Which, by the way, is how long we will be telling your family we have been married?"

"Yes, I don't see why Mr. Todd should reveal the truth to anyone," Samuel said shortly, pulling on his jacket and smoothing down his lapel. The solicitor had raised an eyebrow at the marriage license, but he had not said anything to the new marquess about the date. He'd probably figured it was none of his business, so long as it fulfilled the terms set by the will.

Still, he would have to go back tomorrow with the signed license to prove they had gone through the wedding.

Another layer of lies—but then what did it matter? All would be counterbalanced by the good he could do, would do with Great-Aunt Tessie's fortune.

"Excellent. And how precisely adoring would you like me to be?" Rose said matter-of-factly, sitting on the end of the bed and carefully pinning a few errant curls back into her bun. "You've requested doe eyes for a start." She blinked, her eyelashes distractingly long over her wide, dark eyes.

Samuel's stomach roiled horribly. It was not as though he had not expected there to be a certain... well, businesslike manner about the whole thing. In a way, it was a relief. He would not get attached to her so it would not bother him when she inevitably left with enough money to set her up for life. He should be glad, he knew, that Miss Morgan—that Rose was not begging for his affection and wishing he would fall in love with her. He'd never trust any sentiment from her. Not after he'd seen her acting so up close.

But still. A little begging might have been nice.

"A bit adoring," he said awkwardly. "We are supposed to be newly married, after all."

"We really will be tomorrow," Rose pointed out with a dry smile. "But I understand. And your sister truly is called 'Frank'?"

"Francesca, but she won't answer to it, hasn't for years," Samuel said, his grin becoming sincere now. "And my sister Lilianna isn't here with us. She's with her husband in London."

"You have a large family," said Rose on a sigh, almost a hint of wistfulness on her face.

Samuel laughed. "Oh—forgive me, I am not laughing at you. It's just—well. The Chance family as a whole—there are four branches of us—becomes almost a crowd. When I am just with my parents and siblings, it feels...intimate."

Rose slipped off her shoes and dug her toes into the lush carpet. "That sounds...nice."

He thought about it. He had never had to think about it before. The Chances were just...there. His father, his father's three brothers, and all their wives and all his cousins. Most definitely a crowd.

"You haven't told me about your family," he said mildly. "I should probably know about them, for the pretense."

And the smile disappeared from her eyes like a candle snuffed out not by a breeze, but a gale. "I have no family."

"But you must once have had—"

"Are you coming down for breakfast, you old dog?"

Samuel froze. The previous sentence had been accompanied by a great deal of hammering at his door, something that would not have normally been acceptable in a hotel—but then his brother clearly did not care.

"Who is that?" asked Rose curiously, slipping her shoes back on.

"Get into the washroom," said Samuel in a hiss. *"Now!"*

Panic was rising and his instincts said to hide—hide, in the convenient washroom that was a revelation. A hotel with a washroom for each suite?

Rose stood to her feet with a grimace. "But if that is your family, surely, I should meet—"

"Not him, and not like this," Samuel said firmly, striding toward her and bundling her toward her washroom, trying not to notice the softness beneath his fingertips. "Go on, hide!"

"This is not the most auspicious beginning, you know, *husband*," Rose said sharply as he shut the door in her face.

The door behind him banged open. "What on earth are you doing, Samuel?"

Samuel whirled around and saw his rascal of a brother. "Benjamin!"

"You know that I have been sent up here to get you," his younger brother said with a scowl. "God, you wouldn't know that we are well past one and twenty, would you? It's like being at Eton again."

"I liked Eton," said Samuel mildly, stepping away from the washroom and hoping his brother could not hear the frantic thudding of his heart.

Benjamin snorted. "Of course you did. So come on, what wench has kept you up here?"

There was a sharp twist between his ribs. "No one. Why don't you—"

"Why don't you go to the solicitors today with me?" Benjamin interrupted, throwing himself on the bed and sighing heavily.

"I am certain I could get old Todd—"

"He's not that old," Samuel interrupted, hoping desperately to distract him. "Come on, let's go downstairs."

"I think I could convince him to sign over the money to you without a wife, you know," Benjamin said, pointing a finger at his older brother. "Come on. I'll go with you and we'll see what we could do. We could always bribe him, you know—you'll have enough funds. How about it?"

Samuel hesitated.

Precisely why he did not wish Benjamin to meet Miss Morgan—Rose—he did not know.

Oh, the meeting had to happen at some point. There was not much point in a *secret* temporary wife, not when one needed the temporary wife in the first place to claim money from a lawyer.

But Benjamin... Well, he was a rake, wasn't he? A rogue, the man bedded every serving girl and Society widow he came across—and there were rumors he did not always wait until they were widowed. And that was not the sort of gentleman whom he wished introduced to his wife.

Damn it. To Rose. To his *temporary* wife.

"Samuel, come on," Benjamin said, his voice quieter now. "I know we don't always see eye to eye—"

"Your dirty boots are on my bed," Samuel could not help but point out.

The eyeroll his brother gave him was truly a work of art. He moved his boots off the bed. "Let me come with you to the solicitor's. You can't go alone!"

Samuel opened his mouth, but the next words to be spoken in the room were not uttered by him. They were not uttered by his brother, either.

"He has already gone to the solicitor's to sort everything out," said Rose lightly as she sashayed into the room, her hips swaying and a teasing smile on her lips. "His wife went with him."

Benjamin's jaw dropped. So did Samuel's, but he managed to

close it just in time.

Remember, you are supposed to have been married to this woman for weeks!

"Dear God," murmured Benjamin.

"Manners," Samuel snapped, trying to gain his bearings and keep his younger brother in line at the same time—never an easy task. "A lady is present."

"Yes, she most certainly is," said his brother as he rose to his feet with a most delighted grin on his face. "Your wife, I presume?"

"You presume correctly," said Rose graciously, holding out a hand to be kissed.

Samuel knew he should not mind that she did so. He also should not mind that Benjamin almost tripped over his own feet in his haste to get to her. He most certainly should not mind that Rose's smile widened at the gesture.

"Samuel, you did not tell me you had such a handsome and charming brother," she said in a voice that was so sultry, Samuel was rather surprised the wallpaper did not start peeling off the walls.

Evidently, his brother was similarly impressed. He glanced over his shoulder at the stoic Samuel with a teasing laugh. "Dear God, man, I can see why you kept her to yourself. If I'd had a woman like this in my bedchamber, I'd hardly leave!"

"*Benjamin!*" hissed Samuel, stepping across the room and pulling him bodily away from his—from Miss Morgan. Rose. Damn it.

The nerve of the man!

But Benjamin was laughing. "Just a jest, old man. You mustn't get your drawers in a knot. Well, very pleasant to meet you...?"

For some reason, both his brother and Rose were staring at him. Only after a few moments did Samuel realize why.

"Rose," he said brusquely. "Look, if Mama and Papa and Frank are waiting—"

"Oh, let them wait," said Benjamin with a twinkle in his eye, turning back to the woman in the room and openly appreciating her curves. "Well, how did the two of you meet, then? I must say, Rose, your face, while beautiful, is unknown to me."

Samuel glanced, fear clogging his veins, at Rose. *Blast.* They hadn't yet discussed the finer details and clearly they should have done. He'd anticipated such questions, but he hadn't expected the family to meet her yet. He had thrown out the idea of using his brief trip to Bath to meet an Eton friend newly back in England in mid-December as the where and when, but they hadn't gone over all the details. She would panic, she would say something nonsensical, perhaps overdramatic like an actress might think of. She would—

"I was introduced by a good friend of mine, Lady Packham," said Rose smoothly, as though she could not wait to tell the story. "We met at—now, was it a dinner or a dance?"

"Both," Samuel said hoarsely.

Rose laughed merrily as she stepped around the agog Benjamin and took Samuel's arm. "Oh, yes! You were seated by me at dinner and after an introduction by Lady Packham, you asked for the first country dance. You danced well, I thought."

"He did?" Benjamin snorted.

"I did?" asked Samuel, his eyes blinking rapidly.

Rose flushed prettily and squeezed his arm with an intimacy that made a strange heat soar through his limbs. "I thought so. I was quite taken with him, Lord Benjamin, and so you can imagine my delight when he asked for my hand."

"I can imagine *his* delight, certainly," said Benjamin, leaning against the wall and continuing to admire Rose in, Samuel thought, a most unacceptable manner. "And so you wed? Without telling the family?"

"Well, we wanted to enjoy the first few weeks to ourselves, as I am sure you can imagine," said Rose lightly. "I know he had to get home for Christmas and New Year's and then his cousin's wedding. My friend would have been lonely without me and I had promised to spend Christmas with her, so I kept Lady Packham company and stayed behind in Bath until he could come get me. I made my way to Brighton as soon as he sent word to meet him here instead."

Samuel could not help but stare. It was masterful. She sounded sincere. There was nothing illicit in her words...and yet there was just enough of a suggestion of sensuality to make his spine stiffen and to make his brother laugh.

"You've found yourself a most promising wife, Samuel, I have to say—and I admit myself disappointed. Now I cannot come with you to strongarm old Todd and put you in my debt."

"Putting myself in your debt is not something I ever had in mind," Samuel said forebodingly. "Now, it is high time we went down to breakfast. All of us."

He caught Rose's eye and tried to tell her, without moving a single muscle as Benjamin strode past them toward the door, just how impressed he was.

How could he fail to be? She had been the consummate marchioness. Charming and elegant, but witty and flirtatious enough to match Benjamin's nonsensical energy. How on earth had she known?

"Your brother is a rake," Rose murmured as they stepped out of his hotel room to follow the very same man in question.

Samuel sighed. "I know—but how did you?"

"I am an actress," she whispered, lowering her voice so only he could hear. The fact that in doing so, her breath blossomed against his neck and made him feel most peculiar was neither here nor there. "I can read people."

She certainly could. She had read him as a complete fool, Samuel was starting to realize. The worst of it was, he couldn't completely disagree with her.

Heads turned wherever Rose went. Had he just never noticed, or was it the gown he had borrowed—fine, stolen; it wasn't as if she'd notice it gone, as she'd have never worn it—from Frank thanks to her obliging maid that was doing it? As he and

Rose walked down the corridor behind Benjamin, who appeared to be eager to get to their family so that he could see their faces when the supposed newly married arrived, every male eye turned to the elegant, petite woman in the fine, green gown that showed off her waist, her buttocks, her—

"Excuse me," snapped Samuel at a particularly young man whose jaw had literally dropped as they passed him on the landing. "It's rude to stare!"

"Hush, dear," Rose said companionably, patting his arm as though she were accustomed to this spousal jealousy. "'Tis no crime to look."

It certainly felt criminal, thought Samuel darkly as they slowly descended the stairs into the wide hotel hall. There were even more people here, all staring at Rose.

He glanced at her. She was markedly beautiful, but it wasn't the beauty that was capturing their attention. It was the…the glow. Foolish though it was to think, he could not ascribe it to anything else.

Somehow, Rose had switched on something within her, and she just… Well, she looked like a duchess, not a woman he had quite literally picked up off the street.

Fine. Knocked down, then picked up, then selected. But still.

"Where have you b-been, Samuel?" clucked his mother as the pair approached the table in the hotel dining room. "And wh-who…who is…"

I should have known, Samuel thought wearily as his mother burst into tears.

"Now, now, Florence. The poor dear will make for the hills," said her husband with a smile, placing his arm around her shoulders. "And she hasn't yet, even after being married to your eldest son."

Much to Samuel's horror, his mother's tears only increased in both flow and volume.

"You're wearing my gown," said Frank calmly, seated as she was behind a large drawing of a contraption Samuel hesitated to inquire about. Blast. She *had* noticed.

"I am?" Rose turned to Samuel.

"You are—sorry, Frank," he said hastily, pulling out a chair for his supposed bride and flashing his sister a wink. "Rose had to rush from Bath and I didn't think you'd mind."

"Mind? I'm delighted. She can keep it. It'll be one less gown Mama tries to force me into," Frank said vaguely before turning back to her drawing. Then she looked up again. "Wait. Is this your wife?"

"This is our Sammy's wife," Benjamin said with a grin as he nudged Rose with his elbow. "None of us can believe it. How on earth did he manage to land you?"

"*Benjamin!*" their father shot across the table.

Samuel looked helplessly at his mother, who was still sobbing but who had least been handed a handkerchief by a woman at a neighboring table who obviously thought some great bereavement had been announced, and then he glanced at Rose, who was clearly trying not to smile.

But she was greatly enjoying this, wasn't she? This was the perfect role: a true test of her acting ability.

Well, if the last time she had practiced her acting ability had been anything to go by, this was going to be electric...

"Come now, Lady Aylesbury," Rose said soothingly, stepping around the table and clasping his mother's hand. "No tears! This is a happy occasion."

"It's a *surprising* occasion," muttered Frank.

Samuel purposefully kicked her under the table as he sat down.

"Ouch!"

"It most certainly is, and we are delighted to finally meet you," said their father. He grinned as he too sat down. "Though truth be told, we did not even know of your existence a week ago."

"I know, and I am sure you are most shocked by his behavior," Rose said, rubbing the dowager marchioness's back with one hand and pulling out her own chair with another. Samuel winced. That was his job, if not a footman's. But no one seemed to take note of that. "Come now, sit down—let's get some tea inside you. Yes, we simply could not wait to be married, but after eloping, we were waiting for the perfect moment to announce it, and then, though we had decided perhaps to do so at Christmas, I had to keep my friend company, and then at New Year's, we did not want to steal any attention from your niece, whom we learned was marrying. But your son makes me so happy—"

Samuel's mother burst into a fresh wave of happy tears and Samuel silently thanked Rose for remembering the details of Irene's rushed nuptials. It would have been strange not to bring his new wife home for Christmas season and New Year's otherwise.

Rose poured the dowager marchioness some tea and winked—winked!—at Benjamin. "You look like the sort of rascal who would have some whiskey about his person."

"Why don't you come over here," said Benjamin with wiggling eyebrows, "and search me yourself?"

"Just hand it over, Benjamin," snapped Samuel, his temper seething.

Dear God, she's a master. A mistress? It was a small catastrophe that she had not taken over the London stage. Flirtatious with his brother, cordial with his sister, she was politeness itself to his father and supportive and soothing for his mother.

She was also pouring a large dollop of whiskey into his mother's tea. "There now, something to calm the nerves—I suppose meeting me in person has been a great shock!"

A ripple of laughter moved about the table as Rose sat down not beside Samuel, as he had intended, but instead between his mother and sister.

Well, perhaps that was all to the good. It kept her away from Benjamin, at the very least, and that had to be worth something.

"Tell me," said Frank suddenly, looking up from her blueprint and fixing her new temporary sister-in-law with a stern look.

"What is your view on education? For the lesser sex, I mean?"

Samuel swallowed. It was always a point of contention, and a conversational topic that Frank frequently used as a test. Few passed it.

Rose nodded thoughtfully, then shrugged. "I suppose if we have to educate men, so be it."

The table went quiet.

Frank grinned and turned to Samuel. "I like her. You may keep her."

She disappeared back to her drawing as Samuel inhaled a laugh. "Thank you, Frank, that is most kind of you. Tea, Mi—my dear?"

The slipup was small, but it could have been caught. He cursed himself for making such a categorical error. If Benjamin had been paying attention…

Thankfully, Benjamin was not paying attention. At least, he *was* paying attention, but to the waitress from yesterday, who was most decidedly averting her eye.

Samuel sighed. It was the same old story.

"Yes, thank you, I would love a cup of tea." Rose smiled prettily, fluttering her eyelashes. "He is the most attentive husband, Lady Aylesbury, you have no idea."

"Oh, p-p-please, call me 'M-Mother,' now that w-we are f-family," said Samuel's mother, finally dry enough to put the handkerchief away. "I don't know wh-what came over me. I'm all at s-sixes and sevens!"

"Quite understandable," said Rose reassuringly. "Why, I have heard so many good things about you all and yet I have been most nervous to finally meet you. And there was no need! Although it is a shame that Lady Lilianna is not here."

Samuel just managed to ensure that his eyebrows did not shoot up to his hairline.

Dear God, he had only mentioned his absent sister…what, once, in passing? And yet the woman had remembered. Remembered and managed to slip the fact into conversation as though they had discussed her at length.

She was a marvel.

"Oh, dear Lilianna, I cannot wait for you to meet her," said the dowager marquess with a laugh. "She has quite a temper on her, though, I warn you."

"I am sure I am up to the challenge," Rose said with a beaming expression, directing her glance not at the man who had just spoken, but at Samuel himself.

He inclined his head as he raised his cup of tea as a toast. She most certainly was.

Chapter Seven

ROSE LAY IN the most comfortable bed she could remember in a long time, brushing her fingertips across a genuinely silk bedspread, staring at a ceiling that wasn't cracked or full of mold...and wondered.

Was she truly about to do this?

Oh, meeting Samuel's family had been fine. All she'd had to do was channel the role, and the rest had been easy. It had in fact been rather pleasant, seeing them all tease the tall, charming man who was so easily undone by his own sister.

And now she was lying in bed, in a bed he was paying for, trying to sleep on the night before her wedding.

Her wedding to a man she barely knew.

Her wedding to a man who did not love her.

Her wedding to a man who had already decided how to set her aside.

It was perhaps not the tale that one would tell upon a stage...but was it truly the best story for her?

It was not as though there were copious other roles knocking on my door, desperately begging me to return to the theater, Rose reminded herself forebodingly.

No. It was this opportunity, or the option of begging on the streets.

Rose's stomach turned. Well, perhaps it was not that dramatic. But still. As she lay here, in borrowed finery—precisely how Samuel had perfectly calculated her measurements, she did not like to guess—in a bed that was far too comfortable to sleep in, wondering what the future would bring.

And that was despite knowing quite certainly that tomorrow would bring her wedding.

Do you, Rose Morgan, take this man...

Rose sat up in bed, her stomach now churning so violently that it was impossible to remain horizontal.

Oh, she had acted in plenty of wedding scenes. It was hardly a play if there was not a wedding at the end—or at the very least, in the middle. She had been the bride, more often than not. She had worn the silk gowns, the jewels. She had simpered and smiled and professed joy. She had worn any number of wedding rings...which had all been slipped off and returned to the props master within minutes of the curtains closing.

But not this time.

This time, she would speak her own name in the vows; the ring placed on her finger would not be so easily removed; and the husband she stood before, vowing all sorts of things like honor and duty, would not be a fellow cast member but a real man.

Not that the others weren't real, but—but in a way, they weren't.

And she had never met a man half so real as Samuel Chance.

"Rose?"

Rose started, reaching for the knife that...that was not there. Of course, she had not thought to place it beneath her pillow as she had always done in her rooms before. Well, one never knew who else had a key, even if she was paying the full rate for the room.

"Rose?"

Rose swallowed. She'd almost forgotten she was not alone in here. That there'd be someone to stop an intruder if it came to that, despite her not having her knife. The gentle tapping at the screen that the pair had dragged to separate the bed from her future husband's temporary sleeping arrangements on the hotel sofa would surely not be heard from the corridor, but it echoed around her mind like cannon fire.

"Rose, are you awake?"

This was ridiculous. She could talk to the man. She could always talk to people!

So why was her throat dry and her tongue immovable?

The screen shifted; she could make it out even in the midnight black of the night. It slid slowly, and without any noise, but it was definitely moving.

And she should not have been nervous. Hell, the man had made it perfectly clear that there was to be absolutely none of that sort of thing, or else the annulment would be almost impossible to secure—and it wasn't as though they wanted to actually remain married to each other.

The very idea!

She did not want a man who didn't seem to think her good enough to be his marchioness in the long term.

Still, a flicker of unexpected elation rushed through her as the screen disappeared entirely and Samuel Chance, newly the Marquess of Aylesbury and very soon to be her husband, was outlined in the space left behind.

"Are you awake?" he whispered.

Rose snorted with hardly repressed laughter. "I am now."

"Sorry, I—damn. Sorry."

Her laughter could not truly be described as repressed now. The man appeared to have tripped over her umbrella, one of the few things that had made it through her adventures since she had left home all those years ago. "What do you want, Samuel?"

For a heart-stopping moment, Rose was almost certain he was going to say something salacious—and she would perhaps even allow it.

Well, it had been a long time since she had felt the touch of a man. One whom she *wanted* to touch her, at any rate; all those idiots holding her waist on the stage most certainly did not count.

"Can we... Can we talk?" came his whispered reply.

Rose slipped out of bed immediately. The very idea of talking here, while she was sitting in bed!

No, there was only one direction that led to, and she certainly wasn't going to allow herself to be seduced the...the night before her wedding! Marriage of convenience or not, she was going to allow herself at least a modicum of dignity.

This thought was a tad undermined by the way she slipped on the stockings she had unceremoniously dropped at the side of the bed, but she managed to retain her balance. Just.

"I have a better idea," Rose said brightly. "Are you dressed?"

There was a moment of silence on the other side of the bed. Then, "'Dressed'?"

"You have five minutes."

Five minutes was all she would need, Rose knew, to pull on her thickest gown, find a pair of shoes, and tug on her pelisse. Five minutes was not enough, sadly, to formulate a plan that would make sense to a man who was evidently worldly enough to creep into a woman's side of a screen partition and make such a racket tripping over that woman's umbrella that his question '*Can we talk?*' could surely only have one meaning.

But she did recall a conversation with Miss Margolotta, six years ago. A conversation in which Miss Margolotta, after a whole bottle of red wine, had told Rose the story of how she had managed to distract her third husband...

"I'm ready," came Samuel's whisper. "But where are we—"

"Follow me," returned Rose with a half-smile—one he surely could not see. "And remain silent."

Say what you want about strange men who proposed and planned to pay you a great sum of money to marry him for a year and a day, Rose could not help but think dryly as the two of them crept down the sweeping staircase and out of the front door of the hotel. They knew how to move quietly. Why, Samuel Chance must have crept into dozens of women's bedchambers to—

She pushed the thought out of her mind and slipped her hand through the man's arm. "Right. That's better."

"*Better* is a relative term," muttered Samuel, shivering in the chill night air. "What precisely did you have in mind?"

"Well, I wasn't going to talk to you while I was lying in bed," Rose said. "We put up the screen for a reason, I thought. That could lead to…"

She did not finish her sentence. Unfortunately, the dratted man seemed to notice.

Samuel's face broke into a broad grin. "Lead to what?"

"Never you mind," Rose said firmly, directing him across the empty street toward the sea.

She could always tell where it was. Perhaps it was her wandering nature, her desire to see the world, her inability to stay in one place for very long. Her father had always said—

"What is it?"

Rose swallowed. Somehow, they had ceased walking, and Samuel was looking down at her, his eyebrows drawn together as he studied her.

Dear Lord, what had she done?

As though he could read her mind, Samuel said quietly, "You—You stiffened, all of a sudden, as though you had seen a ghost. Are you quite well?"

'Seen a ghost'? *No*, thought Rose ominously. *I'll never see that man again.*

"Merely an errant thought," she said brightly, as though she frequently reacted bodily to thoughts. She began to walk again, tugging him closer to the sea. "Come on."

"It did not appear to be merely an errant thought," said the irritatingly perceptive man on her arm. "What were you thinking of?"

Rose should not have said it. "Not what, but whom."

There it was: the sea. Even in the darkness of night, she could make out the cresting waves, smell the salt in the air, feel the—

"He hurt you, then."

Rose swallowed. Samuel's voice was… well, strange. He was not demanding a response; indeed, it was a statement and not a question that he had uttered. When she glanced up at him, his face was strangely impassive, as though he were not curious at all but merely making conversation.

And yet as she opened her mouth to speak, hardly knowing what on earth she would say to him, Samuel's nostrils flared.

Rose closed her mouth. She was not about to reveal all her torrid past to a man she hardly knew, and one who would be exiting her life very definitely in just over a year.

No, best to tell him the basics—the absolute truth, no lies, but nothing else—and leave it at that.

Rose inhaled deeply as she pulled Samuel onto the sand. "Yes. My father. I don't see him now, and I have not for a long time."

Strange... Just uttering the words felt like poison was being sucked out of a wound that had been left to fester entirely too long. Had she even spoken about him these last eight years? Had her lips even formulated his name?

Samuel's hand covered her own on his arm. "I did not wish to ask—I mean, about who ought to be giving you away tomorrow."

Rose's laugh was bright and harsh and even she winced to hear it. "Oh, that man gave me away a long time ago."

"He abandoned you?"

Their shoes met with water and Rose halted, desperate to avoid this conversation and yet somehow, there was a trust, an openness she could find with this man that she had never found before.

It was a most disconcerting feeling.

"Rose?"

She did not look at Samuel and pulled her hand from the crook of his arm.

"I apologize," he said softly. "I did not mean to pry."

"I know," Rose said determinedly, not looking at the man standing beside her and instead concentrating on taking off her shoes.

"What... What are you doing?"

She did not need to look up to see the confusion on his face—

it was so potent in his voice. So when Rose did look up, she winked. "I am taking off my shoes and going paddling."

"Paddling," Samuel repeated in a confused tone.

"Paddling," Rose repeated with a bright grin. "In the sea. You've never done such a thing?"

The tall gentleman beside her glanced at the ice-cold waves rushing toward her toes. "Yes, but..."

"Well, stay here if you want," Rose said gaily. "But I'm going in."

Sometimes it was the only thing that helped her brain to reset. Sometimes it was the only place she wanted to be. Rose had always lived by the ocean, or at the very least a river; the water somehow managed to wash away all her pain, all her frustrations, even if she could not go swimming. Sometimes, paddling was enough.

She would have to hope it would be enough tonight.

"Rose!"

Rose ignored him. Gasping with a laugh at the freezing temperature of the water now pouring over her feet, she strode forward, not bothering to hold her skirts up, as it would only be a matter of time before a wave caught at them. The fabric clung to her calves as she luxuriated in the solitude of it all. The sea, herself, and nothing—

"This is absolute madness," said Samuel, his voice short as he shivered, standing suddenly beside her in the ocean. "Absolute madness!"

Goodness. She had not actually expected him to follow her.

Her eyes now accustomed to the darkness of night, Rose took him in. The same handsome face, the broad shoulders, the wide chest—but now his trousers were damp almost from the knees down, and she could just make out his boots on the shore.

And a smile, one she had not known for a great long time, creased her lips. "You're here."

"You invited me," said Samuel simply, though there was a wry look in his eyes. "Not that 'stay here if you want' is the most appealing invitation, but still."

Before she could think what to say, he had slipped his fingers to her hand and interlocked them together. They stood there, staring at each other as the ocean lapped at their legs, the freezing water somehow nothing compared to the strange tension between them.

"Samuel," Rose said softly, hardly knowing what she was about to say next. "Samuel, I—aarghh!"

Her instincts overcame her, launching her into the embrace of the man beside her as a huge wave crashed over them, drenching her skirts almost to the waist and causing Samuel to curse under his breath.

"That's damned cold!"

"Ohhh!" was all Rose could manage as she clung to him, desperate for his warmth. "Ohhh I d-did not s-see that coming!"

She looked up, his charming face suddenly much closer, his immensely kissable lips—

Rose did not exactly pull away, as the man's warmth was far too crucial for that…but she did turn away ever so slightly so that though the man's arms were around her waist and her hands were splayed against his chest, her mouth was not quite within kissing distance of his own.

Not quite.

"There's so little I know about you," came Samuel's quiet words. "But I know you love the sea."

Rose could not help but laugh. "Any water, really. I've not met a river I didn't like."

"You are a strong swimmer, then?"

She nodded. "One has to be, growing up in—"

Just in time, she managed to halt her lips.

No. No, he did not need to know that. Any of that. There was still a chance that he…that they…that some of her family was still there. She did not need the news of her marriage to reach them.

Goodness knows what would happen.

"I learned to swim in Stanphrey Lacey's lake," Samuel said, as though he had not noticed how she had cut off her own speech. "It's very deep at one end. My cousins and I used to dive for pearls."

Rose glanced over. "'Dive for pearls'?"

He laughed, and she felt his laugh move through her, so close were they together in the freezing ocean. "Well, any pebble would do. It was a marvelous game."

"It sounds delightful," she had to admit. "I always wanted siblings."

"You have none?"

"Only one." Rose had spoken before she had realized what she was doing and cursed silently. She had never intended to give the man any information about herself—it was not necessary. It could only end in harm. And now the blaggard knew she did not get on with her father, and that she had a sibling. That was more than anyone had ever known about her since...

She swallowed, hard, but it did nothing to dislodge the lump in her throat. *Damn.*

"I cannot imagine a life with only one sibling. I have three, as you know, and I have over a dozen cousins," Samuel said conversationally, as though she had not revealed a crucial piece of information about her past. "They drive me to distraction at times—my siblings, I mean—but I suppose I would rather have them than not. Most of the time."

Try as she might, Rose could not quite manage to release herself from the man's grip. He was so...so warm. And not warm in a cloying sort of way, the way that a stuffy summer's afternoon in Rome could be. No, he was warm in a...in a *just come in from the cold and the fire was already lit, and a glass of ginger wine has been pressed into your hand by a friend and they are smiling at you* way.

It was an intoxicating way, ginger wine or no.

Rose tried to smile. "You are lucky. To have a family you care about."

"Oh, they have their downsides. Everyone is involved in everyone else's lives, arguably *too* involved, and that gets old remarkably quick," Samuel said ruefully. "But you—you must have a family."

And there it was again. Not a question. The man seemed an expert at asking questions without actually asking questions. Most irritatingly.

"I had a family. They're gone now." Well, it wasn't precisely a lie, Rose told herself encouragingly. She was not a liar. She was just…keeping to the minimum of the truth.

"I am sorry."

"Don't be. I am not," Rose said as radiantly as she could manage. "I have been on my own for so long now, I can hardly imagine what it would have been like to have them alongside me."

"Sounds lonely."

"Well, it is not," she said sharply, pulling away from the man who seemed so eager to tell her what her life had been.

It was not possible. Somehow, Samuel was far stronger than he looked—though now that Rose came to think about it, the sharp angles of the muscles underneath her palm might have had something to do with it.

"You have been on your own for a long time."

Rose glared up at the man. How did this Samuel Chance manage to say so much with so little—how did he ask questions without that questioning lilt in his voice?

It was most aggravating.

"Yes, I have," she said shortly. That was it, confirm the basics and give no additional details. "I have traveled across Europe on my own. I am accustomed to my own company. It will be strange indeed, being married."

"Oh, you won't have to spend that much time with me if you do not wish to," came Samuel's calm and yet somehow teasing reply. Was that a glint of mischief in his eyes? "After all, you will be the Marchioness of Aylesbury. You won't do anything you do not wish to."

It was a darned good thing that Rose was entirely encircled by

Samuel's strong arms, for in that moment, a strong wave roared past them and her knees wobbled.

It was the wave, she told herself firmly, and not the idea of being the Marchioness of Aylesbury that had caused the momentary lapse in concentration. And calm. And strength in her knees.

Dear Lord… The Marchioness of Aylesbury…

"I am sorry that you have had such a hard time."

Rose's expression sharpened. "What do you mean—what have you heard?"

Oh, it was all too much to hope the man would not have found out about her past, wasn't it? And she had worked so hard to keep the truth from those around her, never given her birth name, never allowed herself to truly befriend anyone…

She had escaped, all those years ago, and now—

"I just meant—well, you have no family. You are an out-of-work actress," said Samuel, a crease appearing between his brows. "Being an actress at all, it seems a rather precarious life. Without constant work, I am sure it has been a challenge."

Slowly, slowly, Rose allowed her shoulder blades to relax. "Yes. Yes, being an actress is a challenge. But there isn't anything else I would like to do."

Now wasn't that the truth.

"You have dedicated your life to it," Samuel said quietly.

"I have sacrificed everything for it," Rose returned, speaking the absolute and complete truth for perhaps the first time that day. For the first time in their admittedly brief acquaintance. "Everything."

She would not think of the home she had left behind. She would not think of her mother, the gardens where she grew up, the sound of the wind through the rustling trees.

"And I would make the same choice again, if it were presented to me," Rose continued, half for her own benefit. When she glanced up, it was to see that there was a knowing smile upon Samuel's lips. "What?"

"What?" he rejoined gently.

"You are smiling."

"You make me smile," Samuel said with a shrug of his broad shoulders. "It is not *anyone* who could take me out of a nice, warm hotel room, out into the streets and into the freezing ocean."

Rose scrunched her toes in the salty silt, the sensation grounding her as nothing else ever did. "Well. I am to be your wife tomorrow."

"Today, I think."

The very thought made her pulse skip a beat. *Today.* "Truly?"

"And I suppose we should not linger out here too long, or you shall arrive at the church with a red nose and a sniff," said Samuel with a laugh.

Somehow, his arms were not around her. Rose only realized how much she was enjoying them when they had disappeared.

"Back to the hotel, then," Samuel said brusquely, striding toward the shore. He had not quite reached it before he called over his shoulder, "Come on, wife."

Rose wanted to bristle. She wanted to correct him. She wanted so many things, and yet...

Wife.

Rose snorted as she strode through the waves. "Ridiculous man."

And yet she was the one who in a few short hours would be marrying him.

Chapter Eight

January 7, 1841

SAMUEL CHECKED HIS pocket watch for the ninth time. Then he raised the small mechanism to his ear.

There was a very—very—quiet ticking noise.

Then he shook the timepiece irritably, tapping his foot and ignoring the inconsiderate echoes it made and lifted the pocket watch to his ear once again.

Tick, tick, tick.

The damned thing was definitely working, and even if it was slow, it was most definitely past ten o'clock. So why wasn't she here?

Someone cleared their throat. "She does have the right day, doesn't she?"

Samuel glanced up at the vicar, who was waiting patiently to his right, and tried not to glare. It wasn't the man's fault they were being kept waiting. It was his future bride, whom he had left hours ago in their shared hotel room to dress with assurances she would make her own way, who had decided that timekeeping wasn't a required quality in a future marchioness. "She's coming."

She had better be.

Though it wasn't a consideration Samuel liked the thought of, if Miss Rosemary Morgan did not appear and agree to become his bride, he had simply run out of time to collect the funds that could do so much good to so many people.

Perhaps he should have married her the day after he met her. Yes, that would have been far better: locking down the agreement and marching her to a church.

Samuel's foot continued to tap on the stone-flagged floor.

Actresses! This was why people grew so irate with them: they were flighty, they could not keep to time, they did not even bother to attempt it. Oh, he should have known this was going to go wrong. It was the most outlandish thing he had ever done, and of course it hadn't gone to—

Footsteps.

"Sorry," whispered Miss Rosemary Morgan as she half-strode, half-ran up the aisle of the small church. "Sorry, sorry, sorr—"

"Where have you been?" hissed Samuel, not bothering to keep his ire back or his tongue in check. "You were supposed to be here twenty minutes ago—goodness, you look beautiful!"

She froze, as if surprised to hear him tell her that. But she quickly focused on the task at hand. "I got talking to your mother!" Rose threw back at him through a tight smile as she inclined her head to the vicar and attempted to get her breath back.

Which was not surprising, considering the very tight bust of the blush pink gown she was wearing.

There had been absolutely nothing the woman could say to astonish Samuel.

Nothing except that.

"My—My mother? What were you doing talking to my mother?"

"I ran into her as I was leaving the hotel and she wanted to talk, and I could hardly tell her I was meeting you here *to get married*," Rose said in an undertone, her expression unfractured in a mildly disarming manner.

She inhaled deeply, Samuel averting his gaze and only managing to see the rise and fall of those tremendous breasts from his periphery vision, and then remained silent.

"Umm," said the vicar.

Samuel turned back to the two of them and treated the vicar with a brief grin. "There. Right. Here we go—marry us."

It appeared that was not acceptable. Rose rolled her eyes, her smile somehow became genuine, and she turned to the man and placed a hand on his arm.

"I do not believe we have met, sir," she said cordially, and Samuel was horrified to see her squeeze the vicar's arm in a most... Well. *Comforting* way. "My name is Rosemary Morgan, and I am delighted that you will be the one marrying me."

The vicar's face quickly turned purple. "I—um—not marrying you but marrying you, erm—"

"Oh, I see." Rose laughed delicately and her merriment echoed around the small church and made it...warmer, somehow? "How amusing!"

Samuel stood transfixed as the woman flirted—flirted!—with another man. Another man, right in front of him. Another man right in front of him, when the man in question was a man of the cloth! And married himself! And near eighty!

Besides, they were running out of time.

He pulled out his pocket watch and glared at the hands on the face. They should have been married twenty minutes ago. It was ridiculous that they were standing around, just talking about—

"—and the temperatures really have dropped, haven't they?" Rose was saying conversationally. "Honestly, I thought last week we'd have snow, the way the frost was creeping up the windows in the mornings."

"Can we get on?" Samuel snapped.

Tension shot down his arms like lightning and he hated the sound of his voice, but it was done and he could not take it back.

This is not me.

The thought was unpleasant, indeed, and not one he could ignore. He was never this brusque, this demanding of people's time—but they had agreed to be wed at eleven o'clock, and it was half past the hour. Did she not see that?

Resisting the urge to lift his pocket watch and dangle it before the woman's face, even if his mother apparently carried half the blame, Samuel said quietly, "I mean...I would greatly like to be married. Rose?"

"Oh, yes," Rose said blithely, not even bothering to remove her hand from the vicar's arm. "But the vicar and I were just saying, this weather, isn't it frightfully—"

"Yes, I am sure it is," Samuel interrupted, heat now cascading through him as his irritation grew. "On with the wedding."

Without thought, for thought would surely have prevented him from doing something so utterly foolish, he leaned forward, took Rose's hand off the poor vicar's arm, and grasped it inflexibly.

He had intended to do so as a gesture of readiness for marriage. Was that not what one did, during a wedding ceremony? Hold the bride's hand?

The last few months had provided him with sufficient family weddings to know, after all, and Samuel was almost certain his sister Lilianna had done such a thing with Taernsby.

And yet despite the utterly natural—in his mind—action, Rose was…flushing. *Like an innocent.*

Samuel swallowed. They had not had… well, *that* conversation. They did not need to. He had been perfectly clear that they—that he and she—well, it was not a real marriage. It would not need to be consummated, or at least, it most certainly should not be consummated.

One's previous experience in such matters, therefore, were entirely uninvestigated.

But… Well. Rose was an actress. Everyone knew what actresses were like. Samuel himself had not gallivanted in that direction, but he'd heard his cousin Zander chatter about such things and it appeared that, in London at least, any actress's skirts could be lifted with a sufficient amount of coin.

Rather like what he was doing.

But Rose was flushing like—well, like a debutante. Like an innocent.

Surely not.

"You appear to be a little warm, Rose," Samuel said in a

slightly strangled voice, hoping to give her the chance to fan herself—or at the very least, get her cheeks out of control.

And he'd thought the woman could act! He frowned. *Was this an act?* She didn't need to put on a performance for a vicar they'd never see again, though.

"Oh, yes, a little warm," said Rose gratefully, glancing at the vicar with an embarrassed look and lifting her unencumbered hand to fan wholly ineffectively at her now-blazing-red cheeks.

The vicar smiled indulgently. "A wedding service can take the ladies like this, my lord. Such innocent doves…"

"Well, not for much longer," said Samuel bracingly. "Time to get this over with."

The instant the words were out of his mouth, he realized that they had been the wrong words.

Rose's mouth twisted as her eyes narrowed. "I do not believe we are in so much of a rush that—"

"Yes, we are," Samuel said firmly, trying to communicate with the set of his jaw and the look in his eye that they were most definitely in a rush, and it was her fault they had been delayed in the first place. Well, hers and his mother's. But his mother wasn't here right now to snap at. Not that he would have snapped at her. Not that she would have been here. Oh, it was all just so aggravating!

"But surely, a few minutes won't matter?"

"What is the point in waiting? We just need to—"

"In fact," interrupted the aged vicar with a weary look, his jowls particularly droopy, "the marriage cannot proceed."

Samuel froze. Then he turned, very slowly, on his heels. "I beg your pardon?"

'*Marriage cannot proceed*'? What on earth could be the problem? He had procured the damned license, and a great deal of money and a significant favor it had cost him too, made the effort to find a bride, introduced her successfully to the family—as his wife, to be sure, but that would be rectified soon—so there was absolutely no reason to delay!

"'Cannot proceed'?" Rose's breath hitched. To her credit, she appeared just as disheartened as Samuel felt. "Whyever not?"

"Because, my dear lady," the vicar said sternly, as though they should really have thought of such a thing, "you have no witnesses."

Samuel's shoulders sagged. *Witnesses.* Blast, yes, he had entirely forgotten. The last... Well, all the family weddings he had attended over the last few months had all been packed affairs—it had been a mite difficult to keep people out. Gossiping Society matron Lady Romeril, for example.

But though he had rolled his eyes at the sheer number of attendees Lilianna had invited, there had been a practical purpose.

A wedding needed witnesses.

Samuel caught Rose's eye. Evidently, she had not thought of such a thing, either.

"Witnesses," she said quietly.

"Yes, the whole thing requires—"

"Two people, if I recall?" Rose said brightly, as though she could easily whip up a few people from her reticule. "I remember when I married Romeo—"

"I—I beg your pardon?" the vicar began.

"—and when I married Demetrius, and King Lear too in a very awkward revisionist adaptation," Rose continued as though the vicar were not speaking. "It was always two. Would two witnesses be sufficient?"

The vicar was gaping but just about managed to nod his head.

"Well, that's easy enough—hold your horses, my good sir. I shall return forthwith," Rose said smartly before turning on her heels and marching out of the church.

Samuel's mouth fell open. So, it appeared, did the vicar's, for when he turned around to ask the older man whether or not this whole thing was quite sound, the vicar seemed to be catching flies with his mouth.

"She's... She's quite something, your wife. Your future wife, I mean," managed the vicar. "Where on earth did you find her?"

"You have no idea," muttered Samuel as he stared, boggle-eyed, at the woman now marching back up the aisle.

Rose was flushed, but appeared supremely pleased with herself. "My love, allow me to introduce you to Mr. and Mrs. Howarth."

Samuel stared. They were just...people. A couple in the middle years of their life, smartly dressed, utterly bewildered. It appeared to be a reasonably catching issue around Rose.

"Delighted," muttered the stout Mr. Howarth. "I-I gather, my lord, that you require us? Apparently?"

"Mr. and Mrs. Howarth have agreed to stand witnesses for our marriage, my cherub," trilled Rose with a grin.

Samuel was almost certain that only he saw the wink.

"Right," he said weakly.

"Right," said the vicar.

"Right?" said the rather tall and thin Mrs. Howarth.

Samuel shook his head, as though ridding water from his ears were as easy as ridding all this nonsense from his mind.

He needed to marry Miss Rosemary Morgan.

That was the only thought which should be propelling him at this time. Time was ticking onward, and he needed this wedding to occur as soon as possible. He had paperwork to complete, after all. Letters to solicitors to write.

Fortunes to claim.

Samuel leaned forward and grabbed Rose's hand, most definitely ignoring the spark of heat that poured down her wrist, into her fingers, and into his own. He had imagined it. Probably.

"Vicar, church, witnesses—bride," he said decisively. "Right. Marry us, sir. Immediately."

The vicar, much to Samuel's chagrin, blinked blearily. "'Immediately.'"

"My husband—my future husband is a little eager," Rose began with a sweet smile that twisted Samuel's stomach in a most irregular way. "It is most amusing, actually, last week—"

"No time," Samuel ground out through gritted teeth.

Honestly, it were as though the whole pack of them were conniving to make sure the wedding did not take place at all!

Rose frowned and was looking at him with...was that pain in her eyes? "I just thought that Mr. and Mrs. Howarth would appreciate hearing the story of how charming you could be."

"Well, they don't," Samuel snapped, temper rising. Where had all this anger come from? He was not usually a furious man, but this woman—this woman knew just how to get under his skin!

Mrs. Howarth cleared her throat. "I would like to hear the story."

"No, you don't," Samuel barked, glaring at the woman.

Where on earth had Rose found them, anyway? Had she merely dragged them off the street?

Good God, the name of Chance had sunk low indeed if that were the case...

"Excuse us," Rose said with a saint-like expression.

Samuel blinked. *Us?* What did she mean by—"Ouch!"

It was not, perhaps, the most coherent of statements, but then, it was more a reaction than a political declaration. It was also the only noise Samuel could think to make as Rose grabbed his arm, tugged painfully at his shoulder, and started dragging him to the left.

Feet stumbling, pulse racing, Samuel just about managed to hiss, "What the devil do you think you're doing?"

"Not in a church, thank you," Rose threw over her shoulder as she pulled him into a chapel on the side of the church and released him.

That was, she released his arm from her hand. She then proceeded to pin him against the wall with a glare.

"What is all this about?" Samuel asked, perhaps more defensively than he should have done.

He certainly should have lowered his voice. Blast, why was a church designed to have one's words echo about the place, ensuring that everyone—vicar, Mr. and Mrs. Howarth, anyone else within fifty yards—could hear him?

Rose was still glaring. "You are rushing."

"'Rushing'?" repeated Samuel, eyebrow raised.

"Yes, *rushing*," she said, voice lowering and cheeks flushing as she met his eye. "And I don't like it."

This was all getting a tad ridiculous. *We have come here*, Samuel thought fiercely, *to be married*. Why, precisely, it had to go at a certain speed and with random personages literally dragged off the street, he could not say.

"You will marry again."

Samuel had prepared himself to deliver a long, coherent, and most of all righteous speech, but all the air was taken from his lungs as he stared at the woman before him.

Her whole face was pink now, not just her cheeks, yet her gaze was steady as she stared.

"'Again'?" Samuel repeated in a whisper, hoping to goodness the vicar couldn't hear them.

Rose nodded as the candlelight in the small chapel flickered, casting a golden glow over her.

As though she needed adornment.

"After this is all over, in a year and a day, you will marry again," she said softly—no malice in her words, just plain fact. "I will not. This is the only—the only real wedding I will ever partake in. It may not be true, but it is real. I do not wish for it to be over in a breath merely because you wish to rush."

Samuel swallowed, attempting and failing to ignore the twisting guilt searing through him.

He... He had not thought of that.

But she was right. This may not have been special in the traditional way, but he would have to marry again, if he was to have heirs for the estate. True, his brother and his brother's sons might suffice, but he felt it was his duty to at least try. Especially since he wasn't so sure Benjamin would ever settle down himself.

But Rose—yes, she would be considered unworthy of matrimony, unless the men among the working classes did not care about this charade like a gentleman would, and besides, she would have her portion of Great-Aunt Tessie's inheritance. She would have no need to wed again.

This is likely the only wedding she will ever have.

It was a strange thought. What was even stranger was that Samuel was now filled with a longing to give her the best possible wedding he could.

He pushed the instinct aside as strongly as possible. That was nonsense. There was no time to arrange anything splendid, and there were no funds to do so. That was precisely the point.

Rose was smiling wistfully. "I see you understand."

"I...argh...yes." Why the devil was his tongue so disobliging?

"I am not asking for rose petals up the aisle and a choir of schoolboys singing arias," Rose said, her mouth quirking slightly. "Just for a wedding service that is not rushed."

She tilted her head as she spoke, biting her lip as nerves overcame her.

Pity for her, and something else, something hot and enthralling, surged through Samuel as he stared at her. *The woman deserved arias, and rose petals, and—*

And she is an actress. And she is playing you.

Samuel glared. "You're acting."

"It's working, though, isn't it?" Rose said lightly, straightening up and somehow transforming into a far more businesslike figure. "Besides, I spoke the truth. I don't want this rushed, Samuel. This is my only chance at a wedding. Give me at least an un-rushed service."

Hot anger was trickling through him, mingling with the remnants of the pure pity she had managed to awaken in him. Damned woman was an actress! He should have remembered that, should have prevented her clever wiles from having such an immediate impact on his conscience.

And yet...

Well, he could hardly deny her this. It was such a small request.

Samuel threw up his hands. "Fine! Fine, we'll do it your way."

Rose grinned. "The only way, I think you'll find. Come on, then, dear."

With the last few words, she lifted her voice so that it echoed both around the small chapel and beyond, into the main part of the church. Slipping her hand through the crook of his arm—and precisely when he had formed a crook with his arm, Samuel did not know—the pair of them returned to the gawping Mr. and Mrs. Howarth and the bemused vicar.

"Really, this is all very irregular," the vicar began to say, a censorious tone in his voice.

Samuel's spirits sank. It had been hard enough to find a church who would perform such a ceremony at such short notice. If the man refused to wed them, they would be in trouble, indeed.

"I know, and the Marquess of Aylesbury is very grateful. We both are," said Rose smoothly with a squeeze of Samuel's arm that was more a vise than a caress. "That is why we wanted to discuss the size of the donation that we shall be making to Saint...Saint—"

"Saint Margaret's," the vicar said with eagerness—with avarice, almost, Samuel could not help but think. "Why, that is so generous of you, my lady."

"And we of course have gifts prepared for the two of you, Mr. and Mrs. Howard—"

"Howarth," Samuel hissed, mortified to see the way that Rose could so easily sway those around her.

For they *were* swayed. The vicar was all smiles at the thought of the beneficence that was about to come his way—his church's way—and Mr. and Mrs. Howarth had brightened up considerably after hearing the title 'marquess' of anything.

"Marquess, is it?" Mr. Howarth said enthusiastically. "My-My-My lord, I had no idea!"

"Such an honor, it is," Mrs. Howarth was murmuring, cheeks flushed as she curtseyed so low, she was almost sitting on the church flagstones.

"Such a donation," the vicar was murmuring.

"Such power," Rose whispered in Samuel's ear, practically breathless.

And Samuel hesitated.

This was all getting out of hand. His idea in the first place had been slightly nonsensical, even he could see that. It was rather a miracle that he had managed to get this far.

However far this was, with two strangers genuflecting and a vicar visualizing gold falling into his lap.

Perhaps it would be best if he simply called the whole thing off now. Great-Aunt Tessie's fortune could go to the undeserving cousin, and he could hold his head up high—

Rose planted a searing kiss on his cheek. "Ready to become my husband?"

"Yes," Samuel croaked, his throat moving before his mind could engage.

Blast. How on earth did the woman have such an effect on him? It was most disagreeable, and it had to stop here. The last thing he needed, now that he was the Marquess of Aylesbury and had come into a substantial fortune, was to have feelings for a woman who intended to leave him and could quite clearly play him like a mandolin.

Samuel straightened himself up as much as he could, inclined his head imperiously at the still-lowered Mrs. Howarth, and turned to the vicar.

Well, in for a penny...

"Proceed," he said in what he hoped was a commanding voice.

Rose giggled.

"Dearly beloved," the vicar said, his cheeks flushed and eyes sparkling. "We are gathered here today..."

Chapter Nine

January 9, 1841

R OSE TOOK A long, deep breath.
It was the deepest she had taken these last few days. These last few, whirlwind days.

First the wedding—and that had been a fiasco in and of itself. Honestly, the man was completely impossible, as though he had been purposefully making the whole thing a farce!

And she knew farce. Why, Rose thought smugly as she tugged the blanket more closely around her thighs in the jolting carriage, she had practically *invented* farce. The play she had performed perhaps the best in her life had required *her* to play the role of a boorish gentleman. Or a woman in disguise as one.

The point was, the man was a fool. He was a fool for asking her to marry him, a fool for the way he had behaved at the church, and a fool for agreeing to pay her off in a year.

Not quite a year.

The thought jerked through Rose as the carriage rattled over a cobblestone, both sensations most unpleasant.

Two days had passed since they had wed. Their marriage, such as it was, would now last less than a year.

Precisely why that thought should bother her, Rose had no idea, and she made sure that the flickering uncertainty did not show on her face. It would never do to allow the man in the carriage alongside her to actually see anything that could be mistaken for weakness...

"You look nervous."

Hell's bells, had she lost her touch?

Rose smiled as prettily as she could at the stranger in the carriage with her. For he was a stranger...even if he *was* her husband.

"I am quite well, thank you," she said lightly, as though she had not experienced the oddest few days in her life.

Samuel Chance, freshly made Marquess of Aylesbury, smiled too—though it was more a grimace. "I know things have been...unsettled."

"'Unsettled,'" repeated Rose archly.

It was the best she could do at censoring herself, never an easy task. But how on earth could the man use the word 'unsettled' when the last two days had been...

Well. Absolutely wild.

"Perhaps we should have spoken more about our marriage before we entered into it," Samuel continued as his carriage—*their* carriage—rattled through the streets, which were becoming increasingly busy. "About the practical arrangements, I mean."

Rose did her best not to snort, but it was a very close thing. After all, she knew precisely what he meant when he'd said 'practical arrangements,' and there had been nothing practical about them.

"It's just—well, it is customary for people of my position—"

Something must have shown on her face, for Samuel halted his speech and flushed.

"'People of your position'?" Rose said in a honeyed tone.

"You know what I meant."

"You mean elegant, refined, titled, noble?"

"It is not my fault that I was born as I was," the man said stiffly.

And it wasn't. Rose could not help but feel sorry for the man who had never ventured beyond his class, never experienced life, never seen what the world had to offer people who were willing to leave behind their riches and titles and all that guff to see what else could be found.

Still. The last few days had been a tad tiring.

"It is not the sleeping in different bedchambers that I mind," Rose said, feeling a touch sorry for the man as the carriage rumbled around a corner so rapidly, she was forced to place a hand on the carriage door to steady herself.

"It's not?"

Was the man disappointed there? Rose decided not to look into it too closely. The man she had married was most peculiar: distant and then seeming to want intimacy and then...

"It is the constant temperature changes that I am finding wearing," she said quietly, hoping that he understood.

He did not understand. "Yes, it's certainly more temperate here in London than Brighton," said Samuel vaguely, glancing out of the carriage window. "I tend to find—"

"That is not what I meant."

The journey had been long, and arduous, and...and strange. Rose had experienced her fair share of long journeys—one did not leave Hertfordshire and end up in Rome without a little travel—but the last two days had been most inexplicable.

"I meant," Rose said steadily, as her husband—how strange that was to even think—stared blankly, "that I had not expected to be marched out of a church into a waiting carriage, bundled into it to discover that my belongings had been left behind at Regent's Hotel, to have that information soundly ignored—"

"I apologized for that!" protested Samuel. "I'm not used to having to think about... To having a *wife*. I did write to the hotel once we'd reached the next inn, didn't I? Everything will be sent on to my London address."

"—and to rush straight to the solicitor's to finish the paperwork, and then, instead of heading back to the hotel even *then*, departing immediately on a two-day journey to London, something which had not been mentioned to me previously, to meet your entire family and be presented as your bride to the world at large without even a second gown on me!" Rose's voice had lowered to a hiss with every passing word, and eventually, she found she was glaring.

Well. He does deserve it.

Quite deservedly, Samuel squirmed. "Had I not mentioned we would be coming to London?"

Rose threw up her hands in exhaustion. "And to do the journey in two days!"

"Two days is normal!"

"Only one stop for a luncheon at all the entire trip, forcing us to leave at early hours after rushed breakfasts, and may I say that the refreshments on offer at these so-called inns of yours have been very poor fare!" Now her grievances had started to pour from her lips, Rose was rather startled to find that she could not halt them. "And as for the beds—"

"I gave you the beds!" objected Samuel. "The sofas were not comfortable, let me tell you."

"The beds were no good, either," snapped Rose, exhaustion tugging at her eyes and hunger tearing into her stomach. "I have been unable to wash beyond what I can manage with a small basin—"

"It's not like I've bathed, either—"

"And you expect me to meet your entire extended family and the great and the good of Society as the Marchioness of Aylesbury in a gown I first put on three days ago?" Rose finished with what certainly felt like panic.

And it *was* panic, in a way. She had believed herself prepared, had thought she had known precisely what she'd been getting herself in for.

Marry the man. Become the Marchioness of Aylesbury. Hold court for a few months, enjoy Society, slowly disappear from parties and dinners, then walk away with her head held high and a large wad of cash in her hands.

But traipsing about the country in a carriage with only one gown to her name?

Samuel's face was wooden. "Look, I didn't exactly plan—"

"No, you did not." Just voicing her irritation had bled Rose of most of her anger, and it was mostly pity that remained. "You fool. You aren't thinking more than a single step ahead, are you?"

She had not intended to speak so dismissively, but she could not help it. The man seated opposite her hung his head.

"No," he said quietly.

"May I ask why the rush?" she said, softer this time. "It was bad enough at the church, but once you'd visited the solicitor with the signed license, I thought there was no need to barrel forward with *quite* the same kind of urgency. I'd have asked earlier, but you've been a positively beastly travel companion, I must say. Snapping at everyone and everything in your path."

Samuel winced. "I didn't... I didn't want to go back to the hotel. My parents and siblings were set to leave that afternoon as well, and I'd told them we were leaving before them, after some last business at the solicitor's. I didn't want them to figure out I'd actually spent the morning in a church."

"Your mother did mention that when she caught me. The only reason I finally got away was that I told her I was on my way to meet you for the meeting with the solicitor. But still. I presumed one last trip to the hotel would be in order. I don't have a lady's maid to pick up, but I do have *things*. I may have agreed to play a role for you—and for a substantial amount of time—but I'm not a dog you can just toss inside a carriage to tag along wherever you please without objection."

"I never said that you were," Samuel said softly.

Rose snorted.

"We'll have to get you one."

"A dog?" Rose arched a brow. "They're sweet, but I don't know if I'll be able to care for one after I... after I go back to acting. On the stage." Heaven help her, in a year's time, she'd be able to find another role. At least she wouldn't starve if she didn't. "Unless you intend to keep it."

Samuel swallowed. "No, um... I meant a lady's maid. A marchioness requires one. I suppose I better hire my own valet, too. I've been sharing my father's and going without outside the home, but I suppose a marquess must travel with the proper attendant."

"Right." Rose didn't state what she thought—that she wondered if the woman hired would be fine with working for her for just a year. Even if she left the marriage with a fortune, Rose wasn't sure she'd require a lady's maid on her own. She liked her independence. "I'll leave the hiring of those staff to your housekeeper. I'm a little more worried about *not having a clean dress* at the moment."

Rose steadied her breathing as she looked out of the carriage window. London had not changed in its particulars in the long decade since she had last been here. It was still busy, and dusty, and dirty. It was still full of people, each of them with their own story, each of them with their own worries.

But she could only concern herself with her own.

"Well, I shall simply have to solve this for you," she said with a wry look. "I have the feeling that it won't be the first time."

Samuel blinked. "I—I beg your pardon?"

"As your wife, it will be my responsibility to attempt to keep you in line, and I will work hard at that," Rose said blithely. "After all, as your wife—"

"For now."

"As your wife *for now*, I am quite happy to accept that you are unable to look after yourself," she continued, a spark of mischief heating her, warming her where there had previously been naught but irritation and nerves. "So I shall resolve this for you. First question. To where are we headed?"

Samuel stared as though she had slipped into Italian—something Rose was almost certain she had not done.

"Where are we going?" Rose said, elongating each word and raising her voice. "Exactly?"

"I—I haven't told you?"

The man was going to push her beyond the brink…

"No," Rose said with a smile that she hoped extended to her eyes. "No, the last thing of note you said to me, beyond 'You take the bed, I suppose' and excuses over my lack of trunk was 'In you get.' And I have been in here ever since."

It was not quite a prison—Rose had acted a marvelous role in Milan that required her character to be in a prison, and this carriage was more or less suitable. The blanket was welcome. Her continuous presence within it was not.

But anything would feel like a prison once one had spent so much time within it with absolutely no idea where they were going.

"Ah," said Samuel, his expression awkward. "My apologies, I...we are going to my townhouse. In Mayfair."

Mayfair. It had been a long time since Rose had been in London, but she had not forgotten Mayfair. "Excellent."

"And we will see my family and—"

"Yes, yes, but if we are going to your townhouse, that means I can have a bath," Rose said, words dripping with relief.

A bath. Clean clothes—a fresh gown, even if she had to borrow or send a servant to buy one. A moment to collect herself.

The role itself is not a bad one, she thought darkly as the carriage slowed, *but the wardrobe thus far is disgraceful.*

"And I really did send for your clothes. Or we can buy new ones, any that you want. My family uses a modiste who is... That is..." Samuel's jaw slackened as his eyes widened.

Rose twisted in her seat, attempting to see what he was staring at through the carriage window. "What is it?"

"Oh, hell," Samuel murmured.

Tension jolted across Rose's shoulder blades. It wasn't possible, was it? She had been most clear with Samuel that the news of their marriage was not to be publicized anywhere; she had been definite that there should be no announcement. So how would he know? He couldn't—He *wouldn't* be here.

"Who is it?" she asked, throat tight.

Samuel took a deep breath. "Everyone. They must have estimated our arrival. Maybe even been waiting hours outside in the cold, knowing them."

For a moment, as the carriage was brought to a halt, Rose did not quite understand. *Everyone? Hours in the cold? What on earth does the man mean?*

Only when the carriage door was flung open and cheers started going up outside did she start to have an inkling.

Everyone…

"There he is! My word, we could hardly believe it when Uncle John—"

"The letter was hardly one to believe and yet here she is!"

"Move aside there. I want a look at her!"

"To think, Cousin Samuel is now married! Who on earth will be next? I'd like to…"

The cacophony of sound was unlike anything Rose had ever encountered—at least, outside a theater. Within a theater, she was quite accustomed to applause and riotous questioning and hallooing and chatter and people peering eagerly to take another look at her.

But it had always been her as a character. As Juliet, or Hermia, or Helena.

Not as…herself.

No, Rose reminded herself sternly as about twenty faces attempted to all look into the carriage. Not herself. As the Marchioness of Aylesbury. That was the role she was playing, and she had better be good at it.

Ten thousand pounds and a thousand pounds a year were at stake, and she was not going to lose that.

"I am so sorry," Samuel began hurriedly.

"I don't know what you're apologizing for, Sammy, you dolt," said an imperious woman who had managed to elbow her way to the front of the gaggle. "And what's this I hear about you getting married without my permission?"

Rose stared at the woman, who was magnificent. Dark-chestnut hair was piled up and pinned with what appeared to be diamond slides, her stomach was swollen and rounded and surely would be placing her in confinement any day now, and there was a sharp look in her eyes that told the world she was not to be trifled with.

She would have to practice that look later.

"My sister Lilianna," Samuel said as he rolled his eyes. "She thinks she's head of the family, just because she got married the first of us and set up her own household before anyone else did."

"And don't you forget it, big brother." The aforementioned Lilianna snorted imperiously, a hand on her growing belly. "Come on, then. Out with the pair of you. I want to have a look at this bride of yours."

Rose stiffened.

She had spoken the truth to Samuel only moments ago; it was mortifying traveling with only the gown one had on. It had been three days since she had worn another, and two days since she had been able to have more than a brief moment of toilette. She was not fit to be seen by anyone, let alone her new husband's sister!

And... And everyone else.

"I thought I'd bring the family round, get all the introductions done and out of the way in one go," Lilianna said blithely over the top of Samuel's protestations. "I am almost a mother, you know. I can't stand out here all day! Come on, the sooner you meet everyone, the better! We've been cold out here. We came rushing out of the house when we heard the carriage wheels, but not all of us are suitably attired for this weather."

"My wife is not suitably attired *at all,*" Samuel said quietly.

Rose did everything she could to guarantee that her cheeks did not burn a brilliant red. As it was, her face felt slightly heated...perhaps she was only a delicate pink?

"And why not?" demanded Lilianna. "Good God, man, the least you could do was ensure she was properly dressed!"

And it was the imperious tone of the woman to whom Rose had not properly been introduced that galled her to the point of idiocy.

Or brilliance. The two emotional states were so close together, after all.

"Out of my way, Samuel," Rose said determinedly, pushing the man aside and stepping out into the brilliant winter sun.

There was indeed a crowd of people gathered on the pavement outside what was a truly splendid townhouse. Many of them looked alike, family resemblances appearing in noses and jaws and hair color, and Rose was willing to bet that as many Chances as could be rounded up had been brought here to inspect her.

Well, she could not help but think ominously, *it's too late now. I married him.*

"Lady Lilianna, I presume?" Rose said commandingly, drawing herself up to her full height and ensuring she exuded a powerful presence.

It would have worked, too, if she had not discovered three things.

Firstly, that Samuel's sister Lilianna was easily three inches taller than her, so the other woman had the height advantage without any effort, not to mention the current advantage in girth.

Secondly, that there was a small coffee stain down the front of her own gown. Dear God, when had that gotten there? Why had Samuel not told her?

And thirdly, that being stared at by adoring fans from their seats in a theater was altogether different from being stared at by a bunch of lords and ladies who were all somehow her new family and were now whispering behind their hands at her in a way that told Rose quite firmly that she had in some way disappointed.

Worse. She had failed.

Lilianna raised an eyebrow. "The Countess of Taernsby, actually. And you're Rose, are you?"

Rose swallowed. It was not meant to have been like this. She was supposed to arrive at a pleasant townhouse, be welcomed in by a friendly butler and housekeeper, be introduced to maids who would immediately run her a hot bath and massage her scalp as she washed her hair, find a new wardrobe of elegant gowns waiting for her, and have about fifteen hours sleep in a good bed...before even dreaming of being introduced to a woman as intimidating as her husband's gorgeous sister.

It was not supposed to be like this at all.

There was movement from behind her. Samuel had exited the carriage and now had his arm around her shoulder. His actual arm!

The impertinence!

Never mind that Rose sagged into it with relief, grateful for the steadiness of his frame.

Dear God, am I...

"My wife is very tired from the ordeal of the journey," Samuel was murmuring quietly, "and she needs rest. She can meet the family later."

"But they're all here!" That was Lilianna's voice, Rose was almost certain. It was coming from a very long way away.

"Yes, but Rose, my wife, she—Rose! Rose, can you hear me?"

When Rose next opened her eyes, it was to look at a ceiling with the most spectacular cherub design. She was also lying down.

"Ah, you've come to."

That voice was newly familiar, and her heart contracted with immediate panic.

"Now then, I admit, I was wrong to overwhelm you with so much," Lady Tacrnsby—Lilianna—said matter-of-factly as she pressed what appeared to be a linen cloth bathed in lavender water to Rose's forehead. "I had forgotten that my brother is an absolute arse."

Rose swallowed. Her mouth felt dry and her head felt heavy, and she was lying on what appeared to be a chaise lounge in a room she did not recognize.

Another woman whom she also did not recognize was seated beside her, and she was shaking her head. "Cousin Samuel must have urged you from Brighton at top speed. No wonder you are exhausted."

"How often did you stop on the way?" Lilianna asked brusquely, removing the linen cloth from Rose's forehead.

"Thrice." The word came out softly, but Rose could not speak more strongly. There did not seem to be any strength left in her.

"Only three times a day!" The woman slapped a palm to her chest, her mouth agape.

"Only three times since…since we left Brighton," Rose admitted, feeling strangely like she was betraying Samuel's honor as she did so. "We had dinner and breakfast and spent the nights at two inns, but we rode hard and only stopped one other time for luncheon yesterday." She didn't mention how Samuel, in a sour mood, had seemed to have forgotten lunch entirely on their wedding day.

These family members would never know the seventh *had* been their wedding day.

The two women exchanged looks.

"I told you, Lucy," said Lilianna darkly. "My brother is a complete dolt—but of course you know that, Rose. You married him."

It was all Rose could do not to laugh. "I suppose I did."

It all felt such a long time ago now, yet it had only been two days ago. Or three days ago? How long had she been unconscious?

As though her new sister-in-law could read minds, something Rose would not put past her, Lilianna said brusquely, "You've been out for about twenty minutes. Samuel said that if it went on any longer, we'd have to call the doctor, but—"

"Oh, no!" Rose sat up hastily and the elegant room in which she was located swam before her eyes. "No, I don't wish to be a bother. There's no need for that."

"There's a need for a doctor if I say there is," came a low and oddly possessive voice.

Forcing herself to remain upright and pushing aside the dizziness that threatened to creep into the corners of her vision, Rose glanced over to the left.

There, standing against the wall with one foot leaning against it, concern in every inch of his expression, was...Samuel.

"You," she exhaled, hardly knowing why.

He was kneeling beside her within three strides. "You had me worried there, Rosy," Samuel murmured, brushing away some of her curls from her forehead.

His touch was gentle, and warm, and Rose swallowed with unexpected tenderness. "I-I... I—"

"The poor woman needs rest, Samuel, you complete dolt. Excuse me, *Marquess of Complete Doltedness* now, I suppose," said Lilianna conversationally, as though she frequently chastised marquesses. "You both need rest."

"I may have set the pace too hard," Samuel said quietly, his gaze not leaving Rose, who flushed. "I've managed such a trip in just three stops before when it was just me or a friend and me—and the coachman."

"Yes, well, *wives* are a different manner of traveling companion entirely," Lilianna chastised. "Where was her lady's maid? Her trunks?"

"I—" Samuel swallowed. "I'll make sure she has both soon."

"You'd better," snapped his sister.

Samuel nodded, his chin tucked down like a chastened child's.

This was intolerable! She could not feel tenderness for the man who had engaged her to act as his bride!

Though he was not doing a poor acting job himself, at the moment.

"You must accept our apologies for crowding you," said Lucy quietly. "The whole family, I mean. We had no idea you had been scurried back in such a fashion."

The two women glared at Samuel, who had the good grace to still look abashed.

"I had not thought—"

"Well, you're a husband now, Sammy, you need to start thinking," interrupted his sister with a wide grin. "For perhaps the first time in your life. This woman is a precious creature and we like her already. It's about time you treated her well."

Rose could not help but preen at that.

She'd done it. She'd done it by fainting, apparently, but still, she had done it. She had won over the family.

At least, two of its members...but if she was still as good a reader of people as she had been in Italy, Rose was willing to bet—not all her incoming fortune, but a great deal of it—that gaining the approbation of Lilianna, the Countess of Taernsby, would go a long way to securing the high regard of the entire Chance clan.

She had done it.

Lucy squeezed her hand. "We cannot wait to get to know you properly, Rose."

Rose's smile faded.

But of course, they liked the act. They appreciated a delicate woman who fainted at the first sign of difficulty, and she was pretty. They probably liked that too. But they didn't actually *know* her.

They didn't know of the life she had left behind. Of the secrets she still kept. Of the truth...

"I...I do not know what to say," Rose said, with unexpected honesty.

And much to her surprise, her new sister-in-law gave her what had to be a genuine grin. "Welcome to the family, Rose. It's utter chaos, and there's usually a scandal every other Wednesday...but I think you'll like being a Chance."

Rose's smile returned, though with a flicker of disappointment. "I'm sure as long as I am a Chance, I will enjoy it."

For the next three hundred and sixty-four days.

Chapter Ten

January 11, 1841

SAMUEL TRIED TO speak, but there were so few gaps in the barrage of words being spoken at him over the dining table, he was astonished Rose was still drawing breath.

"—and then Lilianna and I went to her modiste, and what a beautiful set of fabrics that woman has! I was delighted to see that sage green was back in fashion, for it suits me so well, and so I ordered three ballgowns and three day dresses—"

Samuel took a bite of the admittedly delicious partridge, and wondered just how many gowns a woman needed.

Clearly more than six.

"—and your cousin Lucy suggested I buy a fan to match each gown, and it was a rather delightful idea that I had no issue with," Rose said with a wink, pausing only for a moment to take a sip of her wine.

"I spoke to the solicitor—"

"And then we met two of your other cousins at Don Saltero's Chelsea Coffee House, Evelyn and Gwendolyn, and most charming they are too. I had invited your sister Frank, but apparently she was too busy redesigning the world. At least," Rose said with a laugh, "I think that is what she said. And then your mother called on me…"

Most of London Society had called on her, by the sounds of it. Samuel had been out most of the day, meeting with the London branch of the solicitors whom Great-Aunt Tessie had granted permission to distribute funds, and distribute they had. Samuel had never seen such a look on his bank manager's face.

"—and Benjamin called and left a card—"

"You stay away from my brother," Samuel said warningly, just about managing to get his words in before his wife continued.

"—and he and I will be attending the opera tomorrow and you are more than welcome to join us." Rose's smile did not falter, precisely, but it did not grow. "Why are you looking at me like that?"

It was difficult to look at her any other way.

Oh, Samuel had known she was pretty. There was a reason Miss Rosemary Morgan, as she had been then, had caught his eye as he'd stridden through Brighton's streets, beyond the fact that he had knocked her to the ground. She had been pretty.

She was now magnificent. Even with his newfound riches, with the simultaneous hiring of a valet for himself, the addition of a lady's maid to his household had seemed an awful expense, until Samuel had seen just what impressive hairstyles the woman could create with Rose's luscious golden hair. The visits to the modiste had gained his wife two gowns immediately, her measurements—and here he had to swallow—apparently being close to the ideal, and the way the green silk she was wearing tonight skimmed down to her décolletage...

Samuel cleared his throat. "I'm not looking at you any particular way."

"Yes, you are. You've been looking at me strangely since I came down for dinner," Rose said, irritatingly accurately. "Like... Like there's something on my face."

There was something on her face, and it was beauty. Samuel had never realized just how intoxicating it was to listen to a woman speak, but the way Rose laughed and pouted with those red-tinted lips as her brilliant eyes sparkled in the candlelight...

Well, it was a good thing he had striven for decorum and seated the two of them at opposite ends of the long dining table. There was no possibility at this distance that he could reach out and take Rose's hand in his and whisper sweet nothings into her ear.

Not that he would have done that. Obviously.

This is all an act, Samuel reminded himself sternly. *She's acting like this because she is acting. It's all a farce!*

Though why she was bothering to act the noble lady excited over a day of shopping when it was just the two of them, he had no idea.

"I'm just looking at you," Samuel said as jovially as he could manage.

It did not sound jovial. It sounded false, and awkward, and that was because that was exactly what it was.

"Well," Rose said lightly, placing her cutlery down on her empty plate, "I will say that there are some advantages to being the Marchioness of Aylesbury."

Samuel could not help but smile at that. "Just some?"

"Oh, I like the way that people simper at me and stroke my ego," said the irrepressible Rose. "I like being able to buy pretty things and I like your sisters. All your family, in fact. I have yet to meet an unpleasant member."

"Lilianna is a force, to be sure. And Frank has her moments," Samuel said dryly, recalling the time his younger sister had pelted ball bearings at a gentleman caller for daring to speak to her.

"I am sure she does. Everyone does, in their way, but your family... Well, they are some of the nicest people I have ever met," Rose said lightly. "I shall miss them."

And there it was: the ever-present reminder that this, none of this, was going to last. That it was all going to be over and done with within a year. That whatever they were building here was all false, the walls of which would soon tumble down.

It had been his plan. He could not expect a stranger—a woman with a career, no less, no matter how poorly it had been going—to commit to a lifetime with him. Samuel had known this was going to happen...and yet somehow it pained him.

Foolish idea.

"Perhaps it would not be such a good idea to befriend them," Samuel said quietly, glancing at the footman, who immediately began to clear the empty plates away. "If you are not to be a part of their lives this time next year."

"Oh, quite to the contrary," said his wife without a hint of embarrassment. "If I only have a twelvemonth to enjoy their company, I will do so at every opportunity. Oh, ices!"

Her eyes lit up at the arrival of dessert, and Samuel stifled the instinct to grin.

"I remembered how much you enjoyed them at Brighton," he said quietly.

Rose looked up with pure delight in her face and his pulse skipped a beat. "You remembered?"

I remember everything about you, Samuel did not say. What he did say was, "It's only an ice."

"When one has lived in the boiling heats of Italy, one realizes just how rarified and delicious an ice is," Rose said with her eyes shut, lifting a heavily laden spoon to her mouth.

Samuel knew it was inappropriate, knew he should not do it. But all that knowledge did not prevent him from watching eagerly as the spoon neared Rose's plump, wet lips. They parted slowly, decadently, and he was forced to cross his legs under the table. In went the spoon and together came her lips, and the soft moan of delight was enough to stiffen a monk.

And he was no monk.

"It's just an ice," Samuel repeated, his voice half-strangled.

Rose did not immediately reply, for she was too busy devouring the mouthful of strawberry ice. When she finally swallowed and opened her eyes, Samuel was a little surprised that the chair beneath him had not combusted.

"It's delicious, that's what it is," she said in a low, almost husky voice.

Quick, think of something else. Anything else. Anything! "You lived in Italy?"

For some reason, his innocent question wiped the gleeful

expression from Rose's face. "And?"

"And... And what is it like? I only visited Rome on my Grand Tour," Samuel said, wishing to goodness she could be done swiftly with the ice so he could then apply some to his groin. "Did you travel much?"

She was staring as though looking for the catch in a trap. "Travel?"

"In Italy."

There is so much about her I do not know, Samuel could not help but think as he watched her carefully consider what to say—and eat three more lavish mouthfuls of her ice. So much he wanted to know.

And yet what good would that do him? As per the terms of their agreement, Rose would no longer be a part of his life in just under twelve months. She would be gone, never to be seen again.

So why did he want to know so much about her now, knowing he was to lose her?

"I... I traveled in Italy," Rose said eventually, as though she were admitting to state secrets.

Samuel leaned back, his own ice forgotten. "Why did you leave England?"

His wife's eyes narrowed, as though he had asked her a very personal question. "Why do you want to know?"

He shrugged, far more nonchalantly than he actually felt. "We are to live together all year. We may as well know *something* about one another."

"You know everything about me of import," Rose said, her cheeks pink now, as though he had expected a great deal from her. "There is nothing else to know."

Her spoon scraped the bottom of her bowl, and the way her shoulders sagged at the sight of a finished dessert had Samuel do something idiotic.

"Here—take mine." Before he knew what he was doing, he had risen from his chair—*stiff manhood thankfully behaving, finally*—and stepped around the table to offer his wife his own ice.

Rose looked up with a slight frown. "Are... Are you sure?"

"'Sure'?"

"You don't mind going without?"

Samuel was not sure what made him do it. He certainly had not intended to drop down into the seat beside her and take her free hand in his and caress her fingers as he said, "You have gone without before, haven't you?"

Rose snatched away her hand as though she had been burned. "No."

Her answer was far too quick. "There's no shame in it."

"I do not recall any clauses in our bargain that required you to know everything about me, Samuel Chance," she snapped, her focus fixed upon the end of the table where he had, but moments ago, been seated.

Samuel swallowed, discomfort twisting in his stomach that had nothing to do with what he had been eating.

"I... I just thought—"

"No, you *wondered*," Rose threw back at him. "You wondered, you enquired, you asked! You want to know all about me, but you've hardly told me a thing about yourself!"

Samuel blinked. "But—But you've met my whole family!"

Not that he had wished for such a thing to occur, to be sure, but now that it had occurred, he was not entirely against it. What more was there to share, once a woman had met his parents, siblings, uncles, aunts, and cousins? What secrets were there left?

Rose pointed at him sternly with a spoon. Samuel hastily leaned back. "Meeting your family tells me almost nothing about you—though I admit, it does explain why you consider your siblings to be a small number. No, tell me something true."

His frown was slight, but it was there. "Everything I have told you is true."

"I don't mean a dull fact or a statement of what is about to occur," Rose said, a wry smile lilting her lips. "I mean something you haven't told anyone else. Something true, for just us."

Just us.

There is no us, Samuel hastily reminded himself as his loins did that irritating stirring thing they almost always did whenever in the presence of his wife. His actress wife. His temporary wife.

There is no us.

"I... I intend to do a great amount of good with the money I have inherited."

Rose raised an eyebrow. She did not even need to speak to communicate her disdain for what Samuel had said, and he had to admit in the privacy of his own mind, it wasn't that impressive, as secrets went.

"My cousin Thomas runs an orphanage. One for children," Samuel added.

This time, Rose's smile was real. "Yes, I gathered that."

"I intend to supply it with food and clothing for children and staff for years—anonymously, obviously," he said swiftly. "And I intend to pay for Frank to gain access to better equipment. Cables and wires and metal, and things. And I'll double the dowries of the remaining Pernrith Chances."

"'The Pernrith Chances'?"

Once again, Samuel was reminded that Rose was not a member of Society. Otherwise, she would know the full sordid tale of his father's youngest brother.

Half-brother.

"Uncle Frederick, he was... Well, let us say that he was legitimized after his birth. He's half a Chance, really, and his daughters have small dowries," Samuel explained. "Though only two remain unwed. And I want to sponsor artists, like my cousin Evelyn, and bequeath a bursary for the London Archery Club, where my cousin Leopold—"

"And, aside from those fortunate enough to live or work in a Chance family orphanage, do you intend to do anything for those not actually related to you?" Rose asked quietly.

Samuel opened his mouth, realized he had absolutely nothing to say, and closed it again.

"Just a thought," said Rose lightly as she stood to her feet.

"And now I think I shall retire. It is hard work, spending your money, and I need my beauty sleep."

"I think you're doing quite well on the sleep you've already got," were the words that slipped from Samuel's mouth before he could stop them.

The flush of flattery on Rose's cheeks was more than enough of a reward. "Oh. Well. Thank you."

They walked in silence out of the dining room, across the hall, and up the wide, sweeping staircase that Samuel had never realized was about a thousand steps long. Only after an eternity did they reach the top and walk to the left down the corridor that led to their bedchambers, side by side.

They halted outside the bedchamber that Rose had taken the day they had arrived, and a strange sort of awkwardness rose in the silence between them.

"Well," he said.

"Well," Rose echoed with just a hint of a teasing smile.

Samuel hesitated. The whole evening he had been hesitating, teetering on the edge of doing something, he knew not what—save that he should not do it.

The servants were all gone to their evening work or to bed. He and Rose would need to ring the bells to summon the lady's maid and valet before bed. They were alone here, standing just outside the bedchamber door for the marchioness. His marchioness. His Rose.

His wife.

Samuel swallowed. "I... I suppose... Good night, then."

Coward, his mind screamed, but what else was there to do or say? They had entered into an agreement that was quite clear on the complete lack of physical intimacy. He would not touch her. That, he had told himself a long time ago. There was absolutely no good reason to do so. If they consummated the marriage, they would have to aim for divorce, not annulment. And that meant one would have to accuse the other of adultery—really, *he* would have to accuse *her*, as lords were less likely to face the consequences of such an act. And he could not do that to her. Not even to free her from a lifetime with him, like she so stubbornly wanted.

"Good night," Rose said in a low, husky voice as she leaned forward and pressed a kiss on his cheek.

Time stopped for that moment: a time filled with the scent of rosewater and the pressure of her lips and the way her palm splayed against his chest for just a heartbeat as she was mere inches from him. A moment that he reveled in, that Samuel had not known he had needed, but now that it was here, he could never survive its end—

Rose stepped back.

Samuel tried to speak. He really did; his mouth was open, at the very least, and his tongue tried to move, but all that seemed to come out was a low moan.

Not particularly erudite.

She understood nonetheless. Rose's eyes met his own, and she leaned back toward him, her hand once again against him, and this time, Samuel tilted his head at the very last moment and the kiss she intended to press against his cheek brushed against his lips.

They did not brush for long. Samuel groaned, pushing the woman he absolutely should not have been kissing against her bedchamber door and taking possession of her mouth.

Rose returned his ardor, or passion, or need—whatever it was flowing through him, she was in turn possessed with a great deal of it. Her hands were somehow around his neck, fingertips grazing his nape, her body pressed up against him, and it was all Samuel could do not to caress every inch of her with his hands.

As it was, his tongue ravished her lips and parted them, his throat growling at the sweet nectar taste of her mouth as his hands grasped her waist and pulled her into his embrace.

Oh, she was everything—*this* was everything. All he wanted was—

"We shouldn't," Rose panted as she attempted to break the kiss.

Samuel did not permit it. Once again, he captured her mouth, but not before he muttered, "I don't care."

And he didn't. All he cared about, in this moment, was the quivering body in his arms; the way she tasted; the exhilaration roaring through his body.

He had needed her and now Rose was his, marked by his mouth, need soaring between them as his fingers moved lower and—

Samuel halted. The kiss ended. He stepped back.

Rose blinked at him with bleary, confused eyes. "Samuel?"

Dear God, he should not have done that.

That's the trouble with temptation, he thought as he tried not to notice Rose's mussed hair and the bruised pink of her wet lips. It was sweet, indeed, when one indulged, but the instant that the moment was over, one was filled with the bitterness of regret.

And regret that kiss, he did.

"We shouldn't have done that," he said quietly.

Pain radiated through him as Rose grinned awkwardly. "I do believe I said something to that effect when you were kissing me."

"When we were kissing each other," corrected Samuel.

It had been the wrong thing to say. Instead of sadness, fire flashed in Rose's eyes. "Oh, so I suppose I launched myself at you, did I?"

"You were the one who kissed *me!*"

"You wanted me to!" Rose shot back, utterly accurately.

Samuel did not have to admit to that, however. Tugging a hand through his hair and thanking the heavens no one had witnessed him do the unthinkable and actually kiss his own wife—and enjoy it!—he tried to calm his frantically beating pulse and actually think.

It took several seconds, four long, deep breaths, and the reminder that he absolutely could not follow Rose into her bedchamber for Samuel to regain his equilibrium.

He looked at Rose's heaving breasts. The tops of them, anyway.

"We made an agreement," he said curtly. "No amorous congress, no—no intercourse of any kind."

"Yes, because you will take a better wife someday," Rose returned archly. "Someone actually respectable enough for a position such as marchioness."

"So *you* can walk away with a small fortune," Samuel snapped, anger rising. "And I don't need you tempting me—"

"*Me*, tempting *you*!"

She sounded outraged, but Samuel pushed the thought aside. Yes, it was all Rose. *She* had been the one to tempt him. Perhaps she was not the innocent he had guessed. She was an actress, wasn't she? Actresses were not often maids. Maybe she'd found couldn't go an entire year without laying her hands on a man, annulment be damned.

"Yes, you were—" Samuel had lifted a finger rapidly to point it at the woman he very much wanted to bed but halted his speech at her reaction.

Rose flinched.

Flinched. As though he would hurt her. As though he would hurt anyone, let alone a lady.

Let alone his wife.

She covered the moment well, but he surely had not dreamed it.

Samuel cleared his throat. *Focus, man. Focus on what you know.* "You may be unable to keep your hands off me," he said warningly, "but you won't lie with me, you hear? Unlike you, I won't be foolish enough to jeopardize the annulment. Something *you* should be more concerned about than I—"

"'Unable to keep my hands *off you*'?" Rose looked genuinely disgusted at the thought. "That is the very last thing I would want!"

Samuel felt his breath hitch. Dear God, the woman had been

not so much down on her luck, but *down on the street* when he had met her! And now the bed of a marquess was not good enough for her?

"Why on earth not?" he found himself asking.

Rose smiled sweetly and leaned forward, as though to whisper a secret. Samuel most definitely did not follow the curve of her breast as she leaned forward, nor breathe in her scent, which was like honey and rosewater with a hint of salt.

"Because," Rose said in a low voice into his ear, Samuel's heart thundering as her breath blossomed over his throat, "that would mean we couldn't annul the marriage. And I would have to stay married to *you!*"

Before he could say anything—such as how unfair that was, for example, or whether he could inhale her in for the rest of his life—Samuel could only stare in astonishment as the bedchamber door before him slammed…with his wife on its other side.

For at least a full minute, he just stared at the wooden door.

The… The very idea! The mere suggestion that being married to him was *that* unpleasant! It was an outrage!

It was at the very least, a little harsh.

Samuel swallowed. The trouble was, he wasn't the easiest to live with, he knew that. Or at least, his siblings had made that very clear to him over the years, and it was hard to argue with the majority.

But he had tried…he had really tried to be welcoming to Rose. To ensure she appreciated her time as his wife, before all that came to an end.

And besides, Samuel told himself firmly, he had rights. Rights as a husband—rights to her body. It was in the law.

Not that he would ever contravene a woman's wishes in that regard. Dear God, he wasn't an animal.

Samuel reached out, just for a moment, and touched the door before him, placing his palm upon it. On the other side of this door was a woman who could irritate him beyond belief, spend his money like water, and kissed like a harlot.

It's a good thing she's already my wife, Samuel thought fervently as he removed his hand from the door and stepped along the corridor to his own bedchamber. *A wife I cannot touch unless I intended to ruin her with a divorce. Otherwise, I might have done something drastic.*

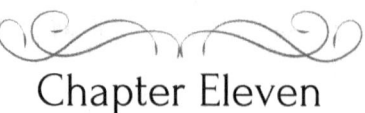

Chapter Eleven

January 13, 1841

THE RING OF the doorbell could be heard all over the house.
"She's here."

Rose looked over at her husband and wondered what on earth she had let herself in for.

Oh, acting as the Marchioness of Aylesbury—that had all sounded like a rather wonderful game. Spending a gentleman's money? *Don't mind if I do.* Wearing beautiful clothes, eating delicious food, not having to worry about getting cold on a winter's night?

She could not wait.

But this—this was the bill she had known would present itself at some point. This was the catch, the flaw in the plan.

This was the first time she was hosting afternoon tea.

"Now, the important thing…" Samuel began, his back stiff and his jaw tight as he stood by the window.

"You have lectured me sufficiently, I am sure," Rose said curtly though through a smile as the sound of footsteps in the corridor below echoed through the house. "I know how to host afternoon tea."

Were those footsteps on the stairs? Had the front door already been opened—was their first guest already in the house?

Samuel was snorting—mostly, Rose was certain, through terror. "Oh, yes, but serving tea as an out-of-work actress down on her luck is not—"

"Are you really going to talk about that here? Now?" Rose

hissed, mortification rising in her like bubbling tar.

Her temporary husband at least had the good graces to clear his throat and look a shade abashed. "No. No, of course not. It's just—"

"I am fully prepared," Rose said smoothly, hoping to goodness she *was* prepared as she sat in the soft, velvet armchair. "You have equipped me well."

"There is no amount of equipping that can ready one for—"

"Lady Romeril, my lady, my lord," intoned their broad-shouldered butler, Arden, as he opened the door and bowed.

Slowly, in no rush but at the same time not hesitating, Rose stood to her feet and examined the woman who had just entered her drawing room.

She was... Well. Not what Rose had expected.

Society spoke of Lady Romeril just as a mouse colony in a barn would speak of the farmyard cat. She was fearsome to behold, and powerful, and deadly. She could ruin a lady's reputation with the merest hint of indecorum. She could end a young man's prospects by merely refusing to approve them.

Lady Romeril, full title unknown, perhaps acquired from a foreign noble husband long gone, had been a central part of Society as long as Society had existed.

Lady Romeril knew everyone's secrets, and if you think she did not know yours, she had just not leveraged it yet.

Lady Romeril...

Rose blinked. Lady Romeril was an older woman with silver, almost-white hair. She was attired in not quite yesteryear's fashions, but yester*decade*'s, and she was leaning heavily on a cane carved from what appeared to be mahogany.

Where was the dragonish creature Rose had been promised?

And then Lady Romeril lifted her gaze, one made of steel and iron, and Rose almost rocked with the weight of it as it questioningly examined her.

Dear God, the woman should have been on the stage in her prime!

"Lady Romeril," Rose murmured, dropping to such a low

curtsey, her knees almost grazed the carpet.

Samuel behind her had done much the same thing—though thankfully, he had not entirely lost his head and started curtseying.

"Hmmph," said Lady Romeril. "You are the new marchioness, then."

In his careful and most persistent instructions on the matter, Samuel had warned Rose that Lady Romeril was not a woman for small talk.

But that was quite acceptable to Rose. She had always been a fan of big talk, as it was.

"I am, indeed. Please, won't you sit down?" Rose gestured to the gaggle of chairs and pair of sofas that filled the drawing room.

In short, hesitant movements as though afraid that one misstep could topple her, Lady Romeril moved forward. And forward. Right at her.

Rose swallowed, left completely speechless as Lady Romeril did not help herself to one of the myriad available seats in the drawing room, but instead pushed past her and settled herself ostensibly quite comfortably…in the chair that Rose had just vacated.

She could have applauded. What a demonstration of power! Rose had never seen anything like it—save perhaps for once, when she had played Lady Macbeth in the Scottish-set play. It had been a mastery of manipulation, it had put everyone ill at ease, and Samuel himself was gaping in abject horror.

Rose smiled. "Ask Mrs. Bailin for refreshments, Arden."

The butler bowed, exiting the room with evident relief on his angular face.

Honestly, was the whole place terrified of this woman? As far as Rose could see, she was merely a strong-willed and strong-minded woman who was not afraid to take what she wanted, even if she were not offered it.

What was not to like?

"It is very gracious of you to accept our invitation," Rose said conversationally as she stepped a few feet forward, turned, and lowered herself into an opposing armchair. "We are mindful of the honor."

"So you should be," shot back Lady Romeril with a leering expression. "And I suppose I too should be grateful in turn that I was the first to receive such an invitation. Half of London is agog to discover what you are like, Lady Aylesbury."

"Oh, please," Rose said with a wave of her hand before her reason could catch up with her. "Call me 'Rose.'"

The silence in the room turned icy.

There was a small, strangling noise behind her. Rose did not need to turn her head to know that Samuel was struggling to breathe.

Well, it was a slip of the tongue—perhaps not the most decorous thing to say in polite company, but it was hardly as though she had revealed a great treachery or admitted to admiring French wallpaper fashions over japanned!

Rose held Lady Romeril's steady gaze with one of her own, ensuring not to drop her chin nor permit her cheeks to flush.

All she had to do was hold her nerve…

The older woman cackled. "*Rose*, is it? Well, Rose, I may tell you that the last time an unknown married into one of the great families, though this one of the Continent, the woman in question found herself unequivocally out of her depth!"

Rose did not take the bait. "Perhaps she and I should take tea sometime."

Or perhaps she had done. Lady Romeril's eyes glittered. "What do you think you're doing right now?"

Behind her, Samuel appeared to be choking. Rose paid him absolutely no heed. "Indeed? Then I am even more delighted to make your acquaintance, Lady Romeril. Tell me, what gossip has occurred in London in oh, the last week, that you think should reach my notice?"

There was a *thunk* by the window. As far as Rose could tell without turning her head, Samuel had either fainted—unlikely—

or been forced by a sudden lack of strength in his legs to sit heavily in the window seat.

"You ought to drink more tea, man," Lady Romeril said blithely to the gentleman behind Rose. "Weakness in the knees is a terrible affliction but can be remedied by strong Earl Grey tea."

"I had always thought coffee most invigorating," Rose said cheerfully as Mrs. Bailin entered the room, the robust and red-faced woman carrying a tea tray. "May I offer you some, Lady Romeril?"

It was a relief, in truth, for a distraction from the melee that she and Lady Romeril were somehow fighting in. Rose broke the connection and turned to the housekeeper, who gulped, seeming wary of even being in the same room as Lady Romeril, and indicated that the tray be placed on the console table beside her.

"Coffee? Not tea?"

"It is the very best blend of roasted beans, I assure you," Rose said lightly, as though she were not contravening all laws of afternoon tea and, presumably, hosting. "I spoke to the lovely manager of Don Saltero's Chelsea Coffee House and ensured this house has a regular supply."

Her guest raised an eyebrow, but it was not a censorious one. "Then yes, I will try some of this coffee of yours."

Rose took great care to maintain strong, not shaking hands as she poured first coffee, then cream, finally dropping a chunk of sugar into the cup before her. "For Lady Romeril, Mrs. Bailin."

Her housekeeper looked at her pleadingly but was forced by the strength of her mistress's glare to pick up the coffee cup on its saucer and traverse the enormous three steps over to their guest.

Lady Romeril took the cup and saucer, sipped at the drink, and her eyebrows rose even further. Rose discovered, much to her chagrin, that her stomach had tightened in a nervous knot.

The older woman smacked her lips. "Very good. Don Saltero's Chelsea Coffee House, did you say?"

The knot in Rose's stomach loosened but did not untie. "Yes, I shall have one of my footmen drop some over for you. Coffee,

Samuel?"

A gargling noise behind her suggested that yes, coffee would be acceptable.

It was a pleasant distraction, pouring out the coffee before passing it to Mrs. Bailin to serve. It was pleasant not to be matching Lady Romeril glare for glare, giving both her eyes and her stomach a rest from the judgment that poured from the doyenne of Society in equal measure.

Well, how was she doing? Rose could hardly consider that she had done well; so far, she had overstepped a boundary of names, suggested coffee over tea, and ignored her husband—though in truth, Samuel was utterly useless at the moment.

After all his talk about ensuring that they were a united front against Society, and Lady Romeril in particular, Rose could not help but think it a tad rich that he had been unable to speak more than two coherent syllables since the woman had entered the room. *Honestly!*

"You truly wish to know the scandals of the Season?" Lady Romeril asked once Rose had dismissed the housekeeper, eying her beadily.

Rose shrugged in a loose manner that managed to release some tensions in her shoulders and make Samuel moan behind her at the same time. "I am new to Society, as you have so delicately pointed out, Lady Romeril. It would behoove me to know of anyone currently being censured, as I am sure you can imagine."

"And you approve of this, do you, Lord Aylesbury?"

For the first time since their guest had arrived, Rose looked over her shoulder at her husband.

She was then immediately forced to stifle a laugh. Samuel was perched on the window seat, clutching a cup of coffee, looking as though he had just been told he would have to live on a boat near the North Pole. Without gloves.

"I—I wouldn't... I don't tell my wife what to do," he said lamely.

It was a complete lie and Rose almost scoffed at the fool, but Lady Romeril was nodding her head approvingly.

"I should think so! The last person to try to tell me what to do was a footman at Almack's. I fear his ankle may never recover."

Rose's eyes widened. "Do you mean to say—"

"As to who is battling scandal at the moment," Lady Romeril continued, speaking over Rose in a commanding way that made the latter think of grand speeches and monologues and ensuring one's voice reached the back of the theater, "I would say that one of the Lloyd girls is going to find herself in trouble before long, and there has been some very vicious chatter about one of the Quintrells, though I will not shame them by saying which one. Very vicious chatter, I must say. The Daltons will be thrilled."

"Indeed?" Rose asked, sipping her coffee, which was most invigorating. *Don't think about it. Don't think about the names you just heard, and how long ago it's been since you last heard them.* "And where did you hear such a thing?"

Lady Romeril's grin widened. "Why, coming from my own mouth, of course."

Every muscle in Rose's body stiffened.

That was the trouble with acting, she reminded herself forcefully as she tried to ensure that the momentary panic was not noticeable. Sit within the role for too long, and you almost forget that you are playing a part.

And you are playing a part, Rose Morgan. Rose Chance—for now. But so is everyone else. Everyone has their agenda. Everyone is looking for weakness in the other.

And you were having so much fun playing the role that you almost forgot what the stakes are.

"In that case," she said aloud as calmly as she could manage, "I shall have to endeavor to seek out these Lloyds and Quintrells, and befriend them."

Samuel dropped his coffee cup.

The resulting smash and curses echoed around the drawing room, but Rose did not look away from Lady Romeril, whose face had turned from genial smile to frozen mask.

"You—You will?"

"Oh, yes, I find it best to ally myself with anyone who is down on their luck," Rose said breezily, sipping her coffee again as though fighting hand-to-hand combat with the best of Society were a casual diversion. "Then when they rise, as they so often do, I can rise with them—with their complete loyalty, of course."

Samuel behind her was babbling something under his breath as a footman hastened over with a cloth, but Rose paid him no heed.

She had gambled, gambled high, and it was not clear yet whether she had won or lost. There was no draw; Lady Romeril was not the sort to permit such a thing.

Either the older woman would relent, beam at her hostess's audacity and consider her an impeccable member of Society...or she would not.

If the former, Rose knew she would have won over the whole of London. Samuel could sleep well at night forever, for his marchioness would be the toast of the town, and together, they could rest easy knowing that their eventual separation would be shocking, but not ruinous.

If the latter...

Well, she could always return to the theater earlier than planned.

Perhaps not in London, but there was always a stage waiting.

Lady Romeril grinned. Sadly, that was no indication of the conversation terminating.

"You," the older woman said slowly, "are very interesting. You know, it's almost as though...we have met before."

It was Rose's turn to drop her coffee—that was, she would have dropped the cup if she had not hastily placed it down on the console table before her.

Pulse racing, lungs tight, panic roaring through her...

No. No, she was not going to let it overcome her. She was not going to allow Lady Romeril to see just how much she had frightened her.

Rose ensured a teasing expression lilted her lips. *Yes, a little regal, a little knowing, but not too knowing...* "I cannot think where we would have met before, Lady Romeril—unless you frequented Bath regularly?"

It was another gamble, but at this point, Rose had few cards to play and little less to lose. If Lady Romeril did recall her... Well, Rose had presumed that most would not recognize her after a decade, but there was always a chance someone would.

Had her act been sufficient?

Lady Romeril's beady gaze did not let up. "On occasion, but I've never found the Bath waters that appealing. But still, you are familiar. Who is your family—what was your name? Before you married His Highness over there, I mean?"

There was a small strangled sound from Samuel, but nothing coherent.

Thanking the heavens that she could at least answer this honestly, Rose said lightly, "Morgan. Not a Society name."

Yes, well, that was true enough.

"Hmmmm." Her guest looked most put out. "You know, I came here this afternoon, Lady Aylesbury, prepared to find a hoyden who had overstretched herself in matrimony who was utterly unable to meet the task. And instead, I find you."

Rose was not sure whether that was censure or praise. "I am as you find me, Lady Romeril."

The older woman snorted. "I very much doubt that—but you make an excellent sparring partner. You could have been an actress, with that amount of gall!"

She laughed, and Rose laughed, and when she glanced over to the wide-eyed husband she had managed to acquire just a week ago, Samuel laughed nervously too.

"An actress!" said the man with an energetic guffaw. "Oh, well done, Lady Romeril! The very idea!"

Rose managed not to roll her eyes. Honestly, the man was a complete cretin!

"And now I really must be going," said Lady Romeril, rising in a sweeping swish of skirts. "This may surprise you, my lord, but there are a great number of people in this town who rely on my notice to feel good about themselves—honestly, I sometimes wonder if it is to feel *anything*—and if I do not make my calls, then I will be inundated with pleading letters tomorrow. And you know how much I hate that."

The glitter in her eye suggested that she was very much looking forward to it.

Rose stood then dropped into a low curtsey. "We are honored by your—"

"Yes, yes, you've already said that," muttered Lady Romeril, gathering her shawl more tightly around herself. "You are most interesting, Lady Aylesbury, and I do not say that about anyone. I must have you to dinner, blast you, and I can work you out that. Aylesbury."

"Lady Romeril," Samuel said hoarsely as the older woman stomped across the room and through the door hastily opened by their footman.

Both Samuel and Rose remained standing, silent, as the footsteps of Lady Romeril made their way across the hall. The slam of the front door was the sign that she had left.

Rose's shoulders drooped as Samuel staggered over to the sofa, promptly lay upon it, and closed his eyes.

"What just happened?" he asked weakly.

It was a question she herself had been about to ask, but she could not permit the man to think she had been undone by such an encounter. Certainly not!

"*You are very interesting. You know, it's almost as though...we have met before.*"

Well, if there was going to be one person in the whole of London who would remember her, Rose had been certain it would be Lady Romeril—that was, after all, why she had invited her first. Beyond the fact that the doyenne would expect to be their first visitor, Rose had to test herself against the very best.

Or the very worst, depending on how one looked at it.

The truth of her past could have come out in that moment, which was surely why her throat was dry and her whole body liable to shiver.

Rose sat down. Then she picked up her coffee, drained the cup, and placed it back on its saucer. "Well. That's over with."

"I do not know how you did that!" Samuel had opened his eyes now and had turned to her, positively beaming. "You beat the old hag at her own game!"

"Samuel!"

"Fine, that was a little harsh. She is not that old," he said with a shrug. "Rose, you don't understand—Lady Romeril has ruined more reputations than a rake. She could have ended this, for both of us!"

Oh, and Rose knew that...far better than he did.

"You just delivered the performance of a lifetime," Samuel said with a wry smile, finally sitting up and shaking his head in wonder. "I have never seen anyone do that."

"Do what?" She had to speak in an airy, nonchalant voice; it was the only way to hide the fact that she was so flattered.

Strange, that a man's approval could make her feel like this. Odd, how Samuel's warm smile and admiring looks could be so...so potent.

Rose shifted in her seat. Not that she was flattered by him. Obviously. "Why did you not mention the Lloyds and Quintrells before?"

"Should I have?" He looked so genuinely confused by her remark, head tilted and mouth twisted, that she decided to let it go.

It should be easy enough to avoid them, after all, whatever she had told the doyenne.

"To see old Romeril beaten at her own game—I never thought the day would come. Not in my lifetime, and for some strange reason, I always presumed the old girl would outlive me," said Samuel with a rueful grin. "I speak the truth only, Rose—you were magnificent. Your acting skills are beyond anything I have seen before on the stage. Truly, I have seen you act in small ways with my family, but that…that was impressive."

Heat was now flushing her cheeks. "You do not have to tease me."

"'Tease' you?" For some reason, Samuel's brow was furrowed. "You think I am teasing?"

Of course he was. Men did not praise acting skills; oh, they liked them in a theater, but they decried them on the street. Men did not like the idea that a lady could pretend, even a little, and Rose had always been most careful to keep her true talents to herself.

At least, when she wasn't declaiming on a stage.

But Samuel… He was looking at her with something akin to ardent admiration, and Rose knew he was a shoddy actor at the best of times.

So was he serious? Was he speaking the truth as he flattered her and praised her?

It was a heady thought.

Rose cleared her throat, ridding herself of all discomposure. "Lady Romeril is just one woman."

"Her opinion will be that of London," her temporary husband pointed out.

Yes, perhaps it would be. *Or perhaps*, Rose thought with a slow smile, *London's opinion will be my own.*

Chapter Twelve

January 15, 1841

SAMUEL ALMOST STARTED out of his chair when Rose carefully but heavily laid a hand on his knee. "What?"

"Stop," his wife said sternly in an undertone that contained resonances that thrummed deep within his soul.

He blinked. "What do you—"

"If you continue tapping your foot like that," Rose said sweetly, "I will tear it off."

Oh. Right.

Samuel looked down at his knee. He had been tapping, he suddenly realized, though he had not consciously been doing so. Was that not what a person did when they were waiting in an office for hours on end for a solicitor to meet them?

He glanced at his pocket watch and cursed under his breath. Fine. Twenty minutes. But it felt like hours.

"You should have brought a book," Rose said serenely as she turned a page of the book she had been prescient enough to bring with her. "Then you would have something to occupy your time."

"I don't need something to occupy my time. I need Mr. Todd to hurry up," muttered Samuel ungraciously.

It was maddening. The letter had arrived only that morning, and the pair of them had rushed to the London officers of Todd, Todd, and Todd—ridiculous name for a solicitors—and yet despite the letter saying that their attendance was urgent, they had been left waiting here for...twenty-two minutes!

"I told you," Rose said calmly, turning another page and not looking up from her book. "I will tear it off."

Samuel looked down at his foot. It was tapping.

With as much control as he could muster, he forced his knee to remain motionless. "It's just irritating."

"Yes, I quite agree," said Rose with a laugh.

Somehow, Samuel did not believe they were speaking of the same thing. "I meant—"

"I know what you meant," said his wife with a heavy sigh that wives seemed to gain at the altar, even when they were temporary ones. "But we do not know that the missive you received is a precursor to bad news."

How could it be anything else? Samuel had known, from the moment he had seen the seal on the letter brought to him on a silver platter by Arden, that it was bad news.

Mr. Todd had no need to see him, no reason to do so. Samuel had presented their marriage certificate to the man in Brighton and the solicitor had accepted it. He had agreed to release Great-Aunt Tessie's funds. It was all finished with.

Why they had been summoned to the solicitor's office, why the Brighton Mr. Todd has made his way to the offices of the London Misters Todd, he did not know. And it was maddening. *Maddening!*

Samuel rose to his feet. "I'm going in there."

"Bad idea, dear," Rose said vaguely as she turned another page of her infernal book.

There was an itching underneath his skin that he would not be able to scratch until he knew what was going on with this damned solicitor, and so Samuel was going to march in there and demand an explanation.

He was a marquess! He was a Chance! He was—

About to be run down by a horde of solicitors who came pouring out of the door he had just been about to open.

"Oh, my lord." Mr. Todd blinked, as though surprised to see him. "What an unexpected honor."

Samuel did not intend to whip out the letter and wave it in the man's face, but it had been a trying day. For example, Lady Romeril had sent her compliments. That never boded well. "You asked me to come here!"

"I did indeed," said a rapidly blinking Mr. Todd, attempting to focus on the rapidly waving piece of paper. "In three days' time."

Samuel opened his mouth to retort, hesitated, then heard the snuffle of laughter from behind him.

Oh, hell.

Steadying the paper in his hand, he glanced down once again at the letter he had read at least six times, attempting to find the mysterious 'three days' that the solicitor had just mentioned.

My lord,

There has been an interesting development in the legacy of your great-aunt, and I would be obliged if you would visit the London offices of Todd, Todd, and Todd in three days, the 18th of January.

I remain your most humble servant,
Allen Todd, Esq.

Oh. Right.

Samuel stuffed the letter into his pocket and hoped he would never have to see it again. "Be that as it may…"

"Ah, Mr. Todd, how pleasant to see you again."

It was all Samuel could do not to gawp as Rose stood, beamed at the now-flushing solicitor, and strode forward with her hands outstretched.

Quite how it happened, Samuel was not sure, how in an instant the blushing Mr. Todd had both Rose's hands in his own as she was saying, "Wonderful to see you again—and the children, they are well?"

How does she do it?

Oh, Samuel's own mother had a certain way about her, but she had always been of a more nervous disposition. Her stutter made her shy and her shyness made her stutter, and so the Dowager Marchioness of Aylesbury had never spent much time in polite Society if she could help it.

But the new Marchioness of Aylesbury?

Samuel stared, transfixed, as Rose thoroughly charmed the solicitor to the point that she was being ushered into the room before himself.

"And tea? I am more than happy to order tea," Mr. Todd said as he pulled out a chair for Rose. His cheeks were still very red. "And cake. We must have cake."

"Mr. Todd," Samuel said in what he hoped was an impressive tone. "We can have cake any time. What I wished to inquire about was the meaning of your letter."

The solicitor scowled, as though being dragged away from serving Rose was a great sacrifice. As, Samuel supposed, it rather was.

"Please, sit," the solicitor said curtly. "And I will have the paperwork brought in."

Samuel sat a tad ungraciously next to his wife as Mr. Todd walked over to the door to mutter instructions to a clerk.

"You could *attempt* to be pleasant," Rose murmured, a hint of a grin on her lips.

I am pleasant, Samuel wanted to say. *I am actually quite a pleasant person all round. Everyone who knows me would say that I am pleasant and that is because I am...when I am not with you.*

Oh, this woman, she... She did something to him. Samuel had not quite worked it out yet, much to his dismay, but something about Rose made him all prickly. He did not want her to be smiling at other men. Men like Mr. Todd. He did not want other men to be pulling out chairs for her, or complimenting her gown, or—or looking at her as they did!

And it was ridiculous. She was an actress. She was only here because he had needed a ready wife!

Samuel swallowed down all the thoughts that had meandered wildly through his mind and managed to say, "'Pleasant.'"

"Yes, pleasant," Rose repeated, inclining her head at Mr. Todd as he returned to the table around which they sat. "It's a lesser known trait of the best people."

Best people, indeed! What did she know about—

"I have asked the two of you here today," Mr. Todd intoned, placing a ream of paper on the table, "because it seems that I have been mistaken in your great-aunt's will and estate."

Samuel's jaw tightened.

He should have known. He should have known it had been too good to be true. All that money? One hundred and twenty thousand pounds, and properties, and all that?

No, a windfall that large simply did not fall into a man's lap, even if he intended to do good with the funds. It was simply impossible...and now he was married to a woman he hadn't needed to drag into this mess in the first place.

"Please explain, Mr. Todd," Rose said gently, her voice modulated at a pitch that soothed Samuel's frayed nerves and somehow loosened his jaw. "There is significantly less money, is that right?"

The solicitor blinked. "Less? Oh, no. No, quite the reverse."

Somehow, Samuel's jaw had tightened again. *'The reverse'?*

"I do not understand," Rose said softly, and without looking away from Mr. Todd, she took Samuel's hand in hers. "The reverse—there is *more* than expected?"

Why did the simple gesture mean so much? Why did the sensation of Rose's hand in his somehow quieten the panic that had been rising in Samuel, her soft skin a balm to his disquieted nerves?

"Yes, quite a bit more," the solicitor said vaguely, rummaging through the papers before him and picking one up. "Yes, here it is. Several properties in Paris, two in Milan, one in Berlin, though I do not believe she had ever been there. Stock and bonds in at least fourteen additional companies, mining mostly, though..."

The man kept speaking. Samuel was almost certain he did because his mouth was moving up and down, and moreover, sound was coming out, but there was no knowing what on earth he was saying because the solicitor's words were coming from a long way away and somehow from under water.

More properties? More stocks and bonds?

How on earth had Great-Aunt Tessie managed to accumulate so much?

"—and that is the problem, you see," Mr. Todd finished grandly.

Rose was nodding as though she fully understood, which was excellent, because Samuel had no idea. "I see."

"You do?" Samuel muttered.

She did not reply—at least, not in words. Her fingers tightened, just for a moment, around his own.

Reassurance, the likes of which Samuel had never known, flooded through his body. Every muscle relaxed, warmth cascading down his spine, and for a moment, absolutely everything was right with the world.

Then his expression sharpened. "Mr. Todd, what do you need from us?"

"Well, as you can imagine, a certain amount of questions have arisen after discovering that your relative was so… Well, *fantastically rich* is the only way I can think to describe her," the solicitor said in what he evidently believed was a delicate tone. "Questions from those who demand answers."

The government, Samuel thought with a sigh. Well, perhaps he should have expected that. One could not become an heir to a fortune fifty times over without attracting some sort of attention.

"We had preferred that the truth stay within the family," Rose said quietly.

Samuel started, staring with wide eyes. What the devil was she talking about? Oh, she played the delicate Society flower, but she surely did not believe she could take on the whole government?

Though if anyone could…

"I quite understand," Mr. Todd was saying, "but the fact remains—"

"And I am certain that you are able to act in this matter with the utmost discretion," Rose continued, smiling at Samuel as though they shared a secret.

Whatever it was, it was not shared.

The solicitor was flushing again. "Oh, anything you wish to tell me, Lady Aylesbury, I would be more than happy to keep quiet."

"Well, then, here is the truth: and as I said, Mr. Todd, we would prefer it if the truth could be shared with as few people as possible. I understand a few government officials may need to be taken in your—into *our* confidence, but we would prefer it if that was the least number of people you can manage. Is that not right, dear?"

Samuel started. "What? Right. Yes. The truth should not be shared."

A truer word had never been spoken. He watched with mounting dread as Rose sighed, shook her head as though she were about to tell a most tragic family tale, and looked beseechingly at the solicitor.

"If the news were to get out... Well, it would truly be a shame for the name to Todd, Todd, and Todd to be so sullied with the fact that you could not be trusted..."

It was very well done, Samuel realized. The hesitancy, the trust, the lingering looks that suggested most strongly that Rose could not wait to tell the solicitor the truth about how exactly Great-Aunt Tessie managed to accumulate a king's ransom...

Yes, it was very clever.

The trouble was, whatever was about to be uttered from those luscious lips was not the truth. How could it be?

So it would be a lie.

"—most honored to be in your confidence—"

"Yes, I know," Rose said with a teasing laugh. "Well, the long and short of it, Mr. Todd, is that at the bottom of this story is an actress."

Samuel's heart stopped.

It stopped for a very long time. At least three heartbeats should have gone by in the time that it halted, and when his pulse started again there was a great pain within him.

Somehow managing to prevent himself from grasping his chest, Samuel wondered how quickly he could get her out of here. If he lifted her bodily, would she still be able to speak? Would she still spill the secret of their connivance?

"An actress?" Mr. Todd repeated.

Rose nodded sagely. "Yes, Great-Aunt Tessie was an actress. Would you like a cough drop, dear?"

Samuel had yelped in a hoarse voice and managed to shake his head as his mute tongue attempted to formulate words. *Any words. Any words!*

Great-Aunt Tessie, an actress? Why on earth did Rose think that this was a sufficiently good lie?

"As I am sure you can imagine, Mr. Todd, being a man of the world, Great-Aunt Tessie's acting exploits gained her a great deal of admirers, and I am led to believe that many of the jewels she was gifted from said admirers were transformed into property over time," Rose was saying blithely, as though lying to the law for a living was something she had not only contemplated, but perfected. "A long career, you know—and the properties one owns can be let out, and they generate money, and that money is in turn invested...you understand."

Samuel understood. He understood that he was going to prison. Was that not the consequence for lying to the government?

Mr. Todd cleared his throat. "I do understand, Lady Aylesbury—and may I say how calmly you can speak of such a profession. An actress, goodness!"

Somehow, Samuel was on his feet, and he was pointing a finger at the flinching solicitor. "How dare you speak to my wife like that?"

"M-My lord, I did not—"

"Hush, Samuel, the man did nothing wrong," Rose said hastily, tugging his sleeve. "Honestly, you are too protective of *your great-aunt.*"

The last few words were intoned sharply, a definite warning in her voice, and Samuel somehow came back to himself.

Ah. Yes. Right. Great-Aunt Tessie.

"Well, with all that cleared up, I have no further questions," said Mr. Todd, his shoulders slumping, as if personally disappointed in himself that he could think of no pretense to keep the beautiful Marchioness of Aylesbury in his office. "Thank you for your, ahem, speedy response to my note."

And it was handshakes and nods and 'Anytime' and 'What a pleasure,' and somehow through that whirlwind, Samuel managed to find himself standing outside the offices of Todd, Todd, and Todd, with Rose's hand looped through the crook of his arm and his carriage before him.

"There," said Rose in a satisfied sort of voice. "That wasn't too difficult, was it?"

Samuel blinked. "Did... Did what I think just happened actually happen?"

"I really have no idea what you are talking about," said his temporary wife happily. "Are you going to help me into the carriage?"

Moving in a dream, utterly unsure what he was doing, Samuel helped into the carriage the brazen actress who had just lied—lied!—to a man whom he was almost sure was a government informer. He followed her into the carriage and sat down, hardly certain who or what he was now.

An accessory to lying?

"You are very quiet," Rose said quietly as the carriage rumbled forward.

Quiet? Samuel did not think he would ever be able to speak again. What was the point, if his newfound wife was just going to lie about everything?

"You are displeased with me."

That got his attention. Eyes sharpening, Samuel looked at the woman seated next to him and wondered how on earth an actress of that caliber had ever been down on her luck.

"I am not displeased, no," he said shortly. "Surprised, certainly."

"'Surprised'?" She was pressed up against him in the carriage, though why, he was not sure. There was plenty of room on her side. "You think a woman should not speak the truth?"

Samuel tried not to laugh, he really did. "Rose, you just told a pack of lies to a man I'm almost certain will tell the authorities."

"'A pack of lies'?" Rose's eyes were wide in mock surprise—at least, he had to assume it was mock surprise. "Why on earth do you think that?"

"Well!" There was little room for Samuel to throw up his hands in the carriage, but he managed it. "All that nonsense about Great-Aunt Tessie being an actress, and jewels being poured into her lap—"

"I'm not sure I exactly said that," pointed out Rose in a far-too-reasonable voice.

"You know what I mean!" Samuel's breath was short and he was almost certain the walls of the carriage were closing in.

Oh, the woman was a marvel, certainly, but the question was: what else could she lie about so convincingly? What did he truly know of her, really?

"I will have you know that the great Contessa Margolotta was a stupendous actress."

Samuel's voice died in his throat as he stared at the flushing but obstinately bold young woman. "I... I... What?"

Rose adjusted her skirts, entirely unnecessarily. "The great Contessa Margolotta. Though she preferred to go by 'Miss Margolotta' for her stage name. Your great-aunt, as your sister Frank told me, and I must say I was astonished to discover the connection. She was a great actress, and I knew that because I shared a stage with her—and the jewels were not poured into her lap, I'll have you know, but pressed lovingly into her hands. When they were not placed around her neck."

It was all Samuel could do to keep his lungs moving. This was nonsense. He was living in a dream world.

Great-Aunt Tessie...an actress?

"You cannot be serious," Samuel murmured.

"After Frank's mention of her name and title, I honestly couldn't believe it myself. I asked that butler of yours for more details of the family tree," Rose said cheerfully, as though temporary wives to premature marquesses frequently rummaged through the family tree looking for scandal. "I was astonished to discover that the two women were one and the same, but there it is."

Samuel blinked. Then he blinked again.

The beautiful, utterly confusing, and *most definitely his wife* woman before him did not disappear.

"You... You knew her?" he croaked.

Rose nodded with a smile. "I did. I also suspected that something of this sort would occur—women, owning property? The very idea. Most men cannot abide it, so I thought it might be useful for me to share that little snippet of family history. Stave off any more serious questioning, that sort of thing. I perhaps should have checked with you first, but there it is."

There it is.

She... She is magnificent. Samuel could hardly believe it, but somehow, Rose had seen off a family scandal, kept his newfound fortune, and done so with such charm and elegance that Mr. Todd was half in love with her already.

Rather like himself.

Samuel pushed the thought away sternly. He could not fall in love with the woman he had hired—yes, hired to pretend to be his wife!

That was, she *was* his wife. But not for long.

"You knew her?" It was still difficult to take in.

"I am rather more surprised that *you* knew her," shot back his wife with a sardonic smile. "She always gave me to understand that she had little time for family."

"She liked me. I visited...oh, once a month? Sandwiches and scones, gossip and rumor, that sort of thing." Samuel had rather enjoyed his monthly visit to Great-Aunt Tessie. It was hard to believe they were over, in a way. "I shall miss her."

"I am sure she loved your company."

"And yet," Samuel could not help but add, "you knew her all this while."

"You... You do not seem pleased." The pleasing smile which had for the earlier part of the carriage journey adorned Rose's lips had disappeared.

"I am very pleased," Samuel managed to say. "Thank you."

Rose's brow crinkled. "You do not *look* pleased."

What possessed him to say what he said next, Samuel would never know. "Then let me show you."

And he was kissing her—kissing her as though his life depended on it, which he rather thought it did. Samuel had expected Rose to draw back, to accept one kiss but then push him away, and he almost groaned with the effort not to crush her against the carriage seat.

His concerns were utterly unfounded. It was he who was pushed against the carriage seat, Rose pressed over him as her hands tangled in his hair and her lips parted to welcome him in.

God, this was everything—*she* was everything. Riding high on passion and pleasure, Samuel allowed his fingers to grasp first her waist, then her buttocks, half-pulling Rose onto his lap as his tongue lavished her own, twisting bliss from each moment as his whole body responded.

"Samuel," she exhaled, and he thought he would come undone.

To hear his name upon her lips, to know that he was the one tugging it from her thanks to his efforts...

How long they kissed for, he did not know. Time around Rose simply did not exist as it did elsewhere. All Samuel knew was that Rose was now the one underneath him, and his mouth was on her neck, worshipping that delicate skin underneath her ear, and—

The carriage stopped. They were home.

"What... What does this all mean?" Samuel breathed against her neck, inhaling her, wishing he could taste her again and again.

He could almost feel Rose's pulse, its thrum taut across her skin, but when she spoke it was in a calm voice that sounded as though nothing interesting had occurred.

"Nothing. It means nothing. Not for you and I."

Samuel straightened, pulling back from the woman whom he had been about to ravish most thoroughly, and cleared his throat. "Oh, right, obviously. Nothing at all."

Nothing at all.

The crash of pain, the jolt in his breath were unwelcome, but expected.

Damn it, but he was a fool. Try as he might to keep his emotions separate from this minx of a gem, he could not.

Rose was beguiling and clever and beautiful, and Samuel had never met a woman like her. He certainly never would again.

And their kisses, full of passion and heat and need and an aching desire to be known...

They meant nothing. As they should. He would not trap her into a marriage she did not want beyond next year. And he wouldn't ruin her with a divorce, either.

Annulment. An annulment was the only way.

Chapter Thirteen

January 23, 1841

ROSE WAS NOT going to think about what she and Samuel had done the last time they had stepped into this carriage. She was not. She was not—

His lips against her mouth and his arms around her and the stiff length of his manhood pressed against her hip...

Rose swallowed.

"Are you quite well?" Samuel's voice was gentle over the rumble of the carriage. "You look a mite pale."

'Pale'? 'Pale'? It's a miracle I look alive, Rose could not help but think. It was astonishing she could walk. It was amazing that she could sleep.

That kiss... Those *kisses*, they had been far too much and at the same time, not enough. Deep was the memory that had wormed its way into her affections, her very soul, and now every time she looked at him, she no longer saw the slightly foolish, money-grasping inconsiderate man she had first met.

No, she saw a man who was passionate and easily inarticulate. A man who, despite being born wealthy, had sought riches, to be sure, but was no miser. A man who was handsome, charming in an aloof sort of way.

A man she could love.

Rose cleared her throat as the carriage drew to a halt. "And whose ball is this, by the way?"

"This one is hosted by the Dalmerlingtons—they have been hosting quite a lot these last few months, now that I come to think of it," replied Samuel with a shrug that she could just make out in the gloom. "Dinners, and balls, and card evenings... Nice people. Solid family."

"But they will not want any hint of scandal. Though we've kept much of the true circumstances of our marriage secret, even our concocted story is sure to get tongues wagging. Perhaps we should not attend."

"Oh, well, gossip of that nature is common when a pretty enough woman enters Society," her husband said with a shrug. "I never pay that much heed. Half the Chances will be here, and the Quintrells, and the Baileys—our cousins—and the Daltons, and the Stewarts... In fact, I'm not entirely sure how they will fit us all in."

If she were truly happy being no more than friends, Rose would have laughed. She would have teased him, suggested that he had something himself to hide, or perhaps hinted that there was a particular young Dalton who had captured his heart.

None of that felt particularly amusing now; not when in less than a twelvemonth, Samuel would be free to pursue any woman he wanted.

The thought of her husband seeking out a second spouse soured in her stomach, though why it should do, Rose could not tell. It was not as though she had any real claim on the man. Not as though he owed her fidelity. Not as though they were anything to each other, besides co-conspirators in a plot to gain wealth.

Rose swallowed. "I see."

Samuel grinned. "Ready for the onslaught?"

It was going to be an onslaught, she knew. Their mantelpiece was groaning with the weight of invitations they had received over the last few days, even though it was marble. Dinners and dances and walks in the park and an art gallery opening and Don Saltero's Chelsea Coffee House had heard that she had praised their blend to Lady Romeril and would she like to visit again, and on and on—

That was *without* the Chances dropping in at every moment.

Rose had never met a family like them; they appeared truly to *like* each other.

Most peculiar.

And all because London Society wanted to meet the enigmatic new Marchioness of Aylesbury.

Rose braved a smile and nodded. Enigmatic, indeed. Well, that was perhaps the correct term for a woman with secrets who had absolutely no intention of telling a soul about them...

Samuel was first to descend from their carriage—*his* carriage, Rose reminded herself sternly—and he offered her his hand.

It was a simple gesture, one that any number of men had made for any number of women in the past. It was hardly a sensual one, either, for brothers had assisted sisters, fathers assisted daughters, friends assisted friends...

But this did not feel like the assistance given to a friend.

A lump formed in Rose's throat as she took Samuel's hand. It was ridiculous that it should feel so hot, his warmth somehow permeating through his and her gloves. It was foolish of her pulse to skip a beat as she stepped forward, idiotic for her knees to feel weak, daft, indeed, that the ground appeared to shift as she stood on it beside Samuel.

Beside her husband. Beside the most handsome man she had ever seen.

Rose forced the thought aside—her eyes must have been playing tricks on her. She had traveled to France and Italy and seen a great number of handsome men. Many had acted on the stage alongside her—though the egos on most of them always diminished their attractiveness in her eyes. Still, it was impudent of her to the extreme to think that Samuel Chance was the most handsome one amongst them!

Utterly oblivious to her consternation, Samuel tucked her hand into his arm as though it were the most natural thing in the world. "Shall we?"

The Dalmerlingtons had obviously invited a great number of people to their ball, for there was an almighty crush in the hall as copious footmen attempted to accept pelisses and greatcoats and hats and scarves and gloves in large numbers.

A gentleman stepped backward right into Rose's path and before she could attempt to move—or if needed, tap the gentleman irritably on the shoulder—Samuel immediately stepped into his path.

Protecting her with his body. His fine, expertly chiseled—

Rose Morgan—er, Chance—you need to get a grip on yourself.

"Awfully busy this, isn't it?" The gentleman guffawed as he turned around. "Awfully sorry, I almost got your—but, Sammy, what are you doing here!"

After a week, Rose was starting to become an expert on the Chance family, and this was most certainly a cousin. She could see it in the sparkle of the eyes.

Her husband smacked the man on the arm. "Why on earth have they let you in, you dog?"

"You know the Dalmerlingtons. No accounting for taste." The man nudged Samuel with his elbow. "Come now, introduce me to this splendid young thing. I suppose he begged you to marry him, did he?"

"He did, in fact." Rose smiled, her stomach jolting with delight as a slight flush broke out on Samuel's cheeks. "But then, he has been so good to me since, I have promised him only to bring it up once a week—and you've filled my quota."

"And for that, I am terribly sorry. Alexander Chance, one of the Cothroms. Have you got us all sorted out yet?" The gentleman wiggled his eyebrows as a pair of ladies pushed past them. "I'm the rogue."

Rose could not help but laugh at that, but she also could not help but notice that Samuel's blush had darkened, his lips growing flat as he clenched his jaw.

Interesting.

"Yes, you are, so go bother someone else's wife," her husband said gruffly.

Lord Alexander Chance winked at Rose. "If you insist."

He disappeared into the crowd and Rose was not unsurprised to find that Samuel squeezed her hand.

"You must ignore him," he said in a low voice as they divested their outerwear into the arms of a frantic footman. "Zander is a rogue, but he is harmless. *Mostly* harmless."

A mostly harmless rogue for a cousin...and he was worried. Rose had always been one for flattery—what actress wasn't—and jealousy was merely another flavor.

But though in a past life, she would have giggled and teased the man she was with and made sure to curtsey low to the next man to ensure that he gained an eyeful of her décolletage, Rose found herself squeezing Samuel's arm. "You mustn't worry. I only have eyes for you."

His gaze caught hers as his lips parted, and Rose found, to her annoyance, that her cheeks were heating.

Hers! As though they had been permitted to do such a thing!

"Shall we go into the ballroom? It's so very hot here," she said hastily.

Whether or not that was a sufficient excuse for her sudden pinkness, she did not know. Either way, Samuel led her forward through a pair of double doors into a room that was both stiflingly noisy and stiflingly hot.

Not a pleasing combination.

"Your cousin was right," Rose murmured in a low voice, bringing her lips close to Samuel's ear so that only he could hear her. "The Dalmerlingtons have no taste."

This many people! Oh, it was unsupportable. How was anyone supposed to even *move*?

"When we host a ball," Samuel replied in a similar murmur, his lips curling upward, "I shall leave all question of taste to you."

A shiver of something hot and spicy trickled through Rose's throat at the mere thought.

A ball, hosted by herself. Hosted by the Marchioness of Aylesbury. Her choices as to music, décor, food, guest list...

And by her side, her husband. Samuel Chance.

Rose tried to remember to smile. "Careful. Do not make promises you do not intend to keep."

And he beamed, and God if he did that too often, she was going to crumble. Rose had made promises to herself, stern promises, about not falling in love with the man who was literally paying her to pretend to the world that she was his happy wife…and now those promises felt a long time ago.

"Goodness, it's busy in here," Samuel said with a laugh. "The poor Dalmerlingtons; they must really want to impress. Come on, over here."

Rose allowed herself to be pulled through the bustling crowd, packed full of clucking mamas and shy debutantes and guffawing gentlemen and a few who looked to be, rather like 'Cousin Zander,' complete rogues. Some were smoking and some were drinking and all were laughing, a dissonance of noise that was almost too much to bear.

And then they were standing in a corner of the ballroom beside a large potted plant that gave them a little coverage from the chaos.

"That's better," said Samuel with a wink. "I get you all to myself here."

Try as she might, Rose could not prevent her heart from singing. That a man should have such power over her—it was ridiculous. And yet this man was charming. And good. So good. Aside from a bit of an occasional impatient streak, there did not appear to be a bad bone in his body, though Rose was perfectly willing to volunteer for the search.

Control yourself, woman!

"Oh, and I thought about what you said," Samuel said without any preamble.

Rose blinked. "You did? I said something?"

"You say lots of things, and I listen to them all," he said with a shrug, as though that were a perfectly normal thing to say. "But I was thinking specifically of when you challenged me to consider what I would do with the money beyond my family."

"I did?" She could hardly remember such a conversation, though that sounded like her.

Oh, of course: the orphanage and the cousins' dowries and Frank's engineering oil...and she had sternly told the man to think about others. Others not living or working at a Chance establishment.

Well, she had never been shy with her opinions, though even Rose had to admit to herself that it was a mite presumptuous of her to dictate how the man should spend his ill-gotten gains.

"Yes, I thought long and hard about it, and I think I have come up with an idea that is perfect," continued her husband with a grin that was almost shy. "I... I wanted your opinion before I put the wheels in motion. Not that it will have wheels."

Rose laughed as a footman—similarly harassed as those in the hall—dashed past them holding a silver platter upon which were glasses of wine. Samuel swiftly grabbed two and handed her one.

After she had taken a sip of the wine that was really very good, she said as lightly as she could manage, "Well, I am always happy to spend other people's money. What are we buying this time?"

"A retirement home," Samuel said, his eyes serious. "For actors and actresses who are down on their luck."

Rose's lips parted.

She must have misheard. Surely, he could not have said that?

"It doesn't have to be a retirement home, as such, I would hardly wish to restrict their professional activities," Samuel was now saying in a rush, his words merging into one another. "No age requirements, no credentials save that they once worked on the stage, or behind the stage, I suppose, and I thought, help with medical problems, and maybe a stage and theater so that they could put on performances, and entertainment, and good food. My sister Lilianna knows a cook who—"

"A retirement home for actors," Rose said weakly.

This was not possible. Men as handsome as Samuel and as charming as Samuel were not this perfect.

"And actresses," he reminded her cheerfully. "I think Great-Aunt Tessie would approve. What do you think?"

"I…" Words were not quite possible, so Rose took a large gulp of wine, coughed, then managed, "I think the great Contessa Margolotta would be delighted her funds could provide a good life for her fellow theatricals."

"Oh, I'm glad. I really am," said Samuel enthusiastically, and he meant it too, gladness radiating from every pore. "But I more meant, what do *you* think? Your opinion… Well, it matters to me."

Rose looked helplessly up at the man she was absolutely not supposed to be falling in love with.

He cared about her opinion. Was there anything more attractive? She had certainly not come across a quality more enticing, more intriguing.

Why else did women the world over pretend to find men so intriguing?

But Samuel was not an actor; this was not a clever trick, or a way to entice her into something, or a placatory gesture from a stage manager who had just given her splendid Act III monologue to another.

This man was genuine, and true, and a far better person than she would ever be.

Rose swallowed. "I think it a most excellent idea."

Samuel's smile was one of relief. "Oh, good! I am so glad. I started sketching out the sort of property we would need, but now you can assist me in drawing up lists of locations, and the staff we'll need—oh, your wine is empty. Let me fetch you another."

"Oh, no, that's—"

He was gone before Rose could attempt to explain that if she was going to retain her head against such a tumult of attractiveness, she would need no more wine.

She sagged against the wall, grateful for the obscuring nature of the potted plant. Well, what on earth was she supposed to say to that? The man was a treasure, worse luck. If only he had been unpleasant and generally spiteful. Then she would not feel so bad for keeping her past a secret and risking his very reputation every time she stepped out into Society…

"…heard she was most pleasant, though somewhat distant."

"Yes, I heard that too."

A pair of women had wandered close to her potted plant, both dressed in resplendent finery, but they must have been nearsighted, for they did not appear to have noticed Rose.

"I thought her pretty, obviously."

"Oh, obviously, but what value will that be in twenty years? That family needs to keep an eye on who joins them in matrimony, that's all I'm saying. One rotten apple will quickly spoil a barrel."

The Dalmerlingtons, Rose thought wryly, *were clearly not as popular as they thought*. Whoever had so recently married into their number was clearly not approved of, if the gossip of these two women was anything to go by.

Poor thing.

"And to give the boy the title! Before his father's dead and buried—"

"Oh, well, the Chances do things differently. The 'dowager duke'—what a remarkably nonsensical title—has been strutting around as if that were a normal thing to be for months."

Rose stiffened. *Blast*.

"But to make him Marquess of Aylesbury, too? 'Dowager marquess' is a thing now as well, I suppose?"

"It's the wife I don't understand," said the other with a shake of her head. "I did not even know Lord Samuel was married."

"No one did! Turned up from Brighton with madam on his arm. No announcement, no banns. Why, I wonder what—"

"Lady Romeril was impressed."

That pronouncement halted the conversation for a moment, and Rose attempted not to breathe. The last thing she wanted was for them to turn around and see her…

"Lady Romeril may well be losing her touch," one of the women said quietly, lowering her voice under the hubbub of the ballroom. "The new Lady Aylesbury, pretty as she might be, comes from no family and with no good blood. That's all I'm saying."

"You're right on that account—oh, there's my daughter. Come on, Geraldine, let me introduce you to the nincompoop she married…"

The two ladies wandered off, leaving Rose flushed behind the potted plant and wondering if that were the worst of the gossip.

That there had been gossip about her, she had known. Well, guessed. There was always gossip about a new member of Society, especially when one had clearly not been in polite Society for quite some time.

But hearing it herself was quite another matter.

"You look a little pink."

Rose started. "Samuel!"

"I told you I'd be back," he said, handing her a fresh glass of wine. "I was worried for a moment that I'd forget where I'd left you, but I could never do that."

She nodded, her thoughts still focused on the two ladies and their conversation. What else were people saying about her? Should she be concerned—was it possible that someone would eventually recognize her?

"Rose."

And if they did, what would Samuel say? Oh, he appeared to be relaxed about the social mores, but then look at how he'd responded when he'd thought she'd said something outrageous to Lady Romeril? He had panicked—the man had barely been able to stand upright. What would he say if he discovered that she had been born—

"Rose?"

Rose blinked. Samuel had stepped closer to her, perhaps far closer than he ought in public, and his brow furrowed as he examined her.

"I lost you for a moment there," he said uneasily. "What is wrong?"

"Nothing is wrong," she said instinctively. Nothing that he could help with. "Thank you for the wine. It is most delicious."

"Do not shut me out, Rose. There's no point, and besides, I... I want to know what you're thinking." Samuel's smile was somehow wistful. "I know we are not long to be husband and wife, but I would like you to trust me."

Trust him.

If only I could, Rose thought darkly. If only her past was not something that others could hold against him. If only she had been brave enough to tell him the truth before they had met at the altar.

As it was...

She exhaled slowly. "I...I overheard a pair of ladies gossiping about me."

The protectiveness she had felt in Samuel's frame in the hall returned with full force as he turned to glare at each and every other guest in the ballroom. "What? Who? Point them out and I will—"

"You will do absolutely nothing! It is common, I am sure, for newcomers to polite Society to be... well, verbally poked and prodded," Rose said hastily. "It's just... Well. I would not wish to shame you with my background. If they were to find out... I do not wish to shame you, Samuel."

There. She had said it.

The trouble was, Samuel did not appear to understand just what a statement she had made.

Of course he did not. How could he, if she did not explain it to him?

"Being an actress is... Well, it is a profession, to be sure, and there are those who are not exactly respectable within it—but I am certain you have always been a most elegant and...and aboveboard sort of person," Samuel said quietly, lifting his free hand to stroke her cheek.

Rose did not flinch this time, but she did hesitate before leaning into his touch, knowing as she did so that she should not but utterly unable to prevent herself. "You are?"

"Naturally. No one could know you as I do and not believe, not be certain that you have never done a bad deed in your life." Her husband's husky whisper tickled her ear.

Oh, she would have to tell him. One day soon, she would have to tell him.

"Now, I need you to drink that wine as quickly as is respectable," Samuel said brightly, pulling back.

Rose started drinking her wine before she could stop herself, halting suddenly and almost dribbling down her own chin. What was wrong with her? Why did her body find it so easy to obey this man?

"Oops, you've got a bit of..." Leaning forward again, Samuel reached out and used his index finger to dab a bit of wine from her lips.

She watched, transfixed, as he then brought that same index finger to his mouth and suckled on the digit.

Dear God, did he know how erotic he looked?

Removing the finger from his mouth casually, as if he did *not* have any idea, Samuel took her glass from her hand and placed both of theirs on a footman's passing platter.

"Now," he said cheerfully, as though absolutely nothing had occurred. "I must dance with you. If we are only to be married for a twelvemonth, I must take every opportunity to have you in my arms."

Saints preserve us...

"'If?'" Rose repeated, unable to help herself.

A shadow passed across Samuel's face. "*Since*. Because we *are* only to be married a twelvemonth. So, shall we?"

What could she say to such a question?

"We shall," Rose said, smiling through the pain as she took his proffered hand and allowed him to lead her to the center of the ballroom.

Just think about dancing. One foot before the other. And another. And another.

Don't think about how charming the man is. Or how good he is. Or how he makes your knees weak, something you had only previously pretended on stage. Don't think about how fervent he makes you, or how his smile makes your heart flutter, or how you've lied to him from the very beginning.

And whatever you do, Rose told herself sternly as the man she was caring more and more for with each passing day twirled her around in a waltz, *do not fall in love with the man who is paying you to only temporarily be his wife.*

Oh, hell. This was never the plan.

Chapter Fourteen

January 30, 1841

"Y OU CAN SURRENDER, you know."

"I am not going to surrender."

"I am just saying..." opined Rose, smiling in that seductive yet mesmerizing way of hers. "You could."

Samuel looked down at the board between them. Then he looked up at his opponent, her gown alluring and her smile far too knowing.

He looked down at the board again quickly before he was tempted to do something he absolutely should not.

"Surrender," whispered Rose with a tinkling laugh.

Samuel refused to notice just how his body stiffened as she'd said that word. It was impossible, yes, but he should at least make the effort. After all, they had played chess before. It wasn't as though he did not know the rules.

The rules that were somehow eluding him, however, were the rules that they had agreed all that time ago in Brighton. God, that seemed a lifetime ago.

A year and a day.

Ten thousand pounds at separation. An annuity of a thousand pounds.

No intercourse.

Three little rules that had seemed obvious and fair and right and now felt like a prison within which he had encaged himself. What the devil was he supposed to do as he sat here on the hearthrug of his drawing room, laughing with a woman as she once again beat him at chess, a woman who made his heart sing and his body fizzle and everything in his mind go blank.

"Samuel?"

After all, Samuel thought feverishly as he tried to spot a way to extricate himself—from the check, not the woman—*we are married, aren't we?* It could hardly be a crime to find his own wife attractive.

Though perhaps not the wife you hired...

"Samuel, if you are not going to make a move," Rose said sharply, "I shall have to discipline you."

Samuel froze. Then he looked up, hardly daring to believe what she had said. *"Pardon?"*

"I absolutely shall," she said sweetly. "Come on. Rescue your king."

His shoulders sagged. *Right, the chess game.* That was what she was referring to. Not some bedroom scene of her having him on his knees, not the inexplicable sexual tension between them, not the knowledge that there was something here, something more. Certainly not the fact that affections had arisen much against their agreement and Samuel was starting to dream of the dratted woman.

Most explicitly.

Rose sighed, leaned forward—displaying an unsettling but most welcome amount of bosom—and tipped over Samuel's king.

"Whoa there!" Samuel protested, almost before he could stop himself.

"You were mated!"

His throat closed up.

Even Rose appeared to have noticed that she had spoken scandalously, for her cheeks were a delicate shade of pink that deepened as she said, "You know what I mean. You'd been stuck there for almost ten minutes. I say that means you have to surrender."

She had folded her hands together, elbows on the table, and

thrust her chest out, clearly delighted at having beaten him once again at the game Samuel had once believed he was more than passable at, and he...

He could not help but grin in return. "Fine. You win this one—but I demand a rematch!"

Rose was already repopulating the board, her delicate fingers moving swiftly in a twisting arc. "Naturally. I am more than willing to beat you three times in a row."

"'Beat' me? That first time you cheated—"

"'Cheated'? It's hardly my fault that you forgot your bishop was there!"

Why, Samuel wondered darkly as they bickered happily, *does this feel so...so right?*

He had played chess with plenty of people before. Friends, enemies, his own brother, who was a mixture of the two. He had bickered before, plenty of times, mostly with his sisters but sometimes with his brother, the lout. He had sat on the hearthrug and drunk wine before with a few university friends. None of these things were new.

But they were now. Sat here, lounging against an armchair as Rose bit her lip, pondering her first move of their new game, Samuel could see that everything shared with Rose became new.

Fresh. Joyful.

It was like discovering that you had been ignorant of a melody all your life, and now music was playing and you could hear the tune of your own soul. The song you had been singing, unbeknownst to you.

And someone else had joined in.

"Who taught you to play chess?" Samuel asked lightly, eating the last of his cheese from the board his footman had left out for them many hours ago.

Rose answered, it appeared, without thought. "My father."

The words had only just left her mouth when red splotches appeared on her cheeks and her gaze darted outward, evident discomfort in her expression.

Samuel was careful to keep things light. *Her father? Interesting.* "Was he very good?"

"No."

He had expected more detail; Rose had never been particularly shy on any topic, regaling him with theater mishaps and descriptions of her European travels, some of her stories most amusing.

What he had not expected was a mere 'no.'

"'No'?"

Rose's eyes had dropped to the chess board. "He was not good at chess, and he was not a good man."

Ah. Right.

"We don't have to talk about him," Samuel said hastily.

"Good," said his wife sharply. "Because he deserves neither the notice nor the time."

Right. Though he noticed she spoke of him in the present tense, despite hinting vaguely that he might have passed on before.

Before he could say anything, Rose had looked up and there was a strange sort of hunted look in her eye. "You must think me an unfeeling daughter."

"No," Samuel said honestly. "I think you sound like a daughter who has endured a great deal of pain."

It was perhaps not the right thing to say—a touch direct, and far more intimate terms than they had ever spoken before. But though his body thrummed with concern that he had been too candid, Rose seemed to relax.

"He... My father. He did not understand—he did not believe acting was a suitable profession for...for me." The red splotches had gone and in their wake was a paleness, an uncertainty in her eye.

Samuel could not help but feel curious. After all, he knew almost nothing of Rose's past; she had been most circumspect with the details of her life before she had begun to travel on the Continent. It were as though she had sprung up, fully formed, an actress ready to take on the world with absolutely no past.

But everyone had a past.

"And your mother agreed with him?"

Rose snorted. "My mother does everything my father dictates—or at least, she did."

Sympathy rose in Samuel. "She died?"

"Perhaps." The woman opposite him shrugged in a manner that was far too nonchalant and studied to be genuine. "I have not heard from them these last eight years."

The very idea of being out of contact with one's family for any length of time greater than a week was startling to Samuel. Why, he had once not seen his mother for ten days, and she had instructed her butler to gain the assistance of the Peelers to batter down his door and ensure his wellbeing.

And that, according to some of his cousins, was an underreaction.

"You are shocked."

"I am—it is not the way my family does things, no," Samuel said honestly. She deserved honesty. "But every family is different."

"My family... My parents, I mean, were very unforgiving. They had no wish for me to be on the stage, and so they cut me off. Or at least, they were about to."

There was something in the way that she spoke, that tilt of her head as she examined the chess board, the careful studied calm with which she spoke.

Samuel gaped. "You ran away."

"I ran *toward*," she corrected, with a little fire in her voice. "I knew what I wanted, and when I want something, I claim it. I don't wait around for someone to give me permission."

Now *that*, he could well believe.

Dear God, it was astounding: the woman had left home and hearth and everything she knew, so desperate was she to gain her heart's desire. Samuel could not recall doing anything so dramatic, anything so violent to his own life.

To leave all stability behind...

Well, that was his assumption, of course. Poor Miss Rosemary Morgan may have left her parents in poverty and built altogether a better life for herself.

"And so you became an actress."

"And so," Rose said with a smile, "I left England behind, traveled the world, earned a pretty penny as an actress to near-universal critical acclaim, returned to England, lost my place at the Grand Theatre, married a marquess...and here I am."

"Here you are," Samuel said, unable to help himself returning her grin. "A marchioness, sitting on a hearthrug, playing chess and drinking wine."

"It's not such a bad life. So tell me," said Rose, leaning back to take a sip of her wine after moving a pawn forward. "You think you are good at chess?"

Samuel gave a laugh as he matched her pawn. "You know, I did. Apparently, I have been mistaken all these years—unfortunate, isn't it?"

"Oh, you shouldn't blame yourself. When we had rehearsals dragging on in Rome, those who weren't in the scene would play chess," his wife said with a shrug that merely emphasized that delightful curve of her breast above her waist. "I'm rather an expert."

"You are?" he challenged.

It was the wrong thing to say. If he knew Rose, and Samuel was starting to wonder if he simultaneously knew her the best and worst of all people in the world, it was that she did not appreciate being challenged.

A mischievous expression curled her lips. "I am. Why don't we make this interesting and find out?"

That was when Samuel should have known to desist. There was no winning in a situation like this, and yet his loins were doing the thinking now.

She was flirting! With him!

She was, wasn't she?

"'Interesting'?" he repeated, slowly moving his knight over his pawns and hoping to goodness she hadn't spotted what he was attempting on the board. "You don't think getting beaten by me will be interesting?"

Her laughter was literal music to his ears. When had he become so...so sentimental?

"Firstly, you will *not* be beating me," Rose said smoothly, unleashing her queen and already promising to do a great amount of damage. "Secondly, there are different variants of chess that can be played that...up the stakes, as it were."

Oh. Samuel was almost disappointed. The Rose he had grown to know over the last few weeks—well, she cared about money, but it was not the only thing that she cared about. To reduce their flirtation to a gamble for money was at the very least...uninspired.

Not like Rose at all.

"Oh, I've got some coins somewhere," Samuel said, more than a little disheartened.

Evidently, that was not the answer she had been hoping for. He had grown to spot the signs: the little furrow between her brows, the way she purposefully did not allow her shoulders to droop.

Perhaps it was the life she had lived as an actress that made Rose rigidly control her body. Perhaps it was this mysterious break with her family, a story Samuel wished to hear much more about but would never ask.

Whatever it was, the woman never let go, not truly. She was always in control, if not of the situation, then herself.

That was something Samuel wanted to change. One day.

"No, I wasn't thinking of playing for money," Rose said distantly. "It's your turn."

Samuel moved a bishop at random. "You weren't? How would you make it interesting, then?"

His wife carefully took his bishop with her queen, holding the piece between two fingers before her face and turning it around and around.

Samuel swallowed. That simple movement was not supposed to be erotic. It wasn't. And yet...

"Well, the way we would make it interesting in Rome," Rose said, her voice still a tad distant, though with a sharpness in her eyes that suggested she was paying very close attention to each word she uttered, "was to play strip chess."

A great deal of things all happened at once.

Firstly, all the breath in Samuel's body was exhaled without his authorization.

Secondly, his hand slipped around the wineglass stem that he had about to lift to his lips.

Thirdly, thoughts of Rose in very little cascaded through Samuel's mind.

Fourthly, Rose laughed.

"You are a prude, Samuel," she teased.

"'P-P-Prude'?" he repeated, sounding unsettlingly like his mother. "No, no, not at all, not a prude, not a prude, just a..."

Precisely what he was, Samuel could not tell. His pulse was hammering, his mouth was dry, and he was swiftly wondering just how many other men Rose had played strip chess with.

The thought was unpleasant, bile in his chest mingling with the soaring hope that he could beat her.

Oh, dear God, if he could take pieces from her and watch Rose carefully remove layer after layer...

"You are game, then?" Rose asked delicately, the bishop in her hand still twirling distractedly near her mouth.

Samuel swallowed hard.

Well, he was hardly going to say *no* to such a desperately interesting proposition. The trouble was his attention was not going to be focused on the game before him, but on the multiple games that Rose had previously played. With other men.

The biting jealousy overtaking him was not so much a surprise, as a disappointment. He had no reason to be jealous. No reason at all.

Except...

Except Rose was *his*. She had become his without Samuel really noticing, and now all he wanted was to keep her for himself for the rest of time. Agreement or not, year and a day deadline or not, he wanted to keep her.

A life without Rose... A life, moreover, *without* Rose after knowing just how wonderful a life with Rose was—no, that could never be borne.

"Samuel?"

And that could only mean one thing, he realized with a sinking feeling that had nothing to do with the half bottle of wine they had consumed since settling down here on the hearthrug by the roaring fire to play chess.

He was in love with his wife.

Damnation!

"Samuel?" Rose repeated, her smile slightly fading.

Well, there's no good time to admit to your hired wife that you've contravened the one rule that's going to prevent disaster, Samuel thought wryly. He may as well play strip chess in the meantime. While he came up with a plan to make the woman fall in love with him in return.

"Strip chess," he said slowly. "I presume the rules are simple?"

"Oh, they have to be, for the people who usually play it are very stupid men," teased his buxom wife, firelight flickering over her face and bathing her in a golden glow. "Yes, the rules are simple. For each piece that is taken, the loser must remove an item of clothing. Winner's choice which."

It seemed simple enough. Samuel cast a careful glance over the woman before him.

So, what was she wearing? A gown, but that surely was in two parts; she would not permit him to remove it all in one go. Under that, a chemise. Under that, another damned layer. Under that...

It would probably take a good streak of playing—or luck—to get her down to her bare skin.

Samuel swallowed as his head swam.

"You are game, then?"

"Oh, yes," he replied without much thought. "Shall... Shall we start the game over?"

"Are you absolutely certain that you wish to play?" Rose was either teasing or remarkably concerned about his welfare, for she looked truly troubled. "I am good at chess, you know."

She was, but Samuel was confident now. He had played two games with the woman, he knew her stratega, her approaches. He knew how she led with the queen and did little with her rooks. Her pawns were all over the place, and as for her knights—well. He had taken both in the last game within five minutes of the first piece moving.

"I don't doubt it," he said aloud, silently doubting it. "But I believe I have little to fear."

Rose's beautiful face smiled. "Then we shall reset the board and commence strip chess."

Lull her into a false sense of security, Samuel told himself silently as the bishop that had previously been blessed with the ministrations of his wife's fingers was replaced on the board. It was that simple. *Let the woman think that she will flatten me, and she will start to make mistakes. Leverage them.*

Take off her clothes.

Samuel's lips curled into a broad grin. "Ladies first."

"It's white goes first, you dolt," Rose said companionably, leaning forward and moving a pawn. A different pawn than last time. "Good luck."

"'Luck'?" He couldn't help but laugh at that. "I don't need luck."

Five seconds later, she took his first pawn.

"Now, I think I would like you to remove your jacket," his wife said, tapping a finger to her lips as she perused him. "Yes, off with it, please."

Samuel chuckled as he removed it. "A lucky start."

"You'll need all the luck you can get, my lad," Rose warned, a glint in her eye that should have warned him far more than it did.

"Shall we continue?"

His pawn forward. Her knight to the left. His bishop forward. Her queen forward. His bishop to the right. Her queen—

"What's your queen doing there?" Samuel looked down in horror as Rose plucked another of his pawns from the board.

"You weren't paying attention," she pointed out, evidently trying and failing not to laugh. "You've got to consider the entire board at all times."

"Yes, yes," he muttered with a laugh. "What will it be, then?"

Rose's gaze raked over him, and Samuel tried not to notice how a trail of heat followed in its wake across his skin. "Your cravat."

Well, it could have been worse, he thought as he removed the inoffensive strip of material. And he was still mostly dressed, after all.

A minute later, his shirt was on the hearthrug.

"I told you that I was good at chess!" Rose protested as Samuel gave her a scalding mock glare.

"You did," he admitted, trying not to revel in the way her admiring eyes were taking in the planes of his chest. "But I am determined to beat you."

Five minutes after that, both of his boots were off.

"And I still call it cheating, the fact that I had to take both of your knights to get both your boots off," Rose said as she sipped at her wine. "The cheek!"

"The cheek is that you managed to completely distract me with that foray with your rook," Samuel returned, half-laughing, half-astonished he had not yet managed to take a single one of his wife's pieces from the board. The damned woman was still fully dressed. "You never play your rooks!"

A sparkle of disobedience gleamed in Rose's eyes. "Ah, but who's to say that I wasn't lulling you into a false sense of security before this game?"

He had to laugh at that, and their mingled laughter filled the drawing room, and a part of Samuel whispered, *Yes, this every day for the rest of my life, please. Please don't leave me.*

It was only a whisper, however. After all, how could he say such things?

He had promised Rose one thing: financial freedom. She would claim it after having served as his wife for a year and a day, and she would be gone.

Gone. Forever.

That line of thinking was surely why within three moves, Rose was taking his queen from the board.

"My queen!"

"If you had wanted to keep her, you should have protected her better," said the minx dispassionately as she placed his queen down with the pile of other white pieces that had said goodbye to the board. "Now, what shall you take off next?"

Samuel swallowed. There was not a great deal for him to take off, in truth. His socks of course—perhaps he would be able to argue that she would have to win two of his pieces to take both of them. That had been the case with the boots, after all. There was his pocket watch; that was still attached to his trousers. There were his trousers themselves, and his underclothing...

And that was it.

The gleam in Rose's eye told him that she had thought just the same. Her laughter was teasing and he could not help but join in.

"You rascal," he teased. "You knew you'd beat me."

"I told you numerous times, *I am good at chess,*" Rose returned, stifling laughter with her fist flitting over her mouth. "You cannot say that I did not warn you."

There were warnings going off in the back of Samuel's mind but he was ignoring them, the giddiness of the game and the sheer proximity of such a beautiful woman and the wine and the evening they had spent together combining to remove any sense.

"Well, you are good at chess," Samuel admitted, lifting his hands in a brief gesture of mock surrender. "But you know, I am good at other things."

Rose lifted an inquiring eyebrow. "Oh, you are?"

This was a mistake. This was foolish. This was something he would look back on and regret.

But dear God, while he was doing it... What euphoria.

Samuel cocked his head in a flirtatious manner. "I am, indeed. Why don't you let me show you?"

Chapter Fifteen

Rose looked up at her husband and tried to remember that 'husband' was perhaps not the best descriptor.

Husband for a time. A borrowed man. A temporary spouse.

The handsome man seated opposite her before the fire lifted his hands, pretending to surrender to her superior chess skills—specifically, her superior strip chess skills.

"But you know, I am good at other things."

"Why don't you let me show you?"

He should not have been allowed to say such things. A man as handsome as that, with that little clothing currently on his body, should not have been allowed to say such suggestive things.

Rose squirmed on the hearthrug. She was probably reading far too much into such a statement. He didn't mean, he *couldn't* mean anything sensual.

Even if that was precisely where her mind went.

Still, she had to match him with the same energy, didn't she? Carefully fluttering her eyelashes in as coquettish and non-serious a manner as possible, Rose said lightly, "Be careful not to tease me. I might misunderstand you."

For some reason, Samuel had clearly not expected her to return with such a statement. His eyes flashed with desire, just for a moment, and it was gone.

Or had she just dreamed the expression in her desperate hope for another one of his scalding kisses?

Rose tried not to inhale sharply as Samuel tilted his head in a teasing way that made her core melt.

"I doubt you misunderstand me," her husband said, his voice promising all sorts of decadent things she absolutely knew he would never deliver on. He gestured at his half-clothed body. "Not when *you* have me here, in such a compromising state as this."

Saints preserve her...

He was teasing. A jest only, Rose knew, and the sort that she would have made if she were the one half-naked before a clothed individual. After all, he was attempting to distract her from the game.

The game she was winning.

Instead of replying, Rose leaned forward—making sure her breasts were almost tipping out of her corset—and took the man's bishop.

Samuel swore under his breath. "I'm trying to seduce you, woman!"

That was only part of the tease, Rose knew. She could not, would not take it at face value. "I think it's time that those trousers came off."

"Rose!"

"You agreed to the rules!" Rose shot back, trying desperately not to think about what could possibly be underneath his trousers.

The man surely wore undergarments...did he not? Oh, she knew there were some gentlemen in Italy who, in the summer months, eschewed any additional layers...but Samuel was an English gentleman. In England. In the middle of winter.

Surely, if she made the man take off his trousers, there would be something to protect his modesty?

Rose rather hoped there was not.

Sighing theatrically as only she could appreciate, Samuel rose to his feet as his fingers moved to the buttons of his trousers. "This is a foolish game."

"Only because you're losing," Rose said, her mouth dry as her eyes refused to leave his fumbling fingers.

Was he truly going to—was he actually—

Samuel allowed his trousers to drop without looking away.

Rose exhaled slowly.

Well, he was wearing undergarments. She would have been disappointed by the long lines of cotton fabric that entirely encased his loins and thighs, except...

Except for the fact that the fabric, while opaque, did absolutely nothing to hide the obvious attraction the man clearly felt for her.

Dear God.

Rose was no expert in the matter—she had usually permitted her opponents to pay a forfeit before actually losing their trousers, and it had only come to that twice in her life—earning her a good secondary income and preventing her from seeing the unpleasant nether regions of her fellow actors.

But... Well, was that part of him not...larger than most?

"You are offended."

Rose started. "Not offended."

Was she incapable of even speaking in full sentences?

Samuel was still standing, gazing down at her with plainly no embarrassment that his rock-hard member was outlined clearly beneath his undergarments. She knew she should look away, knew she should at least *attempt* to preserve his modesty...but well. The man did not appear to mind.

Rose swallowed as her gaze followed the trail of wiry hair that disappeared beneath the waistband of his undergarments. What did that skin feel like? What did it taste like?

And why, for goodness's sake, could she not look away?

"I told you before that I was good at other things," Samuel said quietly, lowering himself onto the hearthrug and lounging—actually *lounging*. "Aren't you curious to know what they are?"

Her mouth was dry and her pulse was thumping in her ears, and Rose was almost certain she did not need to ask to know.

The man was liquid desire. More, he was liquid sensuality, and he was directing it all at her.

They had an agreement. An annulment meant they must never lie together as husband and wife. Rose had not thought much of it at the time, the idea of enjoying amorous congress with a man she'd barely known hardly appealing.

But she knew him now, and everything she knew about Samuel told her that he was a good man. A man who deserved the very best in the world.

Perhaps he could make do with her.

"You... We have an agreement," Rose said, her voice hoarse. "You said it was crucial that we did not...that we never..."

Words failed her, something unusual and most disconcerting. She could always rely on her words, or in a pinch, on the words of a playwright she had memorized. There was always a monologue, or some witty repartee, or a clever insult that she could utilize if her own mind failed her.

But even her memory was failing her now.

Samuel examined her closely. "True, we did have an agreement. But I've come to think, Rose, that... Well, that bending the rules ever so slightly—just while we are married... Well, it would hardly be the worst thing in the world."

Rose leaned forward and picked up her king, desperate for her fingers to have something to do.

This was madness. *Madness!*

If she permitted what he suggested, they would be unable to seek an annulment. They would stay married, forever. Did the man know what he was insinuating?

"And besides," Samuel added, his voice low, a thrum through her body, "anything we share does not need to be communicated to others. It'll be our secret."

Her hopes dropped a few inches within her. *Of course.* Rose had been foolish to think he cared for her in any meaningful way; the man was filled with lust and had no immediate outlet save for herself. That was all.

That was all it ever could be.

"And I..." For some reason, Samuel swallowed and seemed to shrink in on himself a bit. Most unaccountable. "I like you, Rose."

He *liked* her?

In times past, Rose would have sniffed at such a meager declaration of—well, it wasn't even love, was it? Where was the passion? The undying desire? The desperation, the wild statements that if he could not have her, he would die?

Rose looked deeply into Samuel's eyes and saw something more.

Respect. Admiration. Affection.

The very ideas startled her, jolting her so strongly that she almost dropped her king. No man had ever... They had desired her, to be sure, but no man had ever respected her. No man had dwelled in her company long enough to *know* her to admire her. No, they had laughed with Juliet, or Hermia, or Helena. Sometimes even Lady Macbeth. Not her.

And as for affection...

Rose swallowed. "You like me?"

"I know it does not sound like much," Samuel said in a low voice, his attention burning into her. "But there are few people I have a genuine regard for, and you... We fit, don't you see? We work. This is working. And you are so beautiful."

The lust Rose had expected to hear was absent. Not that his tone had no particular timbre to it. It did...but it was not lust.

Desire. Need. *Yearning.*

It was not love. But it was most certainly not lust.

And what did she have to lose? The marriage would be over in eleven months, give or take, Rose reminded herself feverishly as she twirled her king round and around her fingers. The world may not believe in an annulment, anyway, regardless of whether they actually succumbed to this temptation or not.

And she had already lost her heart.

Why not allow herself to be seduced by a man who actually

adored her this time? To a man whom she would always respect, always appreciate, always know to be a good man?

Rose inhaled deeply. "You are asking to bed me."

Perhaps she should not have put it quite so crude a fashion. Samuel winced. "I thought more along the lines of seduction, but yes."

"You might not be very good at it," she said quietly, placing her king back on the board with fingers that were definitely not shaking. She made sure of it. "It would be a shame, indeed, to break our agreement if you have no clue how to please a woman."

The challenge was laid down, and she could never have imagined how eagerly it would be taken up.

Samuel leaned forward, his eyes bright. "Let me show you, then. A little pleasure all for you, before I ask you to remove a single item of clothing."

Her breathing was quicker now. Rose had not noticed when it had happened, but her lungs were tight and her thighs were—

A little pleasure. All for her.

Keeping hold of his stare with her own, Rose slowly leaned forward, inch by inch...and tipped over her king.

Samuel needed no further invitation. With a growl that vibrated through her whole body, making promises she hoped to God he could keep, Samuel scattered the chess board as he lunged forward and pushed Rose's shoulders back.

She shrieked, the movement so swift that she tipped backward onto the hearthrug. *"Samuel!"*

"Be quiet," he warned, leaning over her with his wide shoulders and incredibly attractive chest. "That is, if you can."

It was an intriguing statement, one which would have sounded trite in another's mouth.

Rose tried not to look at the mouth in question as she propped herself up on her elbows. "Samuel—"

"Just lie back," he said with a teasing laugh. "And tell me afterward how *good* you think I am."

Well, the man had confidence. Such a shame that the last time a man had had such self-assurance, it had been such a disappointment.

Rose allowed herself to fall back so that she was lying on the hearthrug looking up at the ceiling and wondered what on earth the man was going to attempt. If he was just going to jam his member within her, she would have something to say about—

Oh, dear God.

"Samuel!" Rose moaned.

She had not intended to moan, but she rather thought no woman would be able to help herself. After all, the man had kneeled between her legs, pushed up her skirts, and delicately slipped down her drawers.

Oh, and so delicately. His fingertips brushed her thighs, sending sparks up her whole body, but there was no roughness, no haste to his movement. Just an inexplicable expertise that softly whispered of previous women adored and satisfied.

Satisfied as apparently she was about to be.

It was on the tip of Rose's tongue to ask Samuel to be gentle with her, but she was forced instead to bite her lip as the man lowered his mouth to her secret place…and kissed it.

She was going to expire. That was the only thing that was going to occur. She was actually going to expire right here before the fireplace.

"So beautiful," came his murmur from between her thighs. "And so delicious."

Another kiss and Rose quivered, not sure whether it was his touches or his words that flickered such heat through her whole body.

She was aching now, and dripping with need, and all she could do was lie back and accept the teasing nibbles that were so exquisite and yet most definitely not enough.

"Samuel," she breathed.

His response was to place his hands on her inner thighs and part her legs, opening her even farther for him, and Rose's hands clenched around the edges of the hearthrug as she fought the instinct to tighten her knees around him.

The man did not deserve to suffocate. Not as his tongue lapped, just for a moment, at her folds.

The curse Rose uttered was undignified.

Samuel chuckled against her flesh and she squirmed, lowering herself into his mouth, but he leaned back, refusing to satisfy her. "Such a hungry girl."

"It's *you* who should be eating." Rose moaned before she could stop herself.

"Oh, you filthy thing," exhaled the man between her legs. "And yet so delicate, and so perfect. So warm, and so wet, and so ready for me."

She truly was going to expire. Precisely why did such praise make her whole body quiver, make the sensations he was bestowing heighten, make her want to get on her knees and worship him?

"I've wanted to do this for days," Samuel said before brushing a kiss over her folds. "No, not days. Weeks."

"Samuel," begged Rose in a hissing whisper, twisting her hips as though to force him to lap at her once again.

"Good girl. Nice and quiet."

She was rewarded with another tongue lapping and Rose was forced to bite her lip to prevent herself from crying out. She would be a good girl, if that gained her another tongue lashing like that.

"You've been very good to me, Rose," Samuel whispered, his thumbs stroking that delicate skin that led to her secret place. His tongue slowly, slowly licked up her slit, making Rose pant. "I want to reward you."

Rose's fingers were growing numb. Her fists were so tightly clenched as she tried not to make a noise.

The man was a god. He certainly had not been jesting when he'd said he knew how to give pleasure.

That tongue of his slowly reached her clit and Rose bucked,

unable to help herself, as it slowly encircled that throbbing nub within her.

It was only to be one thrust as Samuel's hands held her fast against the hearthrug. "That's naughty, Rose."

"*Please.*"

She had not intended to say it, merely scream the single word in her mind, but the aching need within her was growing to a pitch with his teasing that pushed her restraint over the edge.

If only the damned man with his magic tongue could push her over the edge...

"Well, as you asked so nicely and you taste so good..."

And then his tongue was inside her, deep within her folds, lapping and sucking, one of Samuel's hands somehow no longer on her inner thigh but up past her stomach and squeezing her breast, his thumb and forefinger somehow twirling around her nipple, which he had freed. Rose was undone, unable to think, unable to breathe as waves upon waves of bliss were mercilessly poured through her body and his tongue worshipped her clit and—

"Samuel!"

Rose could not help it, but it no longer mattered. She could not be punished because she was soaring, soaring through ecstasy that had not let up and his tongue and his hands and his whole body seemed to be pumping even more through her and when she cascaded down, down through the levels of ecstasy until she was a mere quivering mess of bliss, Rose could do nothing but look up and see...Samuel.

Samuel, leaning over her, smile wide, a breathy look of satisfaction on his face.

She could barely think. Him, satisfied? Was not *she* the one who had been utterly destroyed?

"And that," he said softly, "is the little pleasure I wished to show you."

Rose allowed her head to fall back on the hearthrug as her lungs tried to remember how to work.

'The little pleasure'?

"Rose? I... I did not hurt you, did I?"

It was the concern in his voice that did it. Without that tinge of apprehension, Rose could have shaken hands with the man and walked out of the room.

Well, perhaps not shaken hands with the man. And perhaps not walked. Hobbled. Her thighs might never be the same again, and her knees were weak, and—

The point is, Rose thought furiously, *that now he's had the damned decency to be nice, I really do love him.*

It was most disagreeable.

As it was, there was nothing she could do but sit up, push the man back so that he was now the one looking up at the ceiling, and glare ominously down at him.

"I really wish you hadn't said that," Rose said with perfect sincerity.

Samuel's face was a picture of worry, puckered lips and furrowed brow, and it amused her for a brief moment that the man was so instantly willing to believe that he had acted incorrectly, when all he had done was please her to within an inch of her life.

Perhaps farther than that.

"I didn't hurt you, did I?" Samuel asked weakly as Rose started to do the only thing she could.

Take off her clothes.

"You did not hurt me," she said with a wry expression, her unbuttoned skirt slipping off as she rose to her feet. "Quite the opposite."

The relief was another indication that this man, this impossible man, was a far better one than she had ever presumed. "Oh, that's excellent to hear. And you are removing your clothes...why? In advance of losing our next chess match?"

Rose giggled as she glanced at the board, its pieces dispersed across the carpet. "No, I would have beaten you."

"You would not—"

"It is your time to be quiet. If you can," Rose said softly as her fingers finished untying the laces of her bodice.

The fabric fell to the ground along with her underthings.

It was perhaps not the best angle to view her. Oh, she knew her body was hardly unpleasant to look at, but every actress knew that one's chin did not look so prominent—or double—if viewed from above.

Those in the cheap seats at the front of the stage always saw her with at least five more chins than she actually had as they stared up at her.

That was precisely the angle to which Samuel was being treated now, though Rose had to say that his unabashed stare of admiration as she stood there, utterly naked, was mightily flattering.

"You are the most perfect woman I have ever seen," Samuel said hoarsely.

"That is only a compliment," she said softly, stepping forward and lowering herself to straddle the man still wearing his blessed undergarments, "if you have seen a great many women in the nude. Have you?"

There was no flush in his cheeks, no shame in his eyes as he said, "A fair few."

Rose nodded. She would not have believed him if he had said otherwise; a lord like him, eldest son of a marquess, was sure to have befriended a widow or housemaid or two in his time.

But he was hers now.

The thought rose unbidden, but she could not quash it. Not when it was the truth. "No more after me, please."

"Yes, Rose," Samuel said hoarsely as her fingertips traced the line of his skin where it met his undergarments.

"No one except me," she emphasized, knowing it was foolish, knowing that in a year the new Marquess of Aylesbury would be bedding a fresh widow or even his second wife and Rose would be somewhere on the Continent, never to see him again.

His dark eyes met hers and air caught in his throat as he breathed, "No one except you."

It was not difficult, in theory, to remove a man's undergarments, especially when he was lying so obligingly still and prone. The trouble was Rose's fingers, which were shaking after he had made her what felt like another promise.

Beyond their wedding vows, oaths made to satisfy a vicar and a solicitor, this promise was far deeper. Far more personal.

Far realer.

Rose gasped as the undergarments were flung to one side—not toward the fire—and she saw the full... well, *equipment* that Samuel was working with.

The suggestion through his undergarments had if anything, *underplayed* his hand.

"Oh, goodness," she breathed before she could stop herself.

"Not a disappointment, I hope."

She heard the worry in his voice, the worry that every man experienced by the time he realized he would have to be naked in order to penetrate a woman, though Rose wondered how on earth a man of this... well, *stature* could ever be concerned.

"Not a disappointment, no," she said, the truth once again laced with mirth. "Now be quiet, and do what you are told."

Rose was still so wet from the thorough ravishing that Samuel had given her but minutes ago that it was not difficult at all to lower herself, to spear herself on the throbbing warm manhood.

What *was* difficult was not coming to a peak of pleasure in doing so.

"Oh, God, Rose, you feel so—so—"

It was delightful to see Samuel so equally undone, and Rose tried not to smirk as she slowly rocked on his manhood, drawing herself up over him then thrusting herself back down in a rhythm all of her own making. "I am what?"

Samuel's eyes widened and his lips twisted in unspoken, unspeaking words as he moaned. "Rose!"

And it was charming, wonderful to utterly ruin a man for all other women. Rose tried to keep her own diversion at bay as she slowly, slowly increased the rhythm, sometimes allowing him to thrust deeper within her, sometimes remaining above him for a beat so that Samuel moaned in unsatisfied need—and when he grabbed at her hips and tilted her ever slightly, his manhood slipped deeper within her and Rose's eyelashes fluttered.

"I—I'm close," she panted, unable to keep it to herself.

When she looked down, it was to see Samuel looking up at her with gritted jaw. "Please come soon. I can't—I can't hold on much!"

Rose let herself go, riding him hard and fast, and it did not take long to reach her climax—especially with Samuel's thumb moving to where they joined and twisting around her clit.

"Samuel!"

All thoughts of quiet gone, she lost herself in the experience of being truly at one with another man, a bliss only increased as Samuel swore and thrust upward in a feverish rhythm of abandon.

"Rose—Rose!"

When the pleasure faded, and it could have been an hour, Rose slowly lifted herself off the man and half-lowered, half-*dropped* herself onto the hearthrug beside him.

Their breathing, ragged and uneven, filled the room. It was the only sound Rose could hear as she realized three most inconvenient things.

Firstly, she loved the blaggard.

Secondly, her heart would break when she had to leave him.

Thirdly, they had not used a preservative.

In this moment, she did not know which was worse.

Chapter Sixteen

February 5, 1841

IT WAS ONLY supposed to be once.

Just once. That was what Samuel had promised himself, the morning he had woken up after the evening of strip chess and general debauchery.

Just once. He knew now the taste of Rose Morgan—Rose Chase—the taste of her all over, and he had given her pleasure—five times. One night of amorous congress.

That would have to be enough.

It had not been enough. Samuel had crept into her bedchamber the following morning and woken her up with his fingers, bringing her unadulterated pleasure, and had been forced to stop her screams with a kiss.

That afternoon, she had surprised him by slipping into his study and clambering under his desk, unbuttoning his trousers and—

Well. Suffice to say, he still grew hard each time he thought about it.

The day after that, Samuel had marched into her bedchamber just before Rose had been about to extinguish her candle, and demanded that he ravish her. She had already been naked under the covers.

The day after that, they had enjoyed muffled intercourse after luncheon and dozed the afternoon away, exchanging kisses in their embrace.

The day after that, they had ordered breakfast in bed. It was cold by the time they'd gotten to it.

The day after that, Rose had kissed him warmly as she had entered the dining room for dinner, and the moment had been so natural and so…so right that Samuel had been unable to think of anything except making her cry for mercy until he had done just that, footmen and butler scattering to the winds the moment he had grabbed hold of his wife.

So much for hoping to lie their way to an annulment, should anyone ask the servants.

And now it was today.

Samuel shifted uncomfortably in his seat as he read that day's newspaper. It was ridiculous. They had already enjoyed amorous congress twice before descending for breakfast, and he'd given her a quick fondling just before luncheon, which had made Rose moan in his ear and his fingers feel as though they were magic.

Surely, his loins could not still burn for her.

He glanced up. They still could.

Rose was seated opposite him, lounging in a chair with her legs over the arm. She was reading what appeared to be a very dry Roman play, nothing he had read. The fact that it had come from his own library had been a great surprise.

Her concentration was on the book, not himself, and yet Samuel could not help but feel…feel alive in her presence. There was something truly unique about Rose, something he could not understand and would never cease trying to.

That was… Until she walked out of his life forever.

Would she rather have a divorce, then, than stay with him? If she left England, maybe she wouldn't care if they had to lie and claim her as an adulterer to secure Parliament's approval for the dissolution of the match. She'd be rich. And free.

Samuel forced his eyes back on the newspaper. He would not, could not think of that time. Besides, had they not reached an unspoken yet understood new arrangement?

Why did Rose have to leave at all?

"Anything interesting in there?" Rose's voice was vague, as

though she were still concentrating on her play but was nonetheless curious about his own reading.

Samuel smiled. Her curiosity, that was another thing he loved about her. Not just in the bedchamber, though that was to be sure a great delight.

No, there was nothing Rose was not fascinated by. Perhaps it was her artistic nature. Perhaps it was her creative soul. But the woman was more than happy to discuss almost any topic.

Another most attractive feature.

Samuel rustled the paper as he turned a page. "Nothing much. The Quintrells are giving a ball and the Eatons are hosting a dinner on the same evening."

Rose snorted. "And that's news?"

"It'll be news when Lady Romeril decides which she will attend," he returned with a laugh, lowering his newspaper. "Honestly, sometimes I forget you did not grow up in the same world that I did."

For some reason, there was a strange stiffness in her voice as she replied, "Oh?"

"Yes, these sorts of things can make or break one's reputation. The very idea," Samuel said, warming to his theme, "that one of the families will have to be slighted by Lady Romeril, which is a very disgraceful thing, indeed."

"Yes, I rather gathered that."

He ignored the chill in her voice. "But you don't understand—this could make or break these families. Both of them have daughters, as far as I can recall, looking for husbands. To receive Lady Romeril's disdain—"

"I *said* that I understood."

Samuel lowered the newspaper. Now that was not a chill. That was ice. "Is something the matter?"

There was; he could see it without Rose answering. It was in the way her cheeks had flushed, the way she did not meet his gaze.

But more than that, it was in the way he knew her.

He knew Rose Chase, and she was not happy.

"It's fine." His wife dropped her eyes to her play. She was holding it the wrong way up.

Samuel made to set aside his newspaper but hesitated at the last moment.

Well, it was not as though… They had not actually talked about it. What they were to each other, now. After they had enjoyed each other's bodies so thoroughly.

Still husband and wife, yes, technically. But were they more than that? More than a technicality?

Samuel certainly knew what he wanted, but for the life of him he struggled to read this actress, who knew how easily to twist and change her expression to mean a million and one different things.

Right now, she looked…irritated.

He decided to be direct. "Have I offended you?"

Rose looked up, and there was a wistful expression on her lips that suggested she was rather surprised by his question. "No."

"Are you sure? For I would prefer to know and give you the apology you deserve—"

"Why would you assume an apology would be necessary?" She was laughing now, which was to be preferred, but there was still some distance in her eyes.

Samuel shrugged. "I cannot imagine a situation in which you would be at fault."

Rose opened her mouth, hesitated, then said quietly, "You really mean that, don't you?"

It was a shame she was not seated beside him on the sofa, for he wished he could bring his arm around her and scare away the specter of her father. That was who, Samuel guessed, had given Rose such a disbelief in herself.

"I always tell you the truth," he said simply.

Her grin this time was sincerer. "Well, you have not offended me. Go back to your newspaper."

Rose's attention returned to her play. She blinked. Then she turned the book around so it was the right way up.

Stifling a smile and wondering how on earth he had managed to select this particular actress out of all the actresses who were presumably wandering the streets of Brighton, Samuel returned to his newspaper.

Announcement of an engagement between two people he had never heard of... News of a ship sinking somewhere in the Caribbean... A riot in a town he did not know...

Ah. *The gossip pages.*

It was not a regular habit of Samuel's to read such a thing, but his father had sat him down most seriously when the title had officially been handed over and told him he would have to start doing just that.

"'The gossip pages'?" Samuel had repeated, incredulously.

His father had sighed. "Believe it or not, my boy, who you are, what you do matters now. You are the Marquess of Aylesbury, God help us all—"

"Father!"

"—and that means you need to know whom to speak to and whom to avoid, if I may say so delicately, in public. The gossip pages are your source of information." His father had looked stern. "Not always accurate, but trust me. There is usually no smoke without fire."

Samuel had assiduously obeyed his father's directive and found, much to his dismay, that he rather relished it.

He glanced down at today's pages. A widow in trouble, well, no surprises there. He would just have to hope his cousin Zander hadn't been involved. A brokerage deal gone wrong that would lead to a mill having to close up in Leeds, *dear me.* And a gossiping little paragraph about—

Samuel's heart stopped.

It has come to our attention that a recently joined member of polite Society may not in fact be the lady she appears. A Lady A, who shall remain nameless on our pages for the sake of delicacy, has never claimed noble blood but has not owned that she was an actress, a profession reeking with scandal. Indeed, she may be a new bride, but she is not, however, an innocent one. Lady A is in fact onto her second husband—at least.

His vision was blurry and his pulse had not yet returned to beating. His lungs were tight, aching with the breath he had not taken.

A Lady A, who shall remain nameless on our pages for the sake of delicacy, has never claimed noble blood but has not owned that she was an actress, a profession reeking with scandal.

Well, perhaps he should never have expected to keep that particular piece of information quiet forever. A year and a day had been too much to hope for, clearly.

But it was not that particular sentence that had rocked his sense of stability.

Indeed, she may be a new bride, but she is not, however, an innocent one. Lady A is in fact onto her second husband—at least.

Second husband. *Second* husband.

But—But Rose had never been married before. Had she?

She had never mentioned another husband. He had not asked. Why had he not asked? Should he have asked—did lords generally inquire as to number of previous husbands when propositioning that an actress be their wife for a year and a day?

Samuel forced himself to inhale as lights started popping in the corners of his eyes.

He couldn't believe it. He just... He just couldn't believe it.

It was worse than he could have ever imagined. Rose, married to another? Dear God, was she *still* married—had she made him a bigamist? Who was this man? Why had she married him? Where was he now?

Did this man even exist? Who had reported on this story? Did they really know more about his wife than he did or was it all a lie?

The force of the many questions pouring through his mind threatened to overwhelm, and all Samuel could do was cling to his newspaper and hope the world would soon stop spinning.

This was…impossible. Outrageous. Terrible.

He lowered the newspaper and looked at his wife.

His *wife*. That term had never meant more to him now than it did when he realized he could so easily lose her. His wife—but someone else's wife? Why in God's name hadn't she mentioned this before?

All that to-do at the church, the way she had pointed out that the wedding was to be her only one…

Samuel tried to swallow, but his throat was too dry. And all that had been a lie?

"You look pale." Rose's voice reached him from a great distance. "Did you read something unpleasant?"

Unpleasant? Yes, it was unpleasant to think that the truth and honesty, the openness they had shared for weeks, was in fact merely a façade.

If it was true. But who would dare make up such a story?

Samuel almost laughed. But then, what should he have expected, given that he was paying a woman, an actress, to temporarily be his wife?

"Or something perhaps suggestively scandalous?" Rose's voice was teasing now.

When he blinked and the woman before him came into focus, she was still reading her play, but there was a smile on her lips.

Her lips. Her kissable lips.

He would never kiss them again. How could he, now that all trust between them had been broken? Now that he knew he could never believe a word she said?

Desperate hope that it was a misunderstanding rose within Samuel, swiftly following the panic and attempting to dampen it down.

It was a gossip column—they did not always print the truth, and even if there was a kernel of truth in there, perhaps they had the wrong end of the stick. Perhaps she had been *engaged* once before. Yes, that could be it.

The way he clung to the mere suggestion of a way to explain it all away was worrying in and of itself.

Samuel cleared his throat. "Rose?"

"Hmmm?" She did not look up.

Was he truly going to do this? Was it not better to live in ignorance, never quite knowing, never quite sure, but safe in the fact that he did not know for certain?

Rose looked up and grinned cheekily. "You rascal, I am far too sore to go again. I've never been worn out like you wear me out."

And it was this statement that pushed Samuel over the edge. Had he truly been the only one to love her like that...or was there another husband somewhere who knew just how Rosemary Morgan tasted?

Samuel set the newspaper aside. "Rose, I... I need to ask you something."

"I told you, I'm too sore to—"

"Not that," he added hastily, not sure whether he could bear to hear that again. "No, it's... It's about your past."

He was looking for it this time and so he saw the way her shoulders stiffened, how her whole body tensed then relaxed. She gained control of herself swiftly, he had to admit. But for a moment, just a moment, she was terrified.

Rose placed her book down. "My past?"

"There's..." Samuel tried to inhale, he really did, but it was a challenge. "There is a piece of gossip about you. In the newspaper."

Swinging her legs back down and facing him directly, Rose swallowed visibly as her breath hitched. "In the newspaper—they know I am an actress?"

"They do. How they know, I cannot tell, but that much I know is true."

"And it is my name there, in the newspaper?"

Her urgency did not make sense to Samuel, but he nodded. "Yes. Well, you are described as 'Lady A' and a newcomer to

Society, so I do not think it will take people long. You are also described…as a newly married lady." *Keep calm, man.* "There is something else about your past in there that is very shocking."

The color was draining from her face. "I—I should have told you."

And there it was. Confirmation that he had been right; that was, that he had been wrong to trust his own instincts.

The pain was acute, far sharper than Samuel had predicted. To know that he was the second—at least, for she was an actress, and actresses had fewer scruples about such things—to know Rose intimately was not what hurt, he was discovering. No, he was no prude, and he had taken sufficient women to bed to know that technique was sometimes enhanced by practice.

No, it was the fact that she had kept this from him. Such a crucial part of Rose's life, another marriage, and she had not seen fit to tell him. She had not trusted him.

"Yes," Samuel said quietly. "You should have."

"It was just—it was so long ago, and I hated that it defined me even then," Rose said hastily, her words rushing out of her mouth as though it were a relief to speak them. "And I thought, once you knew… Well, it was exciting, you not knowing. I thought if you knew, you might treat me differently."

He could not help it. His features softened. "Rose."

"You saw me as I was and you chose me," she said with a dry laugh, "and I thought, once you knew that I was nobility—"

Samuel almost fell off his chair. "I beg your pardon?"

Rose stared, her head tilted slightly. "You—You said my past, it was published in the paper."

"It says you've been married before! Not that you are a gentleborn woman—I'm sorry, *nobility?*"

Tugging a hand through his hair and wondering how he hadn't lost a great deal of it in the last five minutes, Samuel stared in utter bewilderment.

Rose, a lady. A noblewoman?

It couldn't be. It wasn't possible!

And yet...even as he sat here, occurrence after occurrence of Rose effortlessly navigating a complex social situation, dancing at balls, laughing at just the right times... Dear God, he hadn't even bothered to tell her how to use a fish knife, and she'd eaten those scallops as though she'd been fresh from the womb and using fifteen different forks.

As though she were born to it.
Dear God.

"You didn't—it doesn't say anything about my father, the Marquess of Dalton?" whispered Rose.

It was a good thing Samuel was seated, for his legs most certainly would have given way under him had he been standing.

Her father. Lord Dalton.

Lord Dalton. Her father.

Her father Lord—

"Look," Rose said firmly, as though only speaking so she could grasp a hold of the conversation. "My father—"

"Lord Dalton," croaked Samuel, his stomach twisting.

"Lord Dalton," she repeated, though her mouth twisted as though his very name were bitter in her mouth. "Though he was the Earl of Burnell when I left home. I... I missed my grandfather's funeral just last year." She swallowed. "My-My father, he never encouraged my acting. He never wanted me to make a 'fool of myself and the family name on the stage,' as he put it."

"But—But...you said your name was Rose Morgan!" What was the world coming to? That a woman could lie so blatantly, and straight to his face!

Rose's expression flickered, her breath hitching again. "And it was. It is Rosemary Chance, Marchioness of Aylesbury now, but when I ran away from home, I—I married a man called Luke Morgan. He... He died just weeks after our marriage." She swallowed, chewing her lip.

Samuel wanted to snap at her, but he felt his chest sting at the signs of his wife in pain. In pain over... the man she'd once loved enough to marry. Without being hired to.

He cleared his throat as she offered no further details. "I'm-I'm sorry for that, but... You mean to tell me you were *Lady* Rose Morgan, not Miss Morgan all that time? You said—at our wedding, you said you'd never been married before!"

This wasn't happening. This was absolutely not happening.

He wasn't the man she loved. He never could be. Could never replace a ghost, a true love gone so soon.

She stiffened. "I said it was the only true wedding I would ever have. Samuel, I eloped. It was not—"

This time, Samuel rose to his feet, unable to take another revelation without standing. "Good God, Rose!"

"It wasn't a lie—you never asked about—I never said that Morgan was my maiden name!" Rose too had straightened and she was standing mere feet from him now.

Tugging another trembling hand through his hair, Samuel shot back, "You are a Dalton! Damn it, Rose, you're from a noble house and I have *paid* you to become my wife!"

"You wouldn't have listened. You wouldn't have understood. It was clear to me you'd only consider a noble lady for your forever marchioness, but I didn't want to be picked for *that* reason. Can you even begin to understand that?"

"I would have at least appreciated the chance to!" Was anything true anymore? Did he know anything about this woman? "Have you even *been* to Rome?"

"Don't be ridiculous," snapped the actress, throwing back her hair, which was coming unpinned in her fury. "Of course I've been to Rome!"

"Well, excuse me, but I just discovered that a noble family with only one daughter who ever came out to Society actually has two! And you are one of them!" Samuel had not intended to raise his voice, but the woman was impossible! He massaged his forehead, scrambling for the details about the Dalton lineage in *Debrett's Guide*, as if he could summon a page he'd only ever glanced at to life in his mind's eye. He did seem to remember the title was a new one, used by the current marquess's father, the first man to have the title, until just last year. "I don't recall what happened to their other daughter."

"My parents lied and said I was ill," she said softly. "That I was sent to the country with a distant relative and I would never debut in Society. At least, that's what they threatened to do if I left. It only makes sense, since they can't exactly scrub me from the family tree."

"Well, how convenient. How convenient for you all, that no one apparently delved too deeply." His words were sharp—*too* sharp—even to his own ear.

"You're just upset because you wanted to think you had been the first to show me pleasure!"

The barb stung, but not as much as the way Rose's face had looked when she had said it.

Only hours ago, they'd been in perfect harmony. And now...

"I am upset," Samuel said slowly, trying to keep his voice level, "because you *lied*."

"I did not lie! And you've got what you wanted, anyway—you've got all the money from Miss Margolotta's will," Rose said forebodingly, folding her arms. "That was all you wanted, wasn't it? I suppose bedding me was just a bonus?"

His shoulders were moving up and down, and only then did Samuel realize that was because he was panting hard.

How could she say such a thing—and to him! How could she accuse him of only being interested in the money, such a miserly thing, indeed!

The fact that it had been almost true until very recently was completely beside the point.

But it wasn't ever as if he felt he needed the money for *himself*. He'd had things he'd wanted to do with it—good things. And his mother had warned him the other possible heir would just waste it.

"I can't hear this," Samuel found himself saying, heart beating frantically and nausea rising.

She was nobility. He had defiled a noblewoman, not with his

body but with his scheme. Dear God, should he have even done it at all, to *any* woman? Here she was, his wife, and he had only married her to claim a fortune.

What sort of man was he?

"You don't *have to* hear it. I didn't want to tell you in the first place!"

"No, I mean I—I can't stay here."

Samuel had stepped across the room before he knew what he was doing, the drive to exit the room and not face the woman he adored and yet clearly did not know overpowering him.

"Samuel!"

He hesitated, one hand on the door. Turning slowly, hoping to goodness he did not lose his nerve by falling to his feet and begging her to forgive him for he knew not what, Samuel looked into Rose's eyes.

They were filled with tears. They were also filled with defiance.

"I have done nothing wrong," she said, though her voice wobbled on the last word.

Christ almighty, he could not remain here. "You can stay here," Samuel said shakily, his voice strangled. "But I can't... All of this is unknown to me now. *You* are unknown to me. I... I have to go."

"Samuel!"

Paying no heed to the cry behind him, Samuel strode forward—out of the drawing room, across the hall, out the front door. He did not stop until his lungs were screaming and his feet ached.

It was dark. He had been gone hours. He was unsure where he was.

And he still had no idea what to do.

Chapter Seventeen

February 7, 1841

ROSE'S STEPS ECHOED uncomfortably on the marble staircase as she descended.

She shouldn't do it. She knew precisely what would happen if she did.

"Samuel?" she said nervously.

Samuel... Samuel... Samuel...

She had liked the size of the townhouse when they had first arrived. Well, what person would not, after having lived in a room in a tenement in Brighton? The Mayfair townhouse was large and spacious and airy. Each room was at least twice the size of her previous lodgings and so splendidly decorated that Rose wondered if there was any marble or gold brocade left in London.

It didn't feel large and spacious and airy anymore. It felt cavernous.

Her footsteps continued to echo uncomfortably as she reached the bottom of the staircase, no rug or carpet to muffle her movements. Not a creature stirred.

Even the servants appeared to be avoiding her.

Which is a nonsensical notion, Rose told herself steadily as she stepped resolutely across the hallway with her head held high. The servants could not possibly have been avoiding her, because no one knew of the break she and Samuel... The argument they had had.

Though now that she came to think about it—and she'd had a great deal of time to think about it over the last few days—they had yelled a great deal.

It was possible the servants had overheard a small amount of what had been discussed…or perhaps more accurately, the servants had been *forced* to overhear the whole damned thing.

Rose's hand hesitated before she entered the library.

It was not that she was not permitted. Samuel had said, when they had arrived here, that she should treat the place like her home.

And he marched out of that door, Rose could not help but think as she glanced over her shoulder. *And he did not come back.* No note, no letter, no appearance of the man who had apparently expected to be told her entire life story for an arrangement. For a job.

He could have been anywhere. He might not even have been in London anymore, though his valet was still at the townhouse last she knew. He'd traveled without one before, though.

And just because the library had been his favorite room in the house…

Rose inhaled slowly, then entered the library.

She immediately regretted it. The place was Samuel, through and through. His favorite cigar smoke still lingered on the shelves. On the table were three books that he had been concurrently reading. Rose lingered for a moment, her fingers brushing the bookmarks. Over there was one of his jackets, evidently cast off while reading and not moved by a servant who clearly supposed their master would not wish for it to be removed.

In a strange sort of way, it was almost as though Samuel had just stepped out of the room, just for a moment. As though he could walk back at any time.

There were footfalls, and Rose turned swiftly with a smile, apologies ready on her tongue and her hands outstretched, ready to take his own—

Arden cleared his throat. "Good afternoon, my lady. Have… Have you heard from the master at all?"

Rose's spirits sank as rapidly as they had risen. "No."

What more was there to say? She had no further information, no knowledge of where Samuel was or what he was doing. She had considered sending a note to his club but realized she could not recall which one he was a member of.

There was so much she did not know about him. Yet everything she did know, she loved.

The butler cleared his throat once again. "And is the master expected back at any particular time, my lady? Or...or day?"

She was not going to cry. Of that, Rose was certain. She was absolutely and completely in control of herself, and that meant she was not going to cry.

The prickling at the corners of her eyes might have suggested otherwise, but she was not going to succumb.

"Are—Are you unwell, my lady?"

"Definitely not," Rose said thickly, turning away from the butler just in time to catch the first teardrop. It and the second were hurriedly dashed away with the sleeve of her gown before she turned back to the servant. "No, I do not know the master's movements. I suppose you...you need him to sign something, or relay instructions to his valet or...or something?"

Goodness, it had been so long since she had lived at home, she had almost forgotten what the master of the house did. From what Rose could recall, it had been her mother who had done almost everything. Not Lord Dalton.

"Is there anything I can do to help?" Rose continued, trying for a smile and probably achieving a grimace.

Arden stepped back. "No, no, I am sure I can manage. Thank you, my lady."

He backed out of the room perhaps a little faster than was polite, but Rose could hardly complain. Not now the tears were flowing without any ability to halt them.

Should she leave? Was it foolishness itself to remain here, in this cavernous townhouse? Did she even have a right to be here, if her husband was at this very moment undoubtedly speaking with Mr. Todd to secure their annulment?

Though a certain lie would have to be told on that score...

Would he instead seek a divorce? On the grounds of her withholding information? No, that might not do it. He'd have to say she had been unfaithful. But she hadn't been.

Would he care if that wasn't the truth, though? He'd seemed as hurt by her explanation of her past with Luke as he might have been had she been talking about a recent lover.

He doesn't want you here. You knew this was always going to be temporary.

Leave, and start again. It would only be the third time she had done it, after all. How difficult could it be?

The very thought weighed heavily on her bones and so sinking slowly into the large leather armchair upon which Samuel had lain his jacket, Rose leaned into it and inhaled.

Samuel.

That was what it smelled like. It was difficult to describe in words, even for an actress like herself who had lived on her ability to speak clearly across a wide theater.

It was...Samuel. His smile, and his laughter, and that way his nose crinkled when she said something outlandish. It was cedarwood, and spices, and a Samuel-ness that was entirely his own.

Rose dashed away a few more tears and, knowing she was being completely foolish, lifted the jacket from the chair and pulled it around her shoulders.

It was too big for her, far too big, but it was like having Samuel's arms around her once again. Rose allowed her eyes to close. If she ignored the reality around her—which was very tempting—she could almost pretend he were there.

Samuel. His strength, and his goodness, his way of looking at the world that was completely ridiculous and at the same time so charming.

Samuel, with his desire to help his family and his ability to learn how to look beyond his horizons and help others. Samuel, with his drive for money that had somehow not tainted his character.

Samuel. The man who had walked out of their home, their pretend life, and only then had Rose realized just how desperately she had wanted it to be real.

She almost laughed, even with her eyes closed, at how ridiculous she must look. Sitting here with her temporary husband's jacket and tear-stained cheeks—

"Am I interrupting?"

Rose's eyes shot open as her legs suddenly unfolded underneath her and she tried to stand up. The trouble was, her feet weren't expecting it and her hands had to shoot out to grasp the chair to prevent her falling down in front of—

Frank.

Samuel's youngest sister blinked at her owlishly from the doorway where Arden had been only moments ago.

Rose stared back.

"Lady Francesca, my lady," said Arden, who stood beside her and bowed before leaving once more. "And no... companion."

Samuel *had* told Rose his youngest sister was rather clever at leaving her chaperones behind. Rose had been so far removed from those kinds of restrictions for so long, she almost hadn't thought twice about it.

Frank glared at the man's back as if he had offended her honor, not letting up until he was out of sight, then she turned back to Rose. "I think it's your turn to say something," Frank said slowly. "I'm almost certain I went last."

Rose sank back into the chair, not bothering to pretend that she was not wearing her husband's jacket. "Come in, do."

Well, what else was she supposed to say? Ladies were expected to be hospitable, and she had been raised a lady. True, she had attempted to escape all that by running off to Gretna Green and marrying a man, a *boy*, really, whom she had barely known, and liked even less the little more she'd come to know him, then she'd run away to Rome and lived her dream as an actress before returning to Brighton and marrying a marquess for a year and a day, if they lasted even *that* long…

But she was still a lady.

Frank closed the door behind her and stepped into the room with her back straight and her eyes wandering this way and that, as if she had no apparent nerves, but a great deal of curiosity. "I'm not sure that's your cut."

Rose blinked.

"Though I admire the effort. I find trousers to be the most troublesome, but I know a tailor," Frank continued conversationally, "who knows the style I like. I can recommend her, if you want."

Rose could only blink.

"The jacket," her sister-in-law said kindly, and a little slowly, as though her hostess were having trouble not only in the hearing department, but in the thinking department as well. "It doesn't fit."

"It isn't mine," was all Rose could think to say.

Frank nodded sagely as she stepped across the library and threw herself into an armchair opposite. "Yes, I find that my brother Benjamin is the closest fit to myself. The poor man doesn't know where he keeps leaving his trousers. Keeps having to make Father's valet purchase new ones."

It was difficult not to laugh. Not at the young woman, who was living up to her name and speaking far more frankly than half the Society in London. No, at the ridiculousness of it all.

Here she was, married to a man who was now perhaps technically missing, and his sister had arrived to see him and had instead found his temporary wife—though she did not know the whole marriage had always been meant to end—dressed in his clothing.

What on earth could happen next?

"Samuel's left London."

Rose's pulse skipped a beat. "I beg your pardon?"

Frank examined her curiously, with no shame in doing so.

"Why did he leave London and leave you behind?"

Leave me behind.

Yes, Rose supposed that was the politest way to say that a husband had abandoned his wife. Though was it true abandonment, if the whole marriage had been a financial arrangement?

She should say something pat and polite. She should say something comforting yet vague. She should say *something*. She couldn't leave Frank to manage all the conversation.

"Do you know where he is?" Rose asked urgently, ignoring all her thoughts.

Frank raised an eyebrow. "I rather supposed that *you* would. The blaggard promised me a new mechanical pencil and it hasn't arrived yet."

It was difficult not to laugh at that. All Samuel's big plans for his family, his hopes and dreams for them; they were all coming to fruition, and all because she had withheld information about her past and married him, anyway.

Rose swallowed through her suddenly dry sore throat. "I am sorry to hear that. Perhaps Arden will know—"

"I know, you know."

"You... You do? Where Samuel has gone?"

Frank rolled her eyes. "No, not that."

Silence descended over the library as Rose stared in horror at the young woman before her. Had she seen the same newspaper that had ruined her happiness? Frank did not elaborate. Eventually, there was nothing for it.

Rose cleared her throat and thrust her nose in the air. "You know something, though?"

"Oh, not the details. Not any of the details, actually. I don't actually *know*, so much as know that there's something to know that I don't know," Frank said calmly. "Something you're not telling me. Not telling anyone."

Rose's shoulder blades relaxed as the hackles on the back of her neck subsided. Oh, well, it was easy enough to sense that something was wrong in the marriage. Newly married husbands did not tend to disappear from their wives' company within a couple of months, after all.

"And you're going to tell me," said Frank.

Slowly lifting an eyebrow, Rose drew on all her years as an actress to say lightly, "Oh, I am, am I?"

Frank nodded matter-of-factly. "Yes. You are."

Rose had never been a card player. Chess was far easier. As long as you could make the pieces do what you want, you could almost ignore the person you were playing with.

Not so with cards. In any card game, you were not just playing the cards, but the player who was holding them. Knowing what they were thinking, or trying to make you *think* they were thinking, was half the game.

Frank would have made an excellent poker player.

Still, it was worth hazarding an attempt. "I am sorry, Lady Francesca, but—"

"I liked you a lot better when you called me 'Frank,'" her sister-in-law interrupted.

Raw nerves from the argument with Samuel reared their head. "And I liked *you* a lot better when you didn't march into my house and demand my secrets."

It had been the wrong thing to say. Frank's eyes widened, her lips parting in evident astonishment.

Or perhaps it had been just the right thing to say.

Because Frank laughed. "Oh, I *do* like you. I hope you and Sammy can make up. There are so few people in my branch of the Chance family who speak how it is—though admittedly, Lilianna can do so a tad too much, once she gets going."

Rose stared. Her family—those of the Dalton estate, she corrected herself—were not people to laugh. They were not people to encourage plain speaking, either, not when only the head of the household was permitted to have an opinion.

But here Frank was, chortling away at Rose's impertinent remark, as though it were the best thing that she had heard all day.

It made no sense.

"Look, I will make no demands of you that I think are unfair," Frank continued, her chuckles subsiding. "Lord knows I keep enough secrets from my family. But you, Rose, are without friends here in London—true friends, I mean. You have no one else to turn to, and it doesn't look to me like Samuel is coming back on his own. And I like you."

A flicker of warmth spread over her shoulders that had nothing to do with Samuel's jacket. "You do?"

Her sister-in-law nodded. "I don't know much about you, Rose, but what I do know, I like. And if your little tiff has anything to do with that nasty gossip I read a few days ago, I hope you won't let it upset you."

The flicker of warmth immediately disappeared.

That nasty gossip. Oh, Frank was well meaning, Rose was sure…but she could not know that she had just described Rose's real life as something nasty and hopefully untrue.

How could she admit to it? If even Samuel's sister who professed to like her would consider Rose's true life story as something to be hidden away or embarrassed by, what was the hope that her husband would ever forgive her?

The smile that had been playing about Frank's eyes was slowly disappearing. When she spoke, it was in a low and most apologetic tone. "Oh, God. It's true. It's true, and I've offended you. Rose, I'm so sorry."

"You have nothing to apologize for," Rose said hastily, wishing to goodness she had thought to ring for tea. Hiding behind a teacup would have been pleasant right now. "You could not have known."

"But why didn't you tell us?"

Her laughter made Frank flush, but Rose could not help it. Intelligent as her sister-in-law was, Rose sometimes forgot just how young and naïve Frank Chance was.

"'Tell you'?" Rose said with a shake of her head. "Tell the Dowager Marquess and Marchioness of Aylesbury that their son was about to marry an actress, one who had run away from her family for a dream of acting and a foolish first marriage that was only ended by the untimely death of her husband?"

Frank's eyes were wide. "And did…did you kill him?"

Rose's snort echoed around the library. "What sort of actress do you think I was?"

It was such a ridiculous suggestion that it made her quite howl with laughter, and somehow, that managed to release a great deal of tension that had been trapped within her for days and days.

Her—kill Luke? Frankly, she was lucky it hadn't been the other way around…

Her guest's expression was rueful. "Sorry. Got carried away there."

"Oh, I don't blame you. My life has been so packed full of melodrama, I am almost surprised there is not a murder in there somewhere," Rose said dryly.

"Wait, though," said Frank, cocking her head. "You said, 'about to marry'? But you didn't meet my parents until you'd been married for several weeks."

Rose swallowed, not realizing until just then she'd let that detail slip. "Yes, about that…"

Frank grinned devilishly. She'd make a good Iago on the stage, tempting Othello into doubting his wife and all he'd believed to be true. "I knew it! I think we all did. Well, maybe not Mama. She *has* to believe her precious baby. But he married only after learning about the terms of the will, didn't he?"

"Yes, well…" Rose did not want to get into the details of that arrangement. "The solicitor is quite aware, so it's all to the good. Look. I am flattered that you came over here to see how I was doing and find out if your…your mechanizing—"

"Mechanical," Frank corrected her, a frown furrowing her brow. "I do hope Samuel ordered the right thing."

"I am sure he did." Even speaking of him was painful, Rose was surprised to discover. A sharp stab in her gut each time his name was spoken, a curling twist of pain in her stomach whenever he was referenced. *Would it ever lessen?* "My point is—"

"The Chance family is one of the noblest, most respected, and most admired in the whole of Society you know," Frank said quietly, as though her response made any sense.

Rose waited for more, but none seemed forthcoming. "Yes, I know."

"We're very good at keeping up appearances," her guest said slowly and meaningfully. "We're even known for breaking the rules. Without suffering any consequences."

Whatever meaning she wanted to convey, Rose was unable to capture it. She knew the Chances were considered eccentric for passing on titles prematurely as they did. But 'keeping up appearances'? Well, she knew all about that. Her father—Lord Dalton had always been focused on impressing the locals in their native Northumbria.

Frank rolled her eyes and leaned back in her armchair. "Land's sakes, Rose! I'm saying that we're good at covering up little escapades and smoothing over little issues! There's absolutely no reason why you and Samuel can't recover from this."

"It's not a *little escapade.*" Not unless obscuring who she was and allowing half-truths to take positions as full-truths could be described as *a little escapade.* "Frank, I appreciate you are trying to help, but you can't. No one can."

"There's something else, isn't there?"

It was most irritating to have someone in the family so intensely clever. Rose had never realized it until now, but it was the clever ones you had to watch out for.

Benjamin? Oh, he had happily accepted that Samuel was married and that was that. No further questions needed. Lilianna had been occupied with her coming child and the Dowager Marquess and Marchioness of Aylesbury had clearly been so astonished and delighted that their eldest son had wed, they did not think to question it. Frank had said they'd almost all guessed at the truth, that Samuel had lied about the circumstances of their marriage, but no one had seemed fit to pry further until now.

But Frank? Frank needed to know things. She needed to take them apart and see how they ticked, Rose was beginning to see with a sinking sensation. And she wouldn't let go of a line of thinking until she had entirely explored it.

Bother.

"There is something else, and you should tell me what it is." Frank nodded, as though agreeing with herself meant it was two votes for truth against Rose's vote for secrecy. "Besides, I'll find out anyway."

Rose's breath caught in her throat. "You... You will?"

"You think that someone won't find out eventually? You're a member of High Society now," her sister-in-law said, with almost a sympathetic expression. "It'll be Lady Romeril, or someone of her ilk, and they won't be kind about it. It'll be everywhere, trust me. Whether it's in a year, or two years, or five—"

"I wasn't even supposed to be Samuel's wife next year," Rose blurted out.

The words had never been meant to be released from her lips and yet the need to confide in someone, *anyone*, had finally overpowered her.

She and Frank sat in complete silence for what felt like forever. All that could be heard was the ticking of the longcase clock in the corner of the library, and the soft, sudden fall of snow just visible through the large bay windows.

Frank uncrossed her legs and leaned forward, looking at her sister-in-law closely. "You love him."

It would have been childish to disagree. Rose nodded.

"And he loves you."

"I don't know about that," Rose began.

"No, I know Samuel. He only runs away from the things that really matter to him—when his heart is truly engaged. Trust me," Frank said warningly. "Both my brothers are complete idiots, but Sammy is usually the less idiotic. The fact that he's run away tells me that he cares too much for you."

It was flattering, indeed, to hear, but Rose could not believe it. Who ran away from the thing they loved?

"So whatever... Whatever scheme it was that the two of you thought up, and honestly, at this point, I don't even care about the details," Frank said darkly, "if you both love each other... I don't see the problem."

Rose's lips curled into a tired smile. "Frank, you—you see the world as a puzzle. As an engineering problem to fix. But you can't fix this."

Her sister-in-law brought her palms together in front of her, her fingertips brushing her lips. "But *you* can."

Chapter Eighteen

February 10, 1841

THIS WAS A monumental mistake.

Samuel had no clue why he'd thought this would be a good idea. It was, perhaps, the most foolish thing he had ever done.

Other than actually marry her, obviously.

"Hot pie, sir?" squawked a man wearing a stained bowler hat and a crooked, toothy grin.

Samuel smiled weakly. "No, thank you."

"I got oyster pie and eel pie and fish pie and—"

"No, truly, I am not hungry," said Samuel as his stomach rumbled.

Another traitorous part of his body. Now his stomach, previously his manhood. Probably at all times his brain.

The pie seller looked disappointed. "Why'd you come to Brighton, then, if not to have fish pie?"

It was an excellent question and not one Samuel thought he could answer. As his attention raked over the horizon, the ocean before him and the scent of salt in the air, he realized he had absolutely no idea why he was here.

Brighton.

It had seemed a good idea at the time. Get out of London, away from the pain of realizing that the woman he had married was still a complete stranger to himself—a ridiculous revelation when he had knowingly married a stranger to begin with—and get back to where it had all started.

Though perhaps in hindsight, his thought process had not been that careful. Now that Samuel came to think of it, he had bundled himself into a carriage that night and ordered the driver to just go to Brighton. Brighton, the place where he had first met Rosemary Morgan.

So not much thought had been involved.

The pie seller had moved along the beach, hoping to entice others with the stack of pies on a tray around his shoulders. In a strange way, Samuel rather missed his company.

It was lonely, standing here on the sandy beach and looking out across the ocean and knowing that he was forever parted from the woman he had been growing to love. Painful, to know that there would never be a connection like it.

"Not a disappointment, I hope."

"Not a disappointment, no. Now be quiet, and do what you are told."

Samuel pulled his mind away from that moment of intimacy and started to trudge along the beach.

There was no particular direction, nothing he was aiming for. Just trudging.

The air was cold, the afternoon fading. The hotel room Samuel had taken had been a mistake, the same hotel where he and Rose...where he and *Lady Rose Morgan* had resided before their ill-fated wedding. Every minute spent there was like a punishment.

Samuel tugged his greatcoat closer as his breath started to appear on the air. The beach was hardly populated at all, most of the residents clearly deciding that they could enjoy the beach view another time.

Like July.

He wondered if he would even still be married come July.

"Damn it, woman," Samuel muttered. "Why did you have to keep so many secrets?"

The fact that he had given her few opportunities to tell him anything was neither here nor there, he told himself firmly. So was the fact that they had not known each other when they'd been married. And that, judging by the look of her face as she had revealed that the Marquess of Dalton was her father, some of her memories were truly painful.

Samuel stamped the beach off his boots as he left the beach and meandered through the Brighton streets.

The trouble was—*the real trouble,* he thought ominously, was that he had attempted to escape Rose and instead, he had come to a place that reminded him of her with every passing corner.

There. That was where they had run into each other. He had knocked her down, Samuel remembered with regret.

Over there. That was where they had lunched, and he had first suggested his ridiculous and most outlandish idea.

There was the part of the beach where they had walked. Samuel had assiduously avoided following in their footsteps, but it was a small town. He could not avoid the sight of it completely.

Samuel cleared his throat and the air blossomed around him.

Damn it. He knew the place he had been avoiding for the last two days, and his treacherous feet had led him right to it.

The Grand Theatre.

He looked up at the façade, wondering if he was brave enough or foolish enough to enter. After all, this had been the last place that Rose had worked her previous life. There were undoubtedly people who were inside right this moment who knew her…perhaps better than he had ever done.

The thought tasted bitter in his soul. Samuel had thought, for just a few days, that he and Rose had come to an unspoken understanding. That night on the hearthrug…he had been sure of it. And now he was sure of nothing.

Well, what did he have to lose?

Stepping forward and trying the handle, he was almost disappointed that it opened easily. The entrance hallway was empty, so he merely kept on walking through doors.

It's like a church.

That was the first thing that rushed through his mind, that the space was like some sort of grand, Continental cathedral.

High ceilings and faraway walls, pillars that made echoes bounce and candles everywhere.

Only when Samuel blinked did he realize that he was standing inside the theater itself. And he was not the only one. The theater was not packed, so this was not a public performance, and Samuel could not help but feel he was seeing something he ought not to.

"Deny thy father and refuse thy name!" cried a woman in a medieval-style gown, striding across the stage with her hand outstretched.

Samuel swallowed, lowering himself as quietly as he could onto a seat right at the back of the theater.

It was a coincidence, that was all. 'Deny thy father'? Yes, that was what Rose had done. Denied her father to the point where she had not revealed her true parentage.

"Or, if thou wilt not, be but sworn my love," continued the woman with a dewy expression, "and I'll no longer be a Capulet!"

That's the strange thing about women, Samuel thought dismally. *They marry, and they take on completely different names. Morgan, indeed.* The man had undoubtedly been a brute. He had no evidence of that, but it was difficult not to take an instant and irrational dislike to a man who had previously wed his own bride.

The bride he had, in essence, paid to wed him.

"Shall I hear more?"

Samuel jolted. He had not spotted the young man in similarly medieval garb, though perhaps he had not been immediately supposed to. The actor was partially hidden by a pretend tree just to the left of the stage.

"Or shall I speak at this?" added the young man in a loud pretend whisper.

"'Tis but thy name that is my enemy," said the actress dreamily, facing in the opposite direction quite on purpose. "Thou art thyself…"

She continued on, but at this point, Samuel's thoughts strayed elsewhere.

This was Rose's world. Strange, to think that she would have known this place better than anywhere else in England. Samuel had never thought much about rehearsals; plays usually appeared fully formed before him on a stage, on the rare occasion that he attended.

But of course rehearsals were vital and would have taken up a great deal of her time. That stage, these very boards, would have been familiar to her.

Samuel swallowed, a knot in his throat still untied. They could have been something special, even though the way they had found each other was...unorthodox.

But now that was over. Gone.

The Juliet on the stage moved toward the center, and she was staring now right at him, though Samuel was unclear whether she could actually see him.

"What's in a name?" she asked in a clear, ringing voice. "That which we call a rose by any other word would smell as sweet."

Samuel stiffened.

Dear God, it was uncanny.

"No, no, no!" An angry voice appeared from the front row.

Samuel had not noticed him before, but a man had stood up from the second row and was shaking his head as though what he had just seen was not only dreadful, but borderline offensive to the acting profession as a whole.

"You really must enunciate, Annabelle—honestly! Rose had a way of speaking that reached the very back of the theater and you are mumbling, Annabelle!"

Juliet no longer looked ethereal and delightful, but greatly peeved, her fists on her hips and a stomp to her feet. "I'm doing my best!"

"Your *best* needs some serious improvement," said the man tartly. "Now, give me that line again."

The actress scowled. "What's in a *name?*" she said, her tone threatening. "That which we call a rose by any other word would smell as sweet."

Samuel flinched. Honestly, the coincidence was almost galling. Yes, Rose was beautiful and charming and lovely no matter what her birth name had been. But that didn't account for... the secrecy. The fact that he hardly knew the woman.

"And again!"

"What's in a name? That which we call a rose by any other word would smell as sweet."

"Again, girl!"

"What's in a name? That which we call a rose by any other word would smell as sweet."

Prickles of irritation were circling up Samuel's spine. He didn't have to listen to this—he could leave at any point he wanted. The fact that he was still sitting here, listening to the repeated reminder that his affection for Rose should not be based on knowing her full history, was neither here nor there.

"Really elongate those vowels, Annabelle!"

"What's in a naaaaame? That which we call a rooooose by any other woooord would smell as—"

"Enough!" thundered Samuel, rising to his feet.

Juliet, Romeo, and the man now standing in the front row all turned to stare.

Samuel cleared his throat. *Well, damn.* "I mean... Pardon me."

"Who the hell are you?" yelled Juliet, her voice losing its delicate refinement and reverting to something more akin to the accent belonging to the pie seller Samuel had met on the beach. "This is a closed rehearsal, I'll have you know!"

"I... I wanted to ask you about Rose Morgan," Samuel found himself saying, stepping down toward the stage and knowing full well that this was a most definite mistake.

What the hell was he doing?

"Rose?" Juliet—or Annabelle—evidently did not appreciate hearing that name again, as her foot was tapping again. "Why? What has she done?"

"She won't have done anything, you silly girl," sniped Romeo, coming out from behind his tree. "He's a patron, ain't he? Looking for new talent?"

"'Talent'? Oh, what a talent," bemoaned the man now seated again in the front row. "I have never seen a woman like it. Oh, Rose, she was a marvel. She could make anyone believe anything."

Yes, Samuel thought darkly. *That is precisely the problem.*

"You know I replaced her?" opined the young woman with a haughty sniff. "She was old."

"She's well under thirty," Samuel could not help but point out.

"Yes, but she was close to it."

"You are a fool if you let her go," said the man whom Samuel had to presume was the manager, or owner, or something. "I let her go and now look at me! Stuck with *her*!"

Juliet theatrically looked behind her, then scowled when she turned back to the seats. "You're a cruel man, Ted. And after I let you take me to bed, too!"

Samuel watched as the two of them bickered. Romeo pulled a pipe out of his pocket and started to smoke it, suggesting that the debate that was currently being run through was one he had both heard before and he no longer bothered to interject into it.

"—but I tell you, Rose was always able to—"

"I don't want to hear any more about Rose!"

Samuel did. It was strange, standing here with three people in this unfamiliar place who had also known her.

He knew her, but in a far different way. These people had lived alongside her for months, perhaps years. He had never inquired as to precisely when Rose had returned from Italy, after all.

They had rehearsed with her, acted with her, celebrated when a play performed well and likely as not commiserated together when it had not. They had seen her joy and her spark, her incredible kindness, for eons longer than he had.

How precisely *they* had let her go, Samuel did not know. The woman had mentioned her age. Good God, that Ted was a fool, if he'd looked at the gorgeous Rose for a moment and considered her too old to play a beauty.

"Oh, go and practice a scene with Romeo here!" snapped the fool in question.

Juliet narrowed her eyes. "Which scene?"

"*Any* scene!" The man threw up his hands. "Just—Just go away and let me speak to this gentleman!"

Juliet—Samuel had already forgotten what her true name was—flounced off the stage in a manner mostly resembling a child. He spotted Romeo rolling his eyes at Ted, and then the younger man sighed heavily, blew out his pipe, tapped it against the pretend tree, and stomped off after his fellow actor.

That left Samuel and Ted.

The latter turned to the newcomer. "Is it true, then? You were looking for Rose because you wanted her to play a role?"

The irony was not lost on Samuel. *Yes*, he wanted to say. *Yes, I want her to play the role of my wife forever and ever and ever. And somehow through her fear and my stupidity and her secrecy and my nonsense, there's a gap between us and I don't know how to fill it.*

"Something like that," was what he actually said.

Ted sighed. "I should never have gone for youth over experience. Honestly, Annabelle is hopeless. I wish Rose had stuck around in Brighton. I would have taken her back in a heartbeat."

Taken her back in a heartbeat.

Samuel tried not to think about how those particular words could be applied to his own life, and instead said, "I wanted to know a little bit about her."

His stomach sank heavily with Juliet's insinuation. Ted had lain with Rose's replacement. Had he ever done the same with Rose?

Strangely, though, he found he would not have been mad at Rose if that were true. He'd just have felt sorry for her. Ted was no prize to be had in bed, by the looks of him.

Ted's eyebrows rose. "She still keeping quiet about her past?

Oh, that's Rose. She never wants her real life to interfere with the roles she's playing."

Now wasn't that the truth.

Samuel gestured to the seats and the two men sat down, the marquess trying not to bash his knees into the other man. "But what do you know of her? Any... Any information would be helpful."

If Ted was suspicious as to his reasoning, he did not seem it. Perhaps it was common in the theater world, Samuel guessed, to come and go without giving much insight into one's past. Perhaps it was just as common for theater owners to inquire into such things.

Either way, the man said heavily, "Look, there's not much I can tell you about Rose. She was, *is*, a clever girl. Smart with her mouth and her mind."

Samuel's whole body went rigid. He didn't like the sound of that. "'Smart with her mouth'?"

"Oh, the way she could rattle off lines without a single fluff, I have never seen the like," Ted said solemnly, clearly utterly unaware of just how suggestive his previous comment had been. "And the way she inhabited a role! I once encountered her just coming off stage as Lady Macbeth, and the look she gave me, I tell you, I fair widdled my—"

"She is an impressive actress, then," Samuel said hastily. He had had a terrible few days. The last thing he needed was to hear of another man's difficulties in that department.

The man sighed and shook his head.

"She wasn't an impressive actress?"

The thought should not have given Samuel hope. Was it possible then that all the encounters they had shared, they had all been true? They had all meant something to Rose? It hadn't all been an act?

"She was the most impressive actress I had ever seen," Ted said, dashing all Samuel's hopes in one fell swoop.

His shoulders slumped. "Oh. Right. Good."

It was *not* good. It was the worst news he had ever heard, but he could hardly be the one to say it, not with this Ted thinking erroneously that he was in the theater business himself.

"But I think what made her truly special," the man continued, "was that all of her acting came from a place of truth."

Samuel blinked. "I don't follow."

"Rose cannot lie," Ted said simply.

There was a strange sort of ringing in his ears. Even after Samuel had shaken his head, it persisted. "I… I beg your pardon?"

"Look, right, most actors, actresses, they're lying on stage, right?" Ted said it as though it were the most obvious thing in the world. "They don't believe what they're saying. They're doing it to be dramatic like."

Samuel was with him so far.

"But Rose… She found the truth *within* the words. She read things, books and things. She looked for the truth in the story, in her character, and she lived that truth on stage." Ted was getting misty-eyed now. "There'll never be another like her."

The man was right. There wouldn't. Hearing how Rose lived, how she found the truth… Was it possible she had found true affection for him?

Samuel had to hope so. There was so much about her that he did not know and whereas days ago, that had filled him with pain, it only sparked enthusiasm within him now. He wanted to know her. He wanted to spend that time getting to know her.

If she would let him.

"And kind, too."

Samuel blinked. "I beg your pardon?"

"Rose. She's kind," said Ted with a wry smile. "She wouldn't allow a man to kiss her unless she liked him, and so there were no kisses given out while she was here. Very kind, in my opinion. Didn't never lead the actors on. Kept it real professional-like with me, too. But somehow, I found I didn't mind. Just looking at her… That smile was enough to keep a man riveted."

Swallowing did absolutely nothing to quieten the strange sort of pounding in Samuel's chest.

But—But she had kissed him. Allowed him to kiss her, and kissed him, and... Well. A damned sight more.

So she liked him?

Was liking enough?

Samuel rose to his feet, eagerness to return to London and put everything right coursing through his body...until one thought occurred to him.

Professional? Not leading men on? But what about her boasts over her chess prowess?

He sank down back onto his seat as Ted eyed him curiously.

"Yes?"

"I... I need to know," Samuel said weakly, knowing he was foolish indeed to even consider asking—but certain he would regret not knowing all the more. "Rose. Chess."

The look on Ted's face was enough—almost enough—without a single word. "Ah. She said the same to you, did she? The strip chess?"

Samuel's heart did not precisely sink; it merely ceased to be. How could he have a heart, after it had been completely broken and destroyed by the knowledge that Rose had lived such a different life to himself?

What she did with her own life, that was her call. He would never censure her for making a living for herself, even if it had required taking her clothes off.

But how could two people with such different journeys travel on together?

Ted was nodding sagely. "Yes, it used to upset people, that did."

"I bet it did," Samuel said hoarsely.

"Everyone did it, of course."

"I'm sure they did," he said weakly, desperately wishing he could escape this conversation.

"And Rose caused such a stink when—"

"I really must be going, I've got a carriage to—"

"—when she wouldn't participate," Ted said placidly.

Samuel had half-risen from his seat, but once again, he lowered himself down slowly. "I... I beg your pardon?"

"Strip chess. You said you were having the same problem with Rose," Ted said patiently, as though Samuel were a very simple man. "Even though it's fairly common among our crowd, she won't play."

"She... She won't?"

"I suppose she's told you the same thing that she told us," continued the man with a shrug. "She said that she could beat everyone in chess without bothering with all that. That she was saving herself for someone special to play strip chess with."

Samuel's gut twisted horribly even as his spirits soared.

That had been a lie, not just a withholding of the truth. She hadn't played it before—because she'd wanted to play it with someone special.

Him.

"I've got to go," he said in a rush, rising to his feet and hurtling through the theater with only one thing on his mind.

He had to get back to Rose.

"Don't you lose her once you've got her!" called Ted after him. "You'll regret it for the rest of your life!"

The man had it right entirely.

Chapter Nineteen

February 12, 1841

A DEQUATELY RESPECTED THEATER *in search of actress with open approach to—*

Rose snorted. 'Open approach.' She knew what that meant. The place would want her to take her clothes off. And only 'adequately' respected? Absolutely not.

Her gaze flickered down the newspaper page that she had been perusing over breakfast, one corner of it sadly tea-stained but otherwise legible.

Acting troupe requires singer, actress, musician for a multitude of roles...

No, that was no good. Her acting skills were impeccable, Rose knew, but her musical ability was second to none. As in, second from the last. It was entirely absent, right next to none. And as for her singing...

No.

Prestigious theater desires a conversation with a suitable actress of international renown.

Rose bit her lip. Well, that sounded more like it. The trouble was, she was almost certain that disgraced nobility need not apply, especially when that woman was twice married, a marchioness, and on the run from her husband.

Slowly, she lifted her focus from the newspaper and looked at the butler just...standing there. Oh, that was what butlers were supposed to do, but still. It was rather disconcerting, in all this wintry silence.

"Thank you, Arden," she said, trying for an imperious and yet aloof tone. "I can help myself to breakfast adequately without you and the others."

The others were the three footmen. And yes, it was probably appropriate for a marquess to eat breakfast with a butler and three footmen in attendance, but her father had always done that, had always insisted on *six* footmen, and—that was, Rose hastily corrected herself, refusing to even think about such a man, she saw no reason to be so encumbered.

The butler raised an eyebrow. "His lordship always—"

"And I am not him," Rose said smartly. *Never a truer word was spoken.* "Thank you."

It was galling to the extreme to notice that the three footmen, instead of accepting her order, looked to Arden.

She smiled sweetly. *"Thank* you."

It was a relief to see them finally start to move. The whole house had felt stifling these last few days, different to how it had been when she and Samuel... When he had both been in it. Without him, somehow, the walls towered over her and the ceilings loomed.

But at least as she sat in the breakfast room all alone, Rose could breathe.

She would find another role. To be sure, the role of marchioness had perhaps been the best one she had ever played... She had certainly enjoyed it the most. And she was a better one than her mother, if she said so herself.

"You are the most perfect woman I have ever seen."

Rose forced the memory away. No, she'd had her fun: she'd hosted the afternoon teas and attended the balls. She'd smiled and laughed and spent the man's money. But it couldn't continue, not forever. It had been foolish of her to think that the whole escapade would last the full year and a day. And to demand the payment when she hadn't made it as long as contracted? She couldn't bring herself to do that.

So: a new role. What was it to be? Acting troupe that traveled the country? Perhaps the globe? A starring actress in a small theater in a town that Samuel and his unexpectedly large family would never visit? Could she risk returning to Brighton?

The notices of employers and employees looking for work were as varied as she had imagined. Rose's attention flickered across the page. The trouble was, she would have to outrun her past.

Both of them.

So, somewhere the Daltons were unlikely to go, and the Chances would probably not venture toward. That did not leave a great number of places...

Rose's eyes settled on a notice that she had not yet read.

Scottish theater looking for actress with believable English accent. Good wages paid. Bring own gowns.

Well, she had the gowns. Samuel—Lord Aylesbury had been more than generous. Rose had to assume the man would not mind if she disappeared with her wardrobe; after all, it was not as though he was likely to find much use out of it.

Until, muttered a most irritating voice in the back of her mind, *he marries again.*

The jolt to her stomach was so severe, Rose was a spot surprised her breakfast did not make a reappearance.

Dear God, the very thought that Samuel...

But he's young, that irritating voice said as it returned with a leer. *And handsome. And rich.* He had a great deal to offer. Of course, he'd have to annul their marriage or divorce her, but she wouldn't fight it. Not even if he had to accuse her of adultery to do it.

And she knew it—knew him better than she had expected in such a short time. She could run away to Scotland, yes, and try to pretend that she was not married, perhaps give him an excuse to sue for divorce by reason of abandonment...but how could she take away the memories?

The scatter of light on the ocean, shining over Samuel's face. The way he laughed, especially when he laughed at himself—one of the most attractive traits in a man. The way his face filled with delight at the thought of helping someone.

Rose swallowed, shaking the newspaper decisively.

She was not going to think about him. *He* was the one who had stormed out of his own house. He was the one who had apparently no interest in discussing her own life with her. He was the one who had thrown a petulant tantrum.

The trouble was, the movement of shaking the newspaper had allowed the mid-morning light to sparkle on a gold band on the fourth finger of her left hand.

Rose stared…at her wedding ring.

It wasn't much. There were no diamonds or sapphires or rubies or emeralds. There had been no grand speeches, save for their negotiations. No expectations, beyond that of wealth.

She had lost something so much greater than money and though a part of her ached to find him, Rose knew that it was impossible.

Where had he gone? Why had he fled at the first sign of difficulty?

"It's foolish, really," Rose murmured to herself, desperately trying to fill up the empty space that had so often been filled, these last few weeks, with their chatter and laughter. "Wearing a ring gifted by a man who does not love me."

The gold gleamed again as she twisted her hand this way and that way. It reminded her of Samuel, of his smile…but not of his love. A ring could not be a reminder of something that did not exist.

Swallowing hard, and knowing that the upcoming action would probably make her cry tears of anger and rage and disappointment, Rose slowly put the newspaper down.

Onto her toast and marmalade.

Not that it mattered. As the sweet, orangery stickiness started to seep through the pages of the newspaper, Rose held her left hand before her and stared at it, attempting to put the image deep into her memory.

She hadn't had a ring last time. This time, she had only worn it for a matter of weeks.

Sighing heavily and hoping to goodness that her sobs would not be audible from the servants' corridor, Rose lifted her right hand and slowly started to remove the only physical evidence that she had ever met Samuel Chance.

"Don't you dare," came a low yet serious voice.

She had barely slipped the ring past the first knuckle and in her surprise, she jammed it back onto her finger and whirled around.

There, standing in the doorway, leaning against the frame as though he had just stepped out of the room momentarily to fetch something, was…Samuel.

Samuel. *Her* Samuel.

Not *my Samuel*, Rose reminded herself severely as she tried to focus on the man before her without rising swiftly just to fall into his arms. He was the Marquess of Aylesbury and he would soon be someone else's husband.

Still, she could not prevent herself from saying, "Samuel."

At least she had some self-control. Rose would have lost all respect for herself if her tone had been welcoming, friendly. No, it was ice cold, frosty, even, permeating a chill into the breakfast room and the few feet between them.

Samuel obviously registered the less-than-warm welcome. His smile faltered, his expression losing a little of that jesting delight.

It pained Rose to do it, but there was no use in getting swept up in their obvious attraction for each other.

They were well suited in that regard, to be sure.

But an actress with a previous husband and a disgraced past—even if it *was* noble—was not the suitable wife for a marquess.

Certainly not one like Samuel.

"I… I have come back," Samuel said, rather unhelpfully.

Rose snorted. *As though she needed someone to tell her that!* "Where have you been?" she snapped.

The actual whereabouts of the man were neither here nor there, really. The fact that he had stormed out, unwilling to have a conversation, gone for days without a word, without a *single* word to let her know that he was well!

Rose swallowed down the torrent of words that threatened to pour from her lips.

He owes me nothing, she tried to remind herself. It was *true* husbands who owed some sort of allegiance and information to their wives.

Not temporary wives who were merely acting the role of marchioness.

Samuel opened his mouth, and Rose just knew it was going to be filled with meaningless patter and nonsense, and if she were not careful, she would be swept up by it. *Thousands of women would be*, she thought darkly, *with his tall stance and those wide shoulders and his intensely kissable lips.*

No, whatever he was about to say, she would have to harden herself to it and not permit herself to be so easily taken in.

Samuel hesitated. Then he said, "I am sorry."

"Oh, that's just the sort of thing I expected from—" began Rose in a heated tone.

Then her voice faltered as her gaze fixed on the man who inexplicably had just said the one thing she could never, in a million years, have predicted.

The breakfast room was spinning. Most unhelpful at a time like this.

"You..." Rose cleared her throat. "You are what?"

"Sorry. Prodigiously," added Samuel, as though that were an adequate measure of apology. "I am sorry, Rose."

Rose. Just hearing her name from his lips was intoxicating. Dear God, she was utterly in the man's thrall. Did he have any idea what he did to her?

No. No, he did not.

And that, Rose thought firmly, *is precisely how it's going to stay.* The absolute last thing she needed was for her own husband to realize just how in love with him she was! That would never do.

The very idea!

"I am, you know."

Her attention snapped back to him. "Are what?"

"Sorry." Samuel even looked sorry, a furrow in his brow and a worry in his eyes that suggested true repentance. At least, repentance of a kind.

Lungs were supposed to breathe air, weren't they? Rose forced hers to get back to work, and the additional oxygen to her brain was most welcome. She had almost forgotten to breathe from the moment the blaggard had turned up again at his own home.

"Ah, my lord." Smiling, Arden appeared from nowhere. "I am glad you have returned from your travels. There are a number of items I wish to draw to your atten—"

"Not now!"

Rose flushed as she realized her yell had not only been intensively rude, but had also been echoed by her husband.

By Samuel. By the Marquess of Aylesbury. Blast it all to hell.

"Not now, Arden," Samuel added, by way of apparent apology. "The marchioness and I have a few things we need to discuss."

Rose scowled at the brute. Oh, so he was going to keep up the pretense, was he? Didn't want the servants gossiping, did he? So why on earth had he thought it was a prudent idea to just disappear off into the great unknown with not even a forwarding address?

"I quite understand, my lord," said the butler, not understanding in the least and showing it by his wide eyes and gaze flickering between them. "I shall be in the servants' hall when you are ready for me."

The man turned and left, and before Rose could say anything about Scotland and borrowing a coach and Samuel never seeing her again, the blasted husband she was lumbered with had stepped into the breakfast room and closed the door behind her.

"There," he said brightly. "Privacy."

"I don't know why you bother," Rose snapped, a stabbing sensation in her gut rising. This was the last conversation she would ever have with the man she loved. "The whole of Society will know soon enough!"

"Yes, I suppose they will. It was inevitable," Samuel said nonchalantly, stepping around the table and seating himself beside her. "Once the gossip column was published."

That the man could sit there and pick up a slice of toast—*her* slice of toast and marmalade from underneath her newspaper!—and eat it as though nothing had happened...

Well, that just proves it, Rose said darkly, desperately trying to repair the wall around her heart as with each second in Samuel's company, another brick came down. He did not understand at all—and moreover, he did not care.

Samuel munched happily. "Goodness, this marmalade is good."

Rose launched herself from her seat, unable to stay still for a moment longer. "Is that all you can say—*that the marmalade is good*?"

Her husband, for the time being, blinked up at her. "Isn't it, though?"

"Of course it's good! It's the best marmalade I have ever tasted," shot back Rose, blinking away tears. Was she truly about to have this conversation with a precursor about marmalade? "That's not what's important!"

"You know, I quite agree. And as you said, the whole of Society will know soon enough. I suppose that means we will have to prepare ourselves for visitors," Samuel said blithely, finishing off his—*her*—piece of toast.

Rose stared at the man, unsure for a moment whether or not he was still in full possession of his wits.

'*Visitors*'?

She was not about to prepare herself for visitors. She was about to leave, head for Scotland, perhaps, as the most unlikely place she would ever run into someone with a surname of Dalton or Chance, and that was all.

There was no negotiation. No debate. Nothing, absolutely nothing Samuel could say that would persuade her to—

"I am desperately in love with you, you know," Samuel said quietly, gazing up at her.

Rose's breath caught.

He was staring like... Well, as though he adored her. No Romeo had ever played it better. No Aramis, or Lysander, or Petruchio.

No, Samuel had outstripped them all and with absolutely no training. It was uncanny.

"You... You cannot mean that," Rose said, her voice hoarse.

Damn it, her projection had always been so impeccable!

"The fact that you cannot believe yourself to be lovable is just another reason why it is my duty to convince you otherwise," her husband said quietly. "Rose, I love you—"

"You don't love me. You don't even know me!"

"I know that you never played strip chess before you came to this house," returned Samuel with a calm that would have been galling, if her mind weren't already distracted by the myriad of other emotions whirling through her.

Rose opened her mouth, hesitated, then closed it again.

Movement, that was what she needed. She needed to move. A scene like this always required using the entire stage.

Striding over to the fireplace and then over to the window, Rose found to her great dismay that the flouncing about had done absolutely nothing to quieten her rapidly beating pulse and had provided absolutely no additional witty remarks.

Blast it all to hell. She usually had a script for this.

But there is, she realized as she glanced over at her irritatingly patient husband, *no script for this. No pat words, no filler lines.*

This was real life, and if she was not careful, it was going to pass her by. The scene would end and not with a kiss, but with a break.

Was that truly what she wanted?

"And I know you were a Dalton, then a Morgan, and now a Chance," Samuel continued, as though there had been no pause in his statements. "And..." His voice cracked. "I know I want you to stay a Chance."

Rose's lips parted, but what could she say?

"I took a chance on you, an actress who was struggling through no fault of her own, just over a month ago," Samuel said quietly, rising to his feet. "And I am so glad I did."

"Samuel," whispered Rose.

He did not let her continue. "Because you have shown me that the world is full of elation, and—and opportunities to help others."

"Samuel—"

"And I know I am not good enough for you, I know that, but I am willing to work on myself." He spoke with a low passion that thrummed in tune with Rose's very soul, but she could not believe it. She could not believe any of this was happening. "You make me want to be better, Rose."

"'Better'?" She had not intended so much disdain to drip from the two syllables, but it was impossible to speak calmly. "You spoke to me so... so..."

"*I am upset because you lied—*"

There were no words to describe just how he had spoken to her other than cruel, but Rose knew she had deserved it. She had lied to him—kept the truth from him, that was.

"And I know I should have told you—" The trouble was, as she tried to articulate that, Samuel interrupted her once again.

"You owed me none of your past."

Rose stared, unsure whether she had heard correctly. "I... I beg your pardon?"

And now he was striding over to her, his immense presence startling her to such an extent that she stepped backward, her knees knocking against the window seat.

"I should never have been so cruel to you. I should never

have spoken so harshly to you," Samuel said hurriedly, lifting a hand but pausing as Rose flinched.

Slowly, silently, her husband lowered his hand.

She swallowed. Try as she might, she had been unable to hide it...and this time, he would surely guess.

Her husband's voice was low and dark, though his anger was quite clearly directed at her. "Was it your father or your previous spouse who hurt you, Rose?"

Rose swallowed. But it was not a betrayal, not really. Not anymore. "My... My husband. Oh, my father is cold and unpleasant and unexpectedly cruel with his words at times, but Luke... He..."

She could not say it.

Samuel swore under his breath. "When you spoke of him dying so soon after your wedding, you looked hurt. I thought it was because he was your true love."

"No. *Never*. I regretted marrying him almost as soon as the ceremony was over." She could speak of it now with calm, as though it had happened to someone else. "Six weeks after we were wed, and about five weeks after I had realized just what a terrible mistake I had made. A... A bar fight. He started it."

Her current husband smiled weakly, looking wounded, but not nearly so much as she had expected. "Well, I suppose I'm beating him then on timing. It took you several weeks to regret marrying me."

"Samuel." Rose did not need to inject the syllables with wretchedness. It came naturally.

Samuel inhaled slowly. "I am so sorry for what you have suffered—and more, I am so sorry you have suffered from my own words. I should never have spoken to you like that."

"You should never have married me," Rose said with an attempt at a laugh.

Her whole body was tingling with the ache of not being touched by him, but it was only as she glanced up and saw the expression on Samuel's face that her pulse truly skipped a beat.

The downturned mouth as he scrubbed a hand over his face.

He was…devastated.

Samuel Chance, Marquess of Aylesbury, probably the wealthiest man in the whole of Christendom and therefore able to choose—or acquire—any woman he wanted…was pained at the very thought of not being married to her.

Did that mean—was it even possible, in a small way, that he truly did…

"You love me," exhaled Rose.

"Of course I do," Samuel said roughly, gazing with such adulation that heat blossomed through her body. "I had hoped, one day that you… That together, we might find some modicum of…"

His voice trailed away as Rose's heart leapt to her mouth.

He loved her. He really did.

Oh, she had been the recipient of a number of love speeches. Being an actress in one's youth, it became an occupational habit, though disturbingly less so in the last twelvemonth or so.

Some of the speeches had been grand. Many of them had been made with sweeping arm movements, one of which had almost knocked her off the stage.

But none of them had been like this: heartfelt, and eager, and tinged with fear.

Fear that the love being expressed may not, in fact, be reciprocated.

Rose reached out for him, but Samuel had already stepped back.

"You are not obliged—I would never demand—"

"Samuel," she said urgently, happiness overwhelming her.

"—and if you choose to forgive me, there are no expectations—"

"Samuel," Rose attempted to interrupt, a smile lilting her lips as joy, joy the likes of which she had never known, flowed through her.

"—quite understand if you do not want to—"

"Samuel!"

Her husband blinked. "I beg your pardon?"

"I... I love you."

Rose had never said it before. At least, she had never said it and meant it, understood it, truly known what it was to love and be loved in return. It had always been an obligation, or a mad attempt to escape her father, or a line on a stage penned by another hand.

It had never been like this: true, and simple, and spoken to a person she truly cherished.

Samuel did not appear to believe her. "But I—I said such awful things."

"And I kept secrets from you, secrets you were entitled to know once I realized I'd fallen in love with you," Rose said wryly. She caught his hands on hers and she could have moaned aloud for the rapture of finally being connected to him again. "I love you, Samuel."

"You love me?" His grin was lopsided, his disbelief palpable.

Rose laughed gently as she pulled him toward her, sighing with delight as his arms encapsulated her, hopefully never to be let go. "I love you. Partly against my wishes, and partly because you are the best man I have ever met."

Now Samuel's disbelief was obvious, his eyes fluttering rapidly. "You are teasing me."

"Just a tad." Rose lifted a hand and caressed the side of his face, marveling at this man who learned as well as loved. "Now, are you going to kiss me or not?"

The kiss was fiery and passionate, eager and desperate, the hunger for each other that had gone unsated for so long propelling them forward.

But it was also sweet, and reverential, and Rose found to her delight that she could be quite happy kissing this man for a very, very long time.

Providing he stopped eating her marmalade toast.

Oh, and there were a few other loose ends to tie up…

Chapter Twenty

February 14, 1841

SAMUEL DREW IN a long, considering breath. "What do you think?"

He wasn't looking at the building. He should have been, he knew; that was the entire reason why they had traveled to this part of London, after all. It had been difficult enough to tear themselves apart and get dressed long enough to step into the carriage.

A smile teased at the corners of Samuel's lips as he thought about that carriage ride. One hand on her breast, another under her skirts—

Rose frowned. "I am not sure."

"You're not?"

"It's... Well, it's hard to imagine, isn't it?" his wife said slowly, her gaze moving from left to right as she took in the building before her. "I suppose one has to rather imagine it like a stage. It's not been properly dressed yet?"

Tearing his eyes away, much to his disinclination, Samuel looked back at the building for which they had traveled to see.

It was large, very large. It took up most of this side of the street, the grand and wide windows reflecting the afternoon sun. There were pillars on the ground floor and copious room inside for what they wanted.

But was it the right location?

"You're not too far from Soho," Samuel pointed out, walking up the steps and letting himself in with the key with which Mr.

Todd had entrusted him. "Walking distance to Hyde Park."

"That *is* good," Rose said as she followed him into the cavernous space. "Goodness."

Goodness was about right. Samuel had visited a number of cathedrals in his time, and a few theaters. Now that he was married to one of the best actresses in the world, by his estimation, he presumed he would be spending a great deal more time in such places.

Theaters, that was. Not cathedrals.

This particular building had similarities, but it was at the same time completely different. Cavernous, yes, but cold. Heartless. It conveyed a sense that great pain had been experienced here, and great loneliness. Somehow that clung to every brick.

"An abandoned building," Rose said with a shiver. "It seems strange. As though ghosts are walking among us."

"After the blaze that gutted the place, it appeared no one wanted the expense of restoring it," Samuel said vaguely, stepping forward with footsteps that echoed unpleasantly around the space. "I suppose it would take a great deal of money to make the place habitable, let alone pleasant. But it is big enough for our plans."

His wife nodded as she looked about her, stepping through a door and starting to explore. "And you think this could be the place?"

"It's hard to think of better," he replied as he followed her into what had once perhaps been a dining hall of sorts. "There are few properties in London this large that ever come up for sale. And it would enable us to get the place ready swiftly. So much of the layout would work for us, don't you think?"

Us. Samuel tried not to puff out his chest as he said the word, the movement surely ridiculous.

Us. Himself and Rose.

It was hard to believe he had considered, even for a moment, not remaining her husband. Letting go of the most beautiful and kindest woman he had ever met? Abandoning the opportunity to build something that truly mattered with this woman who had overcome so much?

He'd been a fool, indeed, to walk out on her. He was fortunate that she had accepted him back.

Accepted him, and loved him.

"You've got that idiot grin on your face again."

Rose's words reached Samuel's ears through a foggy haze, but he managed to concentrate on them.

"I was just thinking about—"

"Me," said his wife with a similarly wide grin. "I know. I know that look."

He did not think, he just acted. Pulling Rose into his arms, Samuel kissed her deeply and passionately, his tongue darting into her mouth at first but then languidly layering on carnality after carnality—

"Ahem."

The pair broke apart, heat blossoming through Samuel.

Mr. Todd looked even more embarrassed than Samuel felt. "So sorry to intrude, my lord, my lady…"

"Please, don't apologize," said Rose smoothly, slipping her hand through Samuel's arm and beaming at the solicitor, as though he were the second-most important person in the world.

Samuel's soul softened. There was a particular smile that she kept just for him.

The solicitor was still flushing. "I thought I would—well, stop by and see what you thought. Whether you wish to purchase."

"'Purchase'?" Samuel repeated, his mind still kissing Rose.

She nudged him hard with her elbow. "The purchase, my dear, of the place to transform it into a retirement home for actors and actresses. The purchase of the place we are standing in right now. As *you* suggested."

Samuel blinked. "Oh. Oh, yes. So I did."

Rose's giggles are not helpful, he could not help but think ruefully. She knew what happened to his brain whenever he kissed her.

Mr. Todd appeared to know, too. "If you wish, I can return another time."

"We'll stop by your office later," Rose said swiftly, much to Samuel's relief. "I suppose there hasn't been a great deal of interest in the property?"

"Perhaps not, but the seller is rather eager. I don't think you're the *only* ones interested in the property."

"Tomorrow, then," said Samuel's wife with a squeeze of his arm. "Thank you, Mr. Todd. Good day."

It was masterful. *Only someone as talented as Rose could have done it*, Samuel thought with a grin. The solicitor drifted out of the building as though on a cloud, just happy to have been noticed by her.

"You have a way with men," he teased under his breath.

Only when the door to the outside world had closed, and with Mr. Todd on the other side of it, did Rose nudge him again in the ribs. "Cheek."

"I'm just saying, you are able to—"

"This place, then," Rose interrupted, forestalling Samuel's monologue on her remarkable powers. "You truly think we can make it into a home?"

His stomach lurched.

A home. He had become so focused on the idea that he should be doing something for the good of those around him, Samuel had almost completely lost sight of the fact that for those who would come to live here, it would be their home.

He glanced about them. The empty space, the slightly stale air, the sense of misery and loneliness that permeated every floorboard...could this place be transformed sufficiently?

"A great deal of money could do it," Samuel said with a nod.

Rose slipped her hand from his arm. "And you have a great deal of money."

He did not miss the slight catch in her voice. It was not censure, not exactly. Rose was too worldly to truly condemn him for being of means.

But there was something in there. Something he had to address.

"I am rich, it is true," Samuel said, taking her hand in his as they walked slowly along what had once been a long dining hall back to the central hallway. "I have you."

Rose rolled her eyes. "Now *that* was worthy of the stage."

"You liked it?" He was almost pleased. "I promise you, I made no preparations."

"That, I can well believe," his wife said dryly as they looked about them in the hallway. "Such nonsense you speak."

"It's not nonsense if it's true," said Samuel, more seriously now. "I thought... I believed completely that money would make me happy. And it's true, I can transform it into happiness—but only when I spend it, and preferably on others."

Rose's smile became a little less sardonic and a little more loving.

"It isn't money that makes me happy," Samuel admitted, almost glad he could rectify this stain on his own character. "It's you."

Her embrace was swift, but warm, and even if it had lasted all day, it would not have been enough.

"So, I suppose we should make a decision," Samuel said with a shiver as they stepped outside. "We could wait for something better to come on the market, but—"

"Rose—Rose? It... It can't be."

Samuel did not need the sudden grasp of his arm to know this was going to be a most tricky situation, indeed.

Standing on the other side of the street, wrapped up against the seasonal cold but most definitely identifiable...were the Marquess and Marchioness of Dalton.

"Oh, hell," muttered Samuel's wife.

"We do not have to speak to them." He turned, standing between the sight of her parents and the woman he loved. "This should be on your terms, if at all. We can turn around and go back inside."

"No." Rose's cheeks were flushed, to be sure, but there was that look of determination in her expression again. Samuel knew it well. "No, it has to happen. It may as well be here, in public, where… Where they cannot…"

Samuel placed an arm around her shoulders and wished to goodness the dratted man had just walked away—but no, he was pulling his wife across the road with him and there was a look of red-faced shock in Lord Dalton's expression he had never seen before.

"Rose," repeated the diminutive Lady Dalton, for it had been she who had called out most indecorously. "It… It is you, isn't it?"

Samuel glanced at his wife. Her gaze was defiant, as he should have known it would be.

"Yes," Rose said in a clipped voice. "Good afternoon, Lady Dalton."

Lady Dalton flinched as though she had been shot. "I—You disappeared—"

"I left home," Rose said firmly, and she stood up straighter as she did so.

Samuel could have crowed to hear her speak so powerfully. Honestly, was there anything this woman could not do?

Perhaps there was one thing: avoid her father forever.

Lord Dalton cleared his throat. "You look well."

Samuel tried not to look at Rose's face as she said, "Yes."

The last thing she needed was to feel as though she had an even greater audience. Thankfully, their little scene was being soundly ignored by the people of London, who evidently had far more important things to do than witness a reconciliation, or whatever this was.

The trouble was, the silence between the trio was growing and there appeared to be no sign that it was about to end.

Samuel cleared his throat, intending to say something, but before he could do so, Lord Dalton's attention snapped to him.

"You," he said curtly. "I suppose it was you she ran off with, you churl."

Samuel raised an eyebrow. Did he really not recognize him, a Chance? Must have been the strange surroundings.

"Monty!"

"Lord Dalton," Rose said in a ringing voice, speaking over her mother. "I would thank you not to speak to my husband like that. The Marquess of Aylesbury is not accustomed to such rudeness."

She should have been a duchess, Samuel could not help but think admiringly. *Or a princess. Or a queen.* The fact that he had only the title of marchioness to offer her was a scandal.

Lord Dalton's lips trembled. "I-I had not realized—my lord, of course. I see that now—"

"And now I think it is time we departed," Rose said smoothly, as though she were a very busy and important person. Which, Samuel thought ponderously, she was. "I am sure we shall see each other in Society now that we are all in London and I hope that we can keep pleasantries front and center...and at a minimum."

It was all Samuel could do not to applaud. The woman had a way of drawing herself up, not as though she were trying to intimidate, but merely as though that were the way she meandered through the world.

Which, now he came to think about it, it was.

Lord Dalton's cheeks were growing redder by the second. "Do you mean to say that you won't be owning us in public?"

"You only wish for my acquaintance now that I am a marchioness," shot back his daughter, her own cheeks equally red. "You had no desire for my company when I was your daughter with dreams and with a passion for the stage, and so I think you should count yourself lucky that I even admit to the acquaintance. Good day, Lord Dalton. Lady Dalton."

A tweak of sympathy grasped at Samuel as he saw the watery eyes, the abject misery in the older woman's face, but there was nothing that could be said. Lord Dalton had already tugged away his wife, and the pair of them strode—or at least, one strode, one struggled to keep up—down the street.

Within half a minute, they had turned the corner and disappeared from view.

"That," Rose said slowly, "was unpleasant."

"But it is done," Samuel said. "And the first meeting was always going to be the worst. Now you have no reason to fear him."

He wanted to protect her, wrap her up in cotton wool and hide her in a tower. He wanted to keep the world from hurting her, wanted to make sure his Rose never came to harm.

His Rose nodded, resolution in her eyes. "Yes. I have no need to fear."

And she can do quite an adequate job of protecting herself, Samuel thought with pride as he saw the way his wife held himself. Dear God, but he was a fortunate man. Where was that carriage? He couldn't wait to get her into it and ravish—

"Oh, Samuel! You've heard the news, then?"

Samuel stiffened, and so did Rose beside him. Though Rose had told him Frank knew more details than most, Samuel and his wife had not made any announcement to the family about the reality of the slightly unorthodox way they had met, and married, and fallen in love.

Not that it was any of their business, of course…but the truth was bound to come out sooner or later.

That was why the fact that his sister was marching over to him, waving what appeared to be a letter, was not exactly welcome.

He turned to his wife. "Do you want to tell Frank about your parents?"

"No," Rose said immediately, reading his mind perfectly. "No. Not yet. She's guessed half my story already."

Samuel gave a brief nod and her returning expression was enough to utterly end him. How had he ended up with such a perfect wife?

"I went to your house, but you weren't there—you look pretty, Rose—your disparaging butler told me where to find you, but look at this, won't you?" blurted out Frank in a long torrent.

Samuel tried not to roll his eyes as he took the proffered letter. "Is that one of Benjamin's shirts you're wearing?"

His sister glared. "I don't think it's appropriate to be asking about a lady's apparel."

The giggle by his side did not help as Samuel attempted to maintain a stern expression. "And where's your chaperone, Frank? As the new head of this family—"

"Oh, damnation to your pomp and ceremony," interrupted Frank with a scowl. "Read the letter!"

Samuel glared back. Then he read the letter.

Victoria and our child unwell once again—won't be coming to Bath. We send all our love.

Cothrom

"'Once again'?" Rose had been reading the note—Samuel was not certain it could accurately be described as a letter—over her shoulder. "Their child has been sick before?"

"He has, indeed!" Frank frowned. "Such a beautiful baby, they say, but I shall not get the opportunity to see him. You will have to get a move on, you two, and make me an aunt for a second time."

Heat scalded Samuel's cheeks. "I don't think we want that quite—"

"And when you have one, you should call it 'Frank,'" said his sister. "It's an excellent name."

"Damn it, Frank, you can't just—"

"I'm off. I've got to find Benjamin. The fool isn't at his club," said his sister, blithely talking over him as she always did. "Bye!"

"Frank, your chaperone! You must stay with us! What are you—"

She rushed off, skirts flying, as Samuel shook his head with a wry expression. "She's a real terror, you know. I have to feel sorry for the poor man she eventually marries. If Mama asks, no, I did *not* see Frank without a chaperone on the London streets and not manage to keep her with me."

It wasn't that he had expected a long reply to his statement, but *some* reply would have been pleasant. But there was nothing. Nothing but silence.

Samuel stuffed the note into his pocket, his sister being so absorbed in her mission to find their wayward brother that she had completely forgotten said mission's purpose and turned to his wife.

Rose was pale. Very pale. Samuel could not recall ever having seen her look so white.

"Rose?" He stepped closer to her, taking her two hands in his own. They were ice. "Rose!"

Rose jerked, her eyes focusing once more, and she stared with bleary confusion. "Wh-What?"

"My dear, are you feeling quite well?" Anxiety pulsated through Samuel along with his blood, each heartbeat only increasing his worry. She did not look at all well. "You look most strange."

Her smile was weak, but it *was* a smile. "Oh, no. I mean, yes."

"Well, which is it?" Samuel urged.

The hustle and bustle of the street continued, but he only had eyes for the woman before him. What on earth could have disquieted her so? There had been nothing in Frank's words, had there, which could have offended? True, there was that quip about the two of them having a child, but honestly, the very idea of that happening so soon was... Was...

Samuel did not know how he was still managing to stand, but he was still breathing because he required enough air to say, "You're not."

"I... I think I might be?" Rose gave a laugh, one of confusion and excitement but also fear. "My courses, they were supposed to come two days ago and I had not thought of it until that moment, but I could be wrong. Two days isn't much of a delay. I could be mistaken—"

"Or you could be with child," Samuel murmured, hardly daring to believe it.

A child. A part of himself, and a part of Rose. A symbol, a walking and talking and laughing piece of evidence of their love for each other.

He squeezed her hands. "You look worried."

"You just said... Well. That we weren't quite—I do not know how you were going to finish that sentence," his wife said weakly, her true concerns painted in her face.

Damn it all to hell.

He'd done it again—spoken hastily for fear of revealing his true feelings, his true desires, and in doing so, he had harmed the one woman in the world for whom he had sworn to care.

"I did not want to seem too eager in front of my sister," Samuel explained rapidly, the two of them stepping back from the road as a trio of pedestrians attempted to pass them. "I did not want you to feel the pressure of—I know children do not always come. My cousin Evelyn—"

"Then you are happy?"

'*Happy*'? There was not a single word that could capture the emotions flooding through him, though Samuel was going to have a good try.

"So happy, I can hardly breathe," he murmured, kissing her swiftly on the mouth before saying, "And if we are wrong, mistaken in our hopes, then perhaps soon—"

"Perhaps soon," Rose repeated, her hands squeezing his own. "But if it doesn't happen—oh, Samuel, you are more than enough for me. *Too* much for me, sometimes. Your love, your affection, I don't deserve—"

Well, he wasn't going to put up with listening to any of that nonsense!

"'Deserve'?" He had not intended his voice to growl, but how could he have let that pass? "You deserve the world."

"And so do you. And I'll give it to you, every day, with my love," Rose said perhaps just as fiercely.

Samuel grinned. "What play is that line from?"

The whack on his chest hurt but was probably well deserved. "Samuel Chance!"

"Rose," he said happily. "My rose. My beautiful, clever, ridiculous Rose."

His wife looked a spot mollified. But only a spot. "And you kissed me in the street, the very idea!"

"Oh, I'm going to kiss you again," said Samuel happily, "Society be damned. And trust me," he murmured, lowering his head to press a kiss by her ear. "I'm going to do a great deal more once we get back inside our carriage…"

Epilogue

March 1, 1841

"Oh! There's a new *Romeo and Juliet* in Brighton, I forgot to tell you."

Rose snorted as she turned the page of her newspaper. "I promise you, once you've been Juliet three times, you can almost recite the entire play."

Her husband's face, just visible over the top of her newspaper, was astonished. "You... You can recite the whole play?"

Rose laid down the newspaper with a grin. "'Two households, both alike in dignity, in fair Verona, where we lay our scene. From ancient grudge break to new mutiny, where civil blood makes civil hands unclean. From forth the fatal loins—'"

"That's enough about loins this early in the morning." Samuel fanned himself with his hand from the opposite sofa. "Not unless you're eager to let me delve into yours?"

"Twice this morning has left me quite... Well, not sore. Let us say, *well-stretched*," Rose said with pinking cheeks, though it was mildly wonderful to be so desired by such a man. "My point is, I could probably declaim the entire thing for you if you wanted. No need to go to the theater."

"I thought you'd be all for it!" said Samuel with a quizzical expression. "You know...back in the theaters you love."

But from the wrong side, Rose almost said but did not quite.

It was difficult to explain. This life, her new life—it was everything she wanted, and sometimes a little bit more.

Yet that did not mean she regretted her old life. Her life on the stage had been wonderful, in its way. Oh, it had been grubby at times, and there had been moments when she had wondered what on earth she had been thinking...

But it had been wonderful—and stepping into a theater not as an actress, but as a patron felt...odd. Not wrong. But not yet right.

"I don't know," Rose said slowly.

And somehow, he understood her. How did he do that, just...just understanding her like that?

"I am more than happy to attend something else. An opera, or a ballet. There's a horse race next week, if you want to get into the country," Samuel said with a shrug as the longcase clock chimed eleven. "And there are plenty of other plays we could see, and right here in London, like *Mac*—"

"Do not utter that name in my presence!" Rose hissed.

She had not known that she was going to say such a thing, but she was married. She was allowed to hiss at her husband, particularly when he was being an idiot.

Samuel blinked. "I thought it was only inside a theater that one should not say *Mac*—"

"Do I have to come over there and stop up your mouth?" said Rose, placing a hand on her chest in mock—well, mostly mock—outrage.

Her husband waggled his eyebrows. "That sounds wonderful, actually."

Rose laughed, and his laughter joined hers to fill the morning room, and she hardly knew how she was supposed to contain so much wonder.

Being with Samuel was...easy.

That was not to diminish the man, far from it. Rose had never encountered anyone, man or woman, who had made her feel so happy, so comfortable, so completely at one with the world that she did not have to look over her shoulder or worry about what was to happen next.

It wasn't just not fearing for her next meal, though that was a lovely consequence. No, it was being with Samuel. His presence alone was reward enough.

Rose left her newspaper behind as she stood from her armchair and stepped across to her husband. Before she could even speak a word, he had grabbed her waist, pulled her down across his lap, and done precisely what *she* had threatened to do to *him*.

Stopped up her mouth…with a kiss.

Melting into his embrace, heart fluttering and pulse racing, Rose parted her lips and wound her fingers swiftly into his hair.

Oh, there was nothing like this: not even a resounding standing ovation could feel like this, the weightlessness of her body, the soaring of her pulse, the way his hands—

"My lord, my lady, there are—ah."

Rose sprang up from her husband's embraces—or more accurately, *clutches*—and tried to smooth her hair down at the same time as her skirts and at the same time as her spirits.

She was not entirely successful.

Arden was pink but kept his gaze resolutely on his master. "As I was saying—"

"We are going to have to introduce some sort of knocking system," Samuel muttered, straightening his cravat with flushing cheeks.

Rose tried not to snort.

"Indeed, my lord," said their butler, now raising his eyes heavenward as though he could receive help from that quarter for his unruly master. "Your family is here, my lord."

"My—My family?"

There was no more that could be said; that was, there was no time for additional words from either Samuel or herself, for the door banged against the wall as a torrent of Chances entered the room.

"—got to do something about it—"

"Utterly disgraceful, he's giving us all a bad name!"

"—and it will get to the papers soon, if we don't do something!"

Rose took a hasty step backward. There was something about a plethora of Chances. Individually, they were all absolute delights—she had yet to meet one that she did not like—but taken all together...

"I h-hope we weren't int-t-terrupting anything," said the Dowager Marchioness of Aylesbury, kissing a stunned Rose on the cheek.

"Nothing at all," lied Samuel rather impressively, Rose had to admit.

One could almost believe him.

Lilianna snorted as she sank heavily down onto a sofa, her hands clutching her large belly. "Less said about that, the better, I say. And to think, I've come out of confinement for this! Right, we'll need at least three pots of tea—"

"This isn't actually your house, Lil," Samuel said with a sigh as he allowed the stated sister to kiss his cheek. "It's Rose's house."

All eyes turned to Rose.

And Rose adored it. If there was one thing she missed about traipsing across a stage, it was the constant knowledge that you were being looked at and admired by a great many people.

The Chance family was its own theater, all on its own.

"Inform Mrs. Bailin we'll have tea and coffee and cake, Arden," she said firmly, indicating that her in-laws should be seated. "Do sit down."

The role of hostess was one she had agreed to play for a rascal of an heir all the way back in Brighton. It had come as a surprise, Rose realized ruefully as she plumped up a cushion for her father-in-law and asked Frank not to spill ink on a cushion, that she quite enjoyed it.

"Now what's all this hubbub?" Samuel said as he attempted to prevent Benjamin from pouring a glass of brandy from his own collection. "It's just past eleven in the morning, you blighter—"

"It's not a hubbub," Lilianna said grandly. "It's a scandal!"

Her husband met her eye and Rose tried not to grin. Her

sister-in-law had missed a trick by not stepping onto the stage herself.

"I am sure it is not that bad," she said aloud as calmly as possible. "Ah, here's the tea."

As Mrs. Bailin and the footmen wheeled in a great number of tea trays—Rose had learned after their last visit that each of the Chance branches required a great deal of cake—the hubbub rose once again.

"—giving all of us a bad—"

"And it's serious this time. There's talk of prosecuting—"

"—n-n-never heard the l-like!"

"Honestly, you're a rabble, not a family," said Samuel with a laugh, handing a slice of cake to Frank, who examined it critically.

"This cake's angle is not symmetrical."

"It'll taste the same," Samuel said as he rolled his eyes, turning to his wife.

Once again, Rose tried not to giggle. "Would you like me to cut you a more symmetrical slice, Frank?"

"Don't m-m-m-mollycoddle her," called her mother over the noise. "And d-don't call her 'Frank'!"

"Here you go," Rose said, cutting a slice very carefully, putting it on a plate, and handing it over to her youngest sister-in-law. "Frank," she added, *sotto voce*.

Frank grinned.

"I h-heard that!"

"I rather think you were meant to," opined Samuel with a laugh, throwing himself into an armchair. "Now, honestly, one of you can surely tell me why you've all marched over here in such high dudgeon?"

"I'm not in high dudgeon," said Benjamin, and Rose noticed as she glanced over at him that he had somehow managed to get a glass of brandy, after all. "I think Cousin Zander should be allowed to live how he wants."

There was a moment's pause.

Just a moment, but it was sufficient. Rose had spent too long attempting to perfect the perfect pause between lines in a scene to know that this was a pause which the family had delivered before.

Samuel rolled his eyes. "Not again."

"He truly is going to disgrace us," said Lilianna smartly. "Don't you think, Arthur?"

Rose started. The man standing behind Lilianna, lounging on the sofa protectively, had not yet said a word and had somehow faded into the background.

"Anything you say, my love," said Earl of Taernsby with a wink to Rose.

"Well, whether or not you approve, Benjamin," said the dowager marquess slowly, "that hardly signifies."

Benjamin bristled. "Papa—"

"It is what Society thinks that matters," continued his father, "and we all know what will happen when the news gets out about his latest unfortunate escapade. And it *will* get out."

Rose swallowed, the sense of foreboding so strong within the room, she could almost taste it. She caught Samuel's eyes as he spoke.

"Ruin," her husband said slowly.

Everyone in the room fell to chattering again, some decrying Cousin Zander in the strongest terms—that was Lilianna—and others laughing about the adventure the man had presumably gotten up to—that was Benjamin. Frank had pulled a protractor out of goodness-knew-where and was carefully measuring the angle of her cake, tongue between her teeth and not a bite of her dessert consumed, and Samuel's parents were talking in hurried whispers about whether they should reach out to his brother William and see if they could delicately assist.

And in all the chatter and confusion, Rose carefully stepped around the room and lowered herself onto a seat beside her husband.

"Well, well," Samuel said quietly. "A ruin. A true scandal."

"Not that we know anything about that," she returned with a smile.

His own expression was so knowing, and yet so loving, that Rose was in half a mind to send the whole pack of them away so she could curl up onto his lap once more.

This husband of hers, he did not spook easily. No matter her past, no matter how she had come into his life, he had fallen in love with her and would stand by her. It was wonderful.

"A letter for you, my lord."

Rose looked up. Their butler's voice was half lost in the din, but he was just about audible.

"Say that again, Arden!" Samuel called out in a loud voice.

His family's voices became murmurs, and then eventually, silence fell.

Arden cleared his throat. "A letter for you, my lord. Erm… For my Lord Aylesbury. The senior. Forwarded from your home."

Rose only caught the moment of mirth for a moment, before her father-in-law steadied his face and held out his hand.

The letter was short, and it was read quickly. When it had been finished, the dowager marquess looked at his wife and sighed.

"My brother requests our help."

"I knew it!" Lilianna had jumped to her feet and was only a little unsteady, her husband's hands jerking out to balance her. "Come on then, Frank. We had better get over there right now. Where are they—the townhouse? Bath?"

"I d-d-don't actually th-think the letter m-meant for *all* of us to g-go," said their mother.

"Come on, then," chortled Benjamin, walking forward with the brandy glass still in his hand. "I wonder if Uncle William still has that marvelous port?"

Rose giggled as Arden just about managed to snatch the glass from the man's hands as he passed him in a flurry of family, the room emptying somehow just as swiftly as it had been filled. There was only the copious cake, mostly uneaten, and the numerous teapots and coffeepots, still mostly full, that remained as evidence that the rest of the Aylesbury Chances had ever been there.

Samuel cleared his throat. "Would you mind taking these back down to the kitchens, Mrs. Bailin? The servants can available themselves of it all. Shame to let it go to waste."

"Very kind of you, my lord," murmured their housekeeper. The footmen and butler stepped in to assist.

And so the room was emptied almost as swiftly as it had been filled.

Rose exhaled slowly. "Well. That was interesting."

"Oh, I hear the name Alexander Chance embroiled in one scandal or another every day of the week. I don't know where the man gets his energy from—and nothing ever really comes of it," Samuel said with a shrug, taking her hand. "Just as nothing came of all that 'Lady A' business. I dare anyone of the *ton* to comment that they guess it referred to you and see what I do to them. Do not think on it. I have far more interesting things to think about."

"You do?"

She should have expected it, yet Rose was still capable of being surprised by this charming, winsome, infuriating man. The way he pulled her swiftly from her seat, however, and tugged her onto his lap… Well, that was impressive. No practiced actor could have done it better.

"Now, where were we?" Samuel murmured, his breath blossoming across her décolletage.

Rose beamed as she looked down at the man she would spend the rest of her life getting to know, and loving more and more with everything she learned. "I think you were about to ravish me."

"Well, then, I had better get to it," her husband, the most brilliant man she had ever met said slowly, "so there is time to ravish you a second time before lunch."

"I wouldn't take a chance on that." Rose laughed, and then she ceased laughing as the man she adored covered her mouth with his own and began a very thorough ravishing, indeed.

A Short Letter From the Author

Hello! Thank you so much for reading *Take a Chance on You*, the eleventh novel in my The Chances series. I truly hoped you enjoyed it and fell in love with Samuel and Rose just as much as I did.

If you've read the first ten books of this series (which I strongly recommend!), then you'll have seen the four uncles fall in love, and now their adult children. I had always wanted to write a series of brothers, but I could never 'meet' the characters who were quite right. After waiting years to meet them myself, I have had a lot of fun writing the four Chance brothers—and now we're diving into their children. Make sure you go back and read them!

If you're desperate to read the happily ever afters of Samuel's siblings, then you'll want to look out for Book 6, *Not a Chance in Hell* (Lilianna's story); Book 18, *Why Take the Chance?* (Benjamin's story); and Book 19, *A Calculated Chance* (Frank's story). Our next Chance adventure is going to jump to a different branch of the Chance family and you'll meet Alexander's true love...

Being an author can be a lonely business, but knowing that there are readers from all over the world who are going to adore my stories makes it all worthwhile. Thank you for your support, and I hope you love reading more of my books!

Happy reading,
Emily

About Emily E K Murdoch

If you love falling in love, then you've come to the right place.

I am a historian and writer and have a varied career to date: from examining medieval manuscripts to designing museum exhibitions, to working as a researcher for the BBC to working for the National Trust.

My books range from England 1050 to Texas 1848, and I can't wait for you to fall in love with my heroes and heroines!

Follow me on twitter and instagram @emilyekmurdoch, find me on facebook at facebook.com/theemilyekmurdoch, and read my blog at www.emilyekmurdoch.com.

www.ingramcontent.com/pod-product-compliance
Lightning Source LLC
LaVergne TN
LVHW011930070526
838202LV00054B/4569